at the clock

She wasn't really going to make a phone call in the middle of the night. But if she was going to use her vacation for a trip to Nicaragua, she needed to find out if Chad still wanted her to come. Maybe this would not be a good time for him....

But through the doubts came the dream of seeing him—her beloved Chad. Her mind wandered off on to thoughts of Chad's arms around her, his kisses. They would make love, and it would be wondrous. And she wanted that with him. No matter what came after, she wanted to have a time of love with Chad.

And what would come after? Would it be easier to make a decision after seeing him again?

All Julie knew was the thought of seeing Chad filled her with longing. Her body ached with it. Her mind focused on images of what could be.

ABOUT THE AUTHOR

As the daughter of an army officer, Indiana-born Anne Henry moved frequently during her childhood. Now she makes her home in Oklahoma, where she edits alumni publications for the University of Oklahoma. Anne is the mother of three grown children.

Books by Anne Henry

HARLEQUIN AMERICAN ROMANCE

ANNE HENRY

BELOVED DREAMER

Harlequin Books

TORONTO • NEW YORK • LONDON
AMSTERDAM • PARIS • SYDNEY • HAMBURG
STOCKHOLM • ATHENS • TOKYO • MILAN

Published June 1990

ISBN 0-373-16347-9

Printed in U.S.A.

Chapter One

There was no mistaking the look on her face. Julie was glad to see him. *Really* glad.

Chad's heart gave an extra thump or two in his chest.

He took a deep breath and nodded at her from his place in line.

She is glad to see me. He felt like letting out a war whoop.

Had a day gone by in the past twenty years that he hadn't thought of Julie Harper at least once?

For years he'd told himself he hated her. But that was because he hurt. God, how he hurt. But after the hurt had scarred over, slowly he began to allow himself to remember her with love.

Chad had talked himself in and out of coming to the reunion at least a dozen times. Then he convinced himself he needed to travel to Houston for other reasons—but he had waited until June to come.

This morning he'd almost lost his nerve and had driven around the high school in his rented car for an hour before getting up enough courage to walk through the front door.

And there she was, sitting at a table in the middle of the lobby beside a familiar-looking woman wearing an outrageous purple hat. A line of people stood in front of the table waiting their turn to register. A group of women across the lobby were struggling to hang a welcome banner over the trophy case. Blowups of several old yearbook pictures were already hung around the room—including one of the state champion basketball team. Chad stared at his own image. He'd been skinny. And young. So young.

The high school looked so much the same, he felt as if he'd gone through a time warp and returned to those days of yesteryear. The wide locker-lined hallways headed off the lobby, where a wall of cases were full of tarnished trophies. The building even smelled the same—disinfectants, sweat, dust.

Chad slipped into line. A couple he couldn't place was in front of him. Kenny Barnsworth and Mary Beth Weber were in front of them—both twenty pounds heavier, married apparently. They'd gone together in high school. Mary Beth glanced his way but either didn't recognize him in his older, heavier, bearded state, or had forgotten him. Another couple got in line behind him, but Chad didn't bother to turn around. The only person he was interested in was sitting at the table at the front of the line.

He hid behind the others, watching Julie greet people, check their names off her list, give out name tags and a packet of information about the weekend. Julie's cheerleader smile was as brilliant as ever, her green eyes as vivid.

Chad used to think she had the world's most beautiful mouth. He'd been right. She still did. Sometimes, over the years, he'd see women who reminded him of Julie, and he'd realize the resemblance was in the mouth. Full lips. Wonderful teeth. Dazzling smile.

A catch in his throat added itself to the pain in his chest. And his knees felt a little soft.

Her dark hair was shorter. He wondered if it still bounced when she walked, if it still shone in the sunshine. She was wearing a yellow sleeveless dress that revealed smooth, tanned arms. Pearls were at her throat. He used to kiss her throat. Her arms.

He used to kiss all of her. It had been glorious.

He remembered the first time he ever saw Julie Harper. She'd been unlocking her locker—that locker there, the third one from the corner—and for some reason she'd looked over her shoulder at him. He must have looked as lost as he was. "Need some help?" Julie asked. Chad stammered out an answer, and she directed him to the office on the second floor and flashed that smile. And he was smitten. Just like that. With one smile. Maybe it was too soon to call it love, but for two years he'd watched her from afar, dreamed about her, rehearsed imaginary phone calls to her, planned imaginary dates with her. And for one glorious year she'd been *his* girl. His basketball letter jacket had graced her slender shoulders. His senior ring had hung on a chain around her kissable throat.

Julie had just finished handing Kenny and Mary Beth their packets when she spotted him in line.

Her eyebrows went up. Her wonderful lips formed his name. Her pencil paused in midair. Then a look of such pure delight came over her face that Chad, at last, could feel glad he had come.

The couple in front of him turned around to stare, then stood back and watched as Julie got up from the table and came around to gracefully slide into his arms, to twine her own arms around his neck, to plant her lips on his.

She smelled of good perfume. Her lips were soft. The feel of her in his arms was sweet beyond belief.

Julie's eyes were moist as she stepped back in the circle of his arms to offer a soft smile.

Chad felt a little dizzy.

"Oh, you darlin' boy," she said. "Why didn't you let me know you were coming?"

He didn't bother to answer. He couldn't answer. All he could do was stand there and smile like an idiot.

"While your mother was still alive I kept up with you, but my goodness, the last I heard you were teaching on some Indian reservation in North Dakota."

"Could you do that again?" he finally managed.

"What?"

"Kiss me."

Several spectators who were grouped around them laughed. "Way to go," Kenny said.

Julie's smile changed to a grin. "We'll see," she teased, then turned and waved toward one of the banner hangers. "Betty Jean, look who's here."

Betty Jean dropped her end of the banner and came squealing across the lobby. "Cha-aad! Chad Morgan. Oh, my goodness. Is that really you behind that beard?"

Betty Jean plowed in between him and Julie to lift her face for a kiss. "You devil. Why, you actually got more handsome in twenty years. You were such a scrawny thing back in high school. I never understood how you had enough energy to run up and down the court. And just look at that beard. My goodness, aren't we sexy?"

"And just look at you," Chad said. "You got…"

Betty Jean giggled and performed a dainty pirouette so he could see her nicely endowed chest from all sides. "Yes, I did, didn't I? The miracles of modern medicine, you know. It took me several years of saving quarters in a jar, but no more double A for little ol' Betty Jean."

Then she stopped and beamed. "I swear, seeing the two of you together again is a sight for sore eyes. We thought you'd dropped off the face of the earth, Chad Morgan. Julie called the Marine Corps Reserve, the University of Texas Alumni Association, several tribal chiefs, the Peace Corps and Lord knows who else. My goodness, boy, where in the world have you been? I think Julie put on this whole reunion just as an excuse to track you down."

Julie actually blushed. "Oh, come on, Betty Jean. High school classes are supposed to have twenty-year reunions. It's tradition."

"Whatever you say, sugar. Well, you two run on and have a cup of coffee—or whatever old sweethearts do after twenty years," she said with an emphatic roll of her eyes. "I'll help Jody with registration."

Chad nodded toward Jody, remembering her now. Jody Johnson. Played in the band. She'd been blond in high school. And hadn't worn a hat.

Then he said hello to Mary Beth and Kenny. Yes, they were married. Three children. He had taken over his father's car agency.

And then others stepped forward. Chad struggled with names. People had changed. Everyone looked like their parents. He wondered if he had changed that much and decided that he probably had. His skin was leathery from the sun. When he smiled, deep creases radiated out from the corners of his eyes. His hairline had receded. His body had filled out with the muscles of manual labor.

It was several minutes before he was able to grab Julie's arm and head toward the coffee shop.

"Did you really try to find me?" he asked.

Julie nodded. And blushed again. Chad felt euphoric.

"Yeah," she admitted. "But I ran out of leads. Didn't you ever hear of forwarding addresses?"

"The people I work for know where I am. With Mom gone, I didn't think anyone else would care."

They took a seat in a corner booth. He hated relinquishing her hand.

"But how did you know about the reunion?" she asked.

"I can count. Like you said, twenty years is tradition. I called the high school and asked if anything was planned. The secretary didn't know, but I was pushy, and she made some inquiries."

"Why didn't you call me?"

"Well, telephoning is difficult at best in my neck of the woods. It took half a day to get a phone call through to that school secretary. Besides, I didn't have the nerve to call you—and I wasn't sure I was really going to come. I still can't believe I did. I kept telling myself it was to visit with stateside colleagues and to see mother's sister, who lives in a rest home in Rosenburg. But poor old Aunt Bess doesn't remember me or anything else—just like the last time I visited her. And I'd never visited Mom's grave since the marker was put in place. But I really came to see you."

"You know about Ross?"

"Yeah. Mom called after it happened and told me. It was while I was still in North Dakota. Tough break. I wanted to write you but wasn't sure how that would seem. After all, none of us parted best friends. But Ross was a decent guy. In spite of all the ugly things that got said there at the end, I never really blamed you for marrying him. He was more your type. I never would have fit in your world."

"Are you married?"

"No. Not anymore. Have you remarried?"

She shook her head no but glanced down at her hand. A very large diamond inhabited the third finger of her left hand.

"Anyone I know?" he asked.

Again she shook her head no.

Silence overtook them. Chad tried to decide how he felt about the ring on her finger. He still didn't fit in her world. All he'd come for was to see her again, he reminded himself, to do what he could to erase the ugly memory of their parting. But he wished the ring wasn't there.

"How are your kids?" he asked. "Twins, right?"

"Yes. They're both starting college in the fall. Sherry wants to major in music. Or maybe nursing. Steve isn't sure. Good kids. Do you have children?"

"No."

Again there was silence. He was blowing it. At no time in his daydreaming about how it would be to see Julie again was he ever at a loss for words. But in his daydreams, she hadn't been wearing an engagement ring.

This time the waitress broke the silence. They ordered coffee.

"I didn't hear about your mother's death until after the funeral," Julie told him when the waitress had gone. "I cried when I realized I'd missed seeing you. I cried about your mother, too. She was such a gentle soul. Oh,

Chad, if you knew Ross was dead, why didn't you contact me years ago?''

"I had nothing to offer, Julie. I turned out to be just
as worthless as your dad predicted. From time to time
Mom would send me your picture from the paper. 'Mrs.
Ross Rhoades Entertains the Symphony League' type of
stuff. There you'd be, wearing a dress that probably
cost as much as I make in a year, standing next to a
tuxedo-clad Ross. Not the sort of life I could give you.''

"So, why did you come now?''

"I just wanted to see you again. I think I would have
felt the same way if Ross were still alive. Reunions are
a place where it's okay to see old girlfriends again. But
I wasn't sure I'd even let you see me. I had visions of
myself peeking out at you from between the fronds of
a potted palm. Other times, I had other visions. I'm not
sure what I wanted or expected. But the knowledge that
there would be a lighthearted opportunity to see you
again was too much for me to pass up. Maybe all I
expected was a dance to the old music—for old time's
sake. That time with you was hard to get over, Julie.''

"For me, too,'' she said softly, reaching for his hand.
"Where do you live?''

He looked at their hands on the Formica tabletop.
Déjà vu. All that was missing was a couple of Cokes
and twenty years.

"Central America,'' he said. "Nicaragua.''

"Why Nicaragua?''

"Because the country is a mess. Do-gooders like me
are needed there.''

"Still into that, huh? Doing good.''

He nodded. "The Nicaraguans called us *tontos
útiles*—useful fools. That's a good term.''

"And what do you do that's useful?''

"Right now I build and repair windmills."

"Windmills?" She frowned. Her face had some creases, too. An older face, the flamboyant prettiness of youth replaced by a quiet loveliness.

"Yeah. Old-fashioned windmills. The eastern part of the country is jungle, but the west is arid and not suitable for most types of agriculture. The countryside reminds me a lot of west Texas. With a water supply, they could raise cattle. I'm heading a pilot program in that area to demonstrate how much difference windmills and education can make."

"Why not do good in Houston, Texas?"

"I'm not sure. It just wouldn't feel the same."

"Is this a life's calling?"

"I don't know. I do know, however, that I'll never own a tux. Hell, I don't even own a necktie. I hope you'll let me in at the banquet tomorrow night without one."

Julie looked uncertain. "Tonight's barbecue at Jody's house is informal. But the banquet is at the country club. Don't men wear ties in Nicaragua?"

"Nope. That's one of the things I like about it."

"Not ever? Not even in the cities?"

He shook his head no and watched her try to digest the knowledge that there was a culture in the world where men never wore neckties. And he knew he should have left well enough alone. Someone wise had once said that you can go back to the place but not the time. His time with Julie Harper was long over. And the knowledge made him feel old and very lonely.

THAT AFTERNOON, after lunch in the same old school cafeteria, with the same meat loaf and banana pudding with vanilla wafers as before, Chad found himself suited up and on the basketball court as Allen High's first, last and only state championship team scrimmaged with the present-day team. Chad had felt a bit smug about his lean, tanned body when he saw what the years had done to some of his former teammates. But before they'd changed into the Allen High jerseys, he'd felt a bit intimidated by their fashionable clothes, their expensive haircuts. Even Eric Warner was well dressed. Chad and Eric had been among the few poor kids at Allen, which served an affluent section of suburban Houston and a few leftover neighborhoods that would soon be gobbled up by developers. But most of all, Chad admired the easy camaraderie of several of the men who had stayed in touch over the years, did business with each other, played golf together, knew each other's families.

And at lunch, watching people pulling out pictures of their kids, talking about additions on houses, family camping trips—well, he'd envied them all a bit.

Their lives were stable. They seemed content. Maybe it wouldn't have been all that bad to have stayed in Houston, married, raised a family, made friends for life. If he and Julie had stayed together, that's probably how it would have been. But they hadn't, and he had changed. He'd joined the Peace Corps, served time in Vietnam, taken up causes, never put down roots. He'd been in Nicaragua longer than he'd ever lived anywhere. And he sometimes wondered if he shouldn't just stay there. He was getting more Nicaraguan with every passing year.

The alumni team lost, of course, but Chad played well enough in spite of his stiff knee, which took away his quickness. But he still had the shot from the corner. He would have played even better if he hadn't kept looking over in the stands at Julie. But he couldn't help himself. She smiled and cheered, just like before.

HER MOTHER'S AGING CADILLAC was parked in front of Julie's house. Julie glanced at her watch. She needed to change clothes and be at the barbecue in less than an hour. What in the world did her mother want?

She pulled into the driveway and surveyed her half-mowed lawn. Steve had either run out of gas or the lawn mower was broken again. They needed a new one. And the sprinkler system was on the blink. But with her bank teller's job, she didn't even make enough to take care of the usual monthly expenses, much less the unusual ones. A lush lawn was no longer high on her priority list, but she wanted to at least keep the grass under control. She couldn't help thinking of how the lawn used to be when she had all the time and money in the world and a yardman to help her two days a week. She'd taken such pride in having a beautiful yard. The grass had been lushly green. Vivid displays of flowers filled carefully tended beds. The shrubs were sprayed regularly and carefully trimmed. Now she and the kids did well to mow and edge. She hadn't bought fertilizer yet this summer. The cedars had bagworms. And the trim on the brick house was in definite need of paint.

Ah, well, several of the other lawns on the street also weren't what they used to be. And one of the houses stood empty with an overgrown, weed-choked lawn. Times were hard. The glory days for Texas oil had passed. It remained to be seen if they would ever come back again. And she had thought that the good times would last forever, that the affluent life-style she and her family had enjoyed for as long as she could remember was some sort of God-given right.

For the thousandth time Julie wished she had sold the house after Ross died—while one could still sell expensive homes.

But she hadn't. Nor had she sold the stock in Texas Central Oil and Gas that had formed the bulk of Ross's estate. Her Daddy hadn't sold his, either. They saw no reason to. Everyone thought that Central stock was good as gold. Then one nightmare of a day the company was declared insolvent, and she could either find a way to keep making the payments on her house or turn it back to the bank and lose everything she had invested in it.

Thank heavens they'd never built the pool Ross had had designed right before he died. The plans were still in his desk. For sure she wouldn't have been able to afford the upkeep on the house if there was a pool in the backyard eating up chemicals and burning up pumps.

Walking in the front door made her feel somewhat better. The entry and living rooms of her spacious home were, for the most part, still the same—a tasteful, elegant mixture of Queen Anne and Oriental, with a contrasting touch of modern glass and chrome. She'd spent a whole year of her life decorating this house, determined to do it herself and not hire some current "in" decorator as most of her friends had done. She'd pored over books and magazines, agonizing over choices, but the end result had been worth it. Stunning, but her own brand of stunning. The rest of the house was a bit lived in, but the living and dining rooms were still company-fresh, still elegant. Of course, she and the children seldom went into either room for fear of soiling the pale beige carpet. Julie used to think nothing of having it professionally cleaned several times a year. Now she couldn't afford to have carpets cleaned and didn't have time to do them herself.

Her mother was in the kitchen. "Hi, honey," Angela Harper called out. "I'm making some coffee. Hope you don't mind."

"Help yourself. What are you doing here? I thought you and Daddy were going to play twilight golf with the Andersons."

Julie put her purse on the hall table, glanced through the mail—mostly bills—and headed for the kitchen.

Angela kissed her daughter's cheek. With her husband no longer vice president of an oil company, Angela had made many sacrifices, but her appearance certainly wasn't one of them. Her hair was frosted and pampered looking. Her red silk shirt and slacks looked marvelous on her athletic figure. Her makeup was a bit overdone but always looked fresh. And Julie couldn't imagine her mother without long red nails. Julie knew the hair and nails were accomplished without the services of a beauty shop these days. And the silk outfit was years old. "I just dropped by to find out how things went today," Angela said. "Where are the children?"

"Steve was going out with Melissa. Sherry's at a rush party. I wish she wouldn't go to those things. I can't afford for her to join a sorority."

"Now, Julie," Angela said in a soothing voice. "You are engaged to a very generous man. I'm sure Kevin won't mind if your daughter pledges a sorority. Wouldn't it be wonderful if she were to become a Tri Delt just like her mother and grandmother? Nothing would make me happier than to go to her initiation, to see her wearing the same pin I wore and you wore."

Being a Tri Delt meant much more to her mother than it did to Julie, who'd only attended college one year.

But her mother never seemed to realize that and kept trying to get Julie to be active in the local alumnae group. "That would be nice, Mother," she said. "But don't count on it. Please."

Julie looked around the kitchen. The breakfast dishes and whatever clutter the kids had left during the day were cleaned up. In fact the kitchen sparkled. No fingerprints on the refrigerator. The window over the sink gleamed. The leaves of the ivy plant shined. The floor was mopped. Her mother had been here for some time. Waiting.

"What's up?" Julie asked suspiciously.

"Can't a mother come to see her only daughter?" Angela said with a pout.

"And miss a round of golf? Okay, Mother, who have you been talking to?"

Angela chewed on her lip for a minute, considering. Then she poured two cups of coffee and carried them to the round kitchen table.

"Your father and I are concerned, dear. We heard that Morgan boy was back in town, and we don't want him causing you any more problems. I couldn't believe it when Rachel called to tell me."

Mary Beth Barnsworth's mother, Julie thought. Ross used to call the woman a mouth with legs. No wonder her own mother had gotten the news so fast.

"Imagine," Angela went on, her voice indignant. "After all the trouble that boy caused! The nerve of some people—and after you worked so hard to make the reunion go smoothly."

"The 'Morgan boy' has as much right to come as anyone else. Chad was a classmate."

"But his being there can only serve to embarrass you. And with you newly engaged to Kevin!"

"Mother, you might as well know that I moved heaven and earth to track down Chad Morgan and invite him to this reunion. When I couldn't find him, I gave up ever seeing him again and decided to say yes to Kevin's proposal. I probably would have anyway, but I wanted to see Chad again to make sure that's what I really wanted."

Angela put a jeweled hand to her throat. "Oh, dear," she said dramatically. "I told your father that you'd never really gotten over that boy, but he didn't believe me. Said you were too sensible for romantic nonsense like that. Oh, Julie, surely you aren't going to do anything to jeopardize your engagement!"

Julie took a sip of coffee before responding. "I don't know," she said honestly. "But I'll tell you one thing—when I looked up and saw Chad Morgan standing there, the old heartstrings sure felt a tug. Twenty years ago, I was really in love with him. You and Daddy wanted to pretend otherwise, but I really was."

"Oh, honey, after all you've been through, your father and I have been so pleased about Kevin. I can't imagine any man more suitable for you. He's responsible and handsome and loves you. Don't throw that away for a ne'er-do-well. With the twins starting college.... Well, you know your father and I will continue to help out all we can, but your father just doesn't make as much at this new job as he did before...."

Julie took her mother's hand. "You and Dad have been great. I don't know what I would have done without you both—financially and emotionally. And I realize Kevin is a dream come true—a wealthy man to make the mortgage payments and pay the tuition."

"A wealthy man who loves you," Angela corrected.

Julie nodded. "Yes, I think he does. And I have grown conveniently fond of him. Although it's hard to sort out true feelings when the bank is threatening to take my home and my children need educating."

"What does Chad do?" Angela asked.

Julie sighed. "He builds windmills—in Nicaragua."

Chapter Two

The Friday evening barbecue was at the home of Jody Johnson Zachery. Jody's husband was in shipping, someone had said at lunch, and rich with a capital R. The barbecue was their treat. A catered affair.

Chad had forgotten how imposing the River Oaks area of Houston was. The homes looked like hotels— elegant, old hotels. Each house obviously had a staff of grounds men to maintain the perfect lawns and lavish landscaping with spectacular displays of flowers. River Oaks was a created world of such beauty and affluence that Chad felt he must be on another planet instead of in another country.

The Zacherys' mansion occupied a huge lot on River Oaks Boulevard right down the street from the sprawling River Oaks Country Club. The mansion spoke of old money and continuing success. The national budget of Nicaragua probably couldn't have touched the place, Chad decided as he rang the bell.

A trim woman answered the door and introduced herself. Susan Something. "The party is out back," she explained with a polite smile.

She seemed older than someone twenty years out of high school, but Chad extended his hand. "I'm Chad Morgan. Should I remember you?"

The woman smiled. "No. I'm the Zacherys' in-house secretary."

Chad was curious enough to ask how many other staff were "in-house."

"Well, there's the cook, the head housekeeper and two assistants, and our butler, who doubles as Mr. Zachery's valet and driver," Betty explained. "And some of our grounds people double as security on evenings the Zacherys entertain," she added, indicating a large man in an ill-fitting dark suit standing in the shadows of the living room.

Chad took a deep breath. He could feed a city in Nicaragua with the money it took to run an operation like this.

He glanced around him at interiors that looked like they had been created for magazine layouts. Did people really *live* in a place like this? Did they put their feet up and read newspapers in those rooms? He was reminded of the White House. All that was lacking were velvet ropes to cordon off the rooms from the tourists.

A full-length oil painting of Jody in an evening dress hung over a marble fireplace. The massive gilded frame looked like something out of a museum. And Jody used to chug-a-lug beer like a linebacker. He imagined she sipped sherry now.

Chad let out a low whistle as he exited into the backyard. It looked like a scene out of one of those evening soap operas. A covered terrace ran the length of the enormous house and overlooked an extravagantly landscaped yard complete with a huge pool, lighted tennis court and putting green. A combo played in a gazebo, and a number of couples—some in Western dress—were dancing on the patio. Uniformed waiters were circulating with trays of drinks, and there was a bar set up at the far end of the terrace.

The Western barbecue motif was carried out with a few bales of hay forming a backdrop for the combo and a cactus centerpiece in the middle of the buffet table. Old-fashioned kerosene lanterns had been electrified and were hung across the yard.

Chad waited his turn to greet the host and hostess. Jody was wearing a Western outfit of satin, denim and sequins. Like many of the guests, she had on boots and a cowboy hat. Her hat had a rhinestone band. Her husband was wearing a sport coat that looked Continental rather than Western. He could have passed for Jody's father.

"Chad's a missionary in the jungle," Jody explained to her husband.

"Which jungle?" Mr. Zachery asked, looking past Chad's shoulder.

Chad tried to clarify that he not only didn't live in a jungle but was not now nor ever had been a missionary. But Jody's industrial magnate husband had already tuned him out, and Jody was gushing out a welcome to someone else.

Chad looked around until he spotted Julie. She was wearing a white sundress. Her only acquiescence to the Western motif was a red bandanna at her neck. She was standing with a tall man several years her senior. When she spotted Chad, she waved him over.

"Chad, I'd like you to meet my fiancé, Kevin McLaughlin. Kevin, this is Chad Morgan. He was an all-state guard on the state champion basketball team our senior year."

That wasn't my only claim to fame, Chad thought ruefully, but obviously Julie hadn't filled Kevin McLaughlin in on some parts of her past history. McLaughlin was about fifty, graying at the temples, movie-star handsome and had the maximum number of diamonds encircling the face of his Rolex watch. His navy sport shirt was silk and bore the Dior logo. His shoes had the look of expensive Italian leather goods. Gucci, probably. The belt, too. Yes, there was a G on the buckle. Whereas Chad was wearing a Nicaraguan shirt—the sort that had tiny rows of tucks down the front and was worn outside of one's slacks. Not only were ties unnecessary in Nicaragua, but he hadn't worn a belt in years. But what was acceptable on even the most formal occasions in Nicaragua made him feel shabby standing beside the elegant Mr. McLaughlin.

"Do you live in Houston?" Kevin asked.

"No. Not since high school."

"Chad and I used to date in high school," Julie explained. She avoided Chad's eyes.

Chad winced. *Date.* Hell, they'd been in love in high school. Really in love. College, too, for a while.

"Really?" Kevin said, giving Chad a second look. "I thought you went with your husband in high school."

"Ross was two years older than I was," Julie said, her voice too high, her words coming in a rush. "We went together my sophomore year and some during junior year after he went off to college. But during my senior year, I went out with Chad. Ross and I got back together at UT, and Chad moved to the Philippines."

"The Philippines? Do you still live there, Mr. Morgan?"

"Call me Chad, please. I'm in Central America now—with an international relief group called One World."

"International relief?" Kevin frowned. Obviously he didn't meet many people with that job handle. "You mean like Red Cross?" he asked.

"Something like that. At One World we like to think of ourselves as picking up where organizations like Red Cross leave off, but we're small-time compared to them. Our mission is to rebuild economies. You know, help people to help themselves."

"How *very* interesting," Kevin said. "A man with a mission."

Chad could tell from the man's inflection that "interesting" really meant weird.

"I like your shirt," Julie said nervously.

"It's one of the ones Nicaraguan men never wear ties with."

Simultaneously the three of them all decided to take a sip of their drinks. Chad was grateful to see Betty Jean flouncing across the terrace. She looked charmingly frivolous in her tight jeans, high-heeled boots and a cowboy hat cocked back on her blond curls.

"Well, Chad Morgan," she said, linking arms with him, "if you're dumb enough to come to this shindig without a lady, I guess you'll have to dance with me. My current boyfriend wouldn't come. Said he'd rather scrape barnacles off a battleship than come to my high school reunion. Can you imagine?"

She tugged Chad out onto the patio-turned-dance-floor. At a safe distance, she said, "I thought it looked like you needed a little rescuing."

"You're a doll. Thanks. But I'm not sure I remember how to dance. It's been a while."

"Don't worry. If you're too bad, I'll lead."

Betty Jean slid into his arms. Chad stumbled a bit, but soon they were doing a reasonable imitation of dancing.

"You're not married, I take it," Chad said. "What happened to Mitch? I thought you two would last forever."

"Me, too. Boy, you really have been out of touch. Mitch got himself killed in Vietnam. I've never quite forgiven him for that—or stopped missing him. I really loved that man. Our son is seventeen."

"And you never remarried?" he asked.

"No. I never met anyone who could fill Mitch's shoes. Now I've decided not to look at their feet. Donnie is going off to college in another year, and I'm not one of those women who wants to live alone."

"The current boyfriend, what's he like?"

"Boring. I fear the days of our relationship are numbered. While I do like an occasional baseball game, I happen to think there's more to life than sporting events—live and televised. But when Bobby takes me out, we go to a baseball game or a basketball game or a football game, depending on the season. We've also gone to golf tournaments and a rodeo. When we stay home, we catch those events on TV."

"You keep looking. You deserve the best."

Betty Jean kissed his cheek. "Thanks, sugar. Ditto for you. You've got the look of a lonely man. Kind of sad around the eyes."

"What do you think of Kevin?" Chad asked.

"What do I think of Kevin?" Betty Jean repeated, wrinkling her nose while she decided how to answer. "I think he's very urbane. The sort of man who intimidates maître d's and can carry on with the wine steward for fifteen minutes about the merits of each wine on the list. I suspect he wishes Julie would hang out with people more dignified than yours truly. He'd flip if she ever showed up in jeans that showed off her fanny," she said, slapping her own tightly clad fanny for punctuation. "But in all fairness, I think he cares about Julie, and he'll treat her well. She's had a rough time of it since Ross fell off that mountain in Colorado. The oil company that Ross's and Julie's daddies founded bellied up several years back. Mr. Harper is a vice president of some small outfit now, but he's not wealthy anymore. A lot of the oil crowd in Houston are facing 'reduced circumstances' these days. The people who are still rich either sold off in time or were diversified, like Jody's husband."

"Are you saying that Julie's marrying McLaughlin for his money?" Chad asked.

"Don't sound so judgmental. She's about to lose her house and has two kids who want to go to college. But even so, Julie wouldn't marry a man she didn't care about. And the twins like Kevin. He bought them both cars for highschool graduation presents."

"Then why did she want me to come to this reunion?"

Betty Jean sighed. "She really chewed me out for spouting off like that this morning. But I swear, it was the gospel truth. She even talked about hiring a private detective to search for you but couldn't afford the expense. You see, after she got over the shock of Ross's death, she started thinking about you again. Actually, I don't think she ever stopped thinking about you, but it was something she chose not to deal with. I guess most people have an old sweetheart they think about from time to time. But she and Ross were happy enough. Of course, that man had a wild streak that Julie had a hard time accepting. Every so often Ross would go off to Vegas and gamble too much, drink too much and Lord knows what else. And he wrecked several cars. She never said, but I imagine he'd been drinking when he skied the last run of his life. Julie and the kids were skiing behind him. It was one bad scene, I guess.''

The music ended and Betty Jean took Chad's arm and led him to a table by the pool. She grabbed a couple of beers as they passed by a waiter.

''Anyway,'' she resumed as she seated herself, ''she'd talk about you some, wonder where you were, what you were doing, get a faraway look in her eyes. You know how women talk. We wonder how it would have been if we'd married the guys we didn't. And she thought about how it would be if she ever saw you again, how it would feel. But then she couldn't find you, and Kevin was pestering her to announce their engagement. You saw the ring, I take it?''

''Yeah. Some rock.''

Betty Jean took a sip of her beer, then asked, ''So, what are you going to do?''

''Do? Ask her to dance, then slink back to my little corner of the world.''

''Oh, so you're going to be noble,'' Betty Jean said, primly folding her hands in front of her. ''That's nice.''

''Do I detect a note of sarcasm?''

''Moi?'' she said, rolling her big blue eyes. ''Never. She can marry Kevin McLaughlin, be rich and pampered, entertain beautifully, get her picture on the society page of the Houston *Post* with great regularity. You can go back and play Albert Schweitzer in the boonies. And both of you can spend the rest of your

lives wondering how it might have been. Sounds good to me.''

''Albert Schweitzer was a doctor in Africa. I help farmers in Central America.''

''Same difference. I'll bet Albert was running away from romance, too.''

''Betty Jean, you're more of a romantic fool than I am. It won't work. Church mice are richer than I am.''

''Good grief!'' Betty Jean said with a toss of her head. ''You two have been carrying the torch for twenty years. Doesn't that count for something?''

Chad took a long draft of his beer, staring at the rear of the mansion. There were lights in every window. Back home, where electricity was a precious commodity, he counted himself lucky if the lights stayed on long enough for him to see the evening news on television.

''Sitting here behind this temple to the ultra-rich, I feel pretty silly,'' he said, ''but it does give me a new perspective on things. Strange as it may seem, I love my life, Betty Jean. *Really* love it. I love Nicaragua, the people, the job. There are no houses like this in Nicaragua. No Rolex watches. No Mercedes-Benz in circle drives. No swimming pools in backyards. Just gentle people who manage somehow, in spite of war and deprivation, to be dignified and cheerful and clean.

''The older I get, the more I thank Mr. Harper and circumstances for seeing to it that I didn't marry Julie and struggle to be upwardly mobile in Houston, Texas. There's nothing the matter with that, mind you, but I personally would have been miserable in a three-piece suit, always knowing that I hadn't been true to myself, that I'd somehow missed the mark. Julie and I might even have ended up hating each other.

"As it is, my life has been rich and full, interesting and useful. But I've paid a certain price, and that price is lonely nights. Not always. I've been in love a time or two. Married for a while. But I've used my memories of Julie to get me through the lonely times, especially after I heard that Ross had died. When I dream, it's Julie's face I see. But my fantasies were always of walking with her along a moonlit beach, sharing candlelight dinners, making love. Never once did I really try to project what it would be like with her in my day-to-day life or me in hers. Coming back here makes me realize that. Julie and I—we're worlds apart. We always were, I guess. Maybe I'm finally old enough and wise enough to figure it out."

Betty Jean touched his arm. "Maybe what you say is true, but as long as you're here, at least go dance with her. Tell her she's beautiful. Tell her you dream about her. A girl needs to hear those things from the first man she ever loved."

"You forget. Ross came first."

"In high school? She didn't love Ross then. She felt something for you that she never felt for Ross."

"She married Ross."

"Yeah, but what did you expect?" Betty Jean asked indignantly. "When you wanted her to drop out of college, join the Peace Corps and go with you to the Philippines, she got scared. Girls like Julie and me were raised to want things. A beautiful home. Designer clothes. Junior League. Social standing. Children who take music lessons and play Little League ball. A standing appointment at the beauty shop. A safe, careful life with no surprises. The joke was on us, though. Ross and Mitch died. We have to fix our own hair. If we wear anything designer, it comes secondhand off the racks of the consignment shop. But anyway, when you started wanting something other than the careful life for Julie, her parents panicked. Lord, they were scared to death you'd take their only child off to live ten thousand miles from here. Her daddy especially. His pampered little girl off with *natives* half a world away!"

"But I backed down," Chad insisted. "I told them I'd stay in school. I told them I'd do anything they wanted. I'd even change my major to business. But they didn't think I was good enough for her. My mother took in ironing and foster kids. My dad had split. I was poor. But I didn't blame them. I didn't blame Ross. But I did blame Julie. You can't imagine how it hurt."

"You expected too much of a spoiled little rich girl. Way too much. You always made it so hard for her. Refusing to rent a tux for the prom and making her feel different. Refusing to have anything to do with all the parties and social life at college. Insisting on taking her around in that old car of yours instead of her pretty new one. Oh, I know you didn't have any money, but then you refused to let her daddy help you out. Then, just because you got hurt and couldn't be the basketball hero anymore, you came up with the ultimate test of her love, insisting that she turn her back on her parents and the only life she'd ever known and go someplace so far away that you'd have her all to yourself. I couldn't believe you'd even suggest that Julie Harper, homecoming queen, go off and live in a shack with outdoor plumbing. You were an idiot, Chad Morgan, and a selfish one. You got just what you deserved!"

BETTY JEAN STAYED by Chad's side while they mingled. The word about him had spread. Everyone wanted to come up and shake his hand, visit a bit. He was a cu-

riosity. Windmills in Nicaragua. What seemed normal
to him seemed insane to others. He wished he'd never
mentioned the windmills. Part of his job was educational—updating breeding practices, discouraging
overgrazing of pasturage, encouraging farmers to try
new feed crops for their herds. And he had administra-
tive duties, looking after One World's widely scattered
activities in Nicaragua. He could have called himself an
administrator, but that would have been misleading,
and he'd always prided himself on being honest. To say
he was an administrator would conjure up images of
offices and secretaries. All he did was drive around
every couple of weeks, checking on people, delivering
their modest pay envelopes along with whatever supplies he'd been able to obtain, and offer encouragement. Although gasoline was in short supply, it was
usually necessary to contact his people in person. The
phones were undependable, the national mail service a
disaster. Sometimes he used an electronic mail service
that a friend of his had started. The friend was French.
Michel. Another "useful fool." Michel's service de-
pended on the telephones, but the computers were pro-
grammed to start dialing at two o'clock in the morning
when there might be a free line. And the computer
didn't mind dialing three dozen or more times until a
line became available. Then the next morning there
would be a message waiting on a computer in another
city.

One World was a haphazard organization at best.
People drifted in and helped out in whatever way they
could for as long as they wanted to. Worldwide, the organization was known to be apolitical. It made no
judgment about political situations; it simply tried to
help get people back on their feet after wars or earth-

quakes or famine. After a year or two in Nicaragua, Chad's people usually went back home, wherever that might be. Burn out was common. The little war-torn country was frustrating. Teachers got frustrated with no books, no paper, no pencils. The health-care folks couldn't get medicine. Agricultural consultants couldn't get fertilizer, or pipes for irrigation, and couldn't change generations of poor practices. Consumer goods were often impossible to obtain, unless one was willing to pay black-market prices. One nurse finally gave up when she couldn't find any mousetraps. Her mother would mail her packages with mousetraps, makeup, spices, candy and other sorely missed items, but the packages would never arrive. When the nurse finally found some traps through black-market contacts in Managua, they were stolen out of her house along with her television, her clothes and her kitchen sink. Everything was stolen in Nicaragua. Thievery was the only industry that was thriving. The nurse came to him in tears. "I can put up with bugs. I can put up with no hot water, Hershey bars and all the rest. But mice, Chad! That's the last straw. I just can't live with mice."

The only amenities in Nicaragua were a slower lifestyle, a kindly climate, the most beautiful beaches in the world and a higher percentage of gentle, friendly people than most parts of the world could offer—people who'd decided to enjoy life no matter what. As for the thievery, Chad supposed he'd steal, too, if it meant the difference in feeding his family or not. But that was too much to explain with party small talk. So he stopped trying. Let them think he was an Albert Schweitzer clone if it made them happy.

Eventually he made his way back to Julie and her fiancé. Betty Jean made it easy for him. She commandeered Kevin into dancing with her. And finally, after so many years, he was dancing once again with Julie, his first love, the woman to whom he'd compared all others.

It was difficult not to pull her close like he used to, difficult not to close his eyes, but propriety demanded that he hold her lightly. He was aware of Kevin watching around Betty Jean's cowboy hat. He wondered if he would dislike the man even if he wasn't engaged to Julie and decided that he would.

He put his cheek against Julie's sweet-smelling hair. His arm was around her slim waist. Her dress was low cut enough that the tips of his fingers could stray up to bare skin. Amazing how tantalizing that was—just fingertips on skin—*her* skin. He allowed them to caress, just a bit.

Then he pulled away to see her face. "Remember how we used to dance?"

She smiled. "Oh, yes. I remember well. The slow dances. They never played enough slow dances. I'm not sure how decent we were by the end of the evening, but it felt mighty fine."

"By the time we got to the car, I thought I'd die if I didn't kiss you right that instant."

"We did steam up a few car windows."

Chad laughed. "I'd forgotten about that."

"How long have you had the beard?"

"A few years. Razor blades are sometimes in short supply, and I kept cutting myself with one of those old-fashioned straightedges. I guess I should have had a shave before I showed up this morning. Beards are obviously not in. They all think I'm strange enough the way it is."

"It makes you look older."

"I am older. Look, Julie, the music will stop playing in a minute, and I'll have to relinquish you. I doubt if your... if McLaughlin would think kindly if I danced with you a second time, and this isn't good enough— one dance with that man glaring at me. I'd like to see you, talk to you. This morning was nice, but I was so nervous. I want to know how you are, *really* are. I want at least to hold your hand and touch your hair. I want..."

She shook her head for him to stop. "Lunch. In a public place. I don't trust either one of us alone."

"You're pretty committed to that Kevin guy?"

"Yeah. Pretty committed. But that doesn't mean I don't want to have lunch with you."

"With the boy you *dated* your senior year."

"Sorry about that. Kevin is the jealous type. How long are you staying?"

"Just a few days."

"Sunday, then. At Ouise's on Sunset. Noon."

"And tomorrow evening. After the banquet. Will there be dancing?"

"Yes, there will be an orchestra."

"Will the place be as well lighted as Jody's back-yard?"

"No, I don't think so."

"And when I dance with you, can I hold you close?"

She frowned and glanced over her shoulder. Betty Jean was still dancing with Kevin. "Oh, Chad, this is so damned hard. If the reunion had been last year, I would have dragged you out of here by your beard and found some car windows to steam. But now, promises have been made. I'm very obligated."

"Betty Jean told me. He bought your kids cars."

"And will pay their tuition. Make it possible for them to have nice clothes, to enjoy college."

"You're marrying him for your kids?"

"No. I'm marrying him for me. He's a good man, and I really care for him. And I'm tired of debts, of being afraid every time I pick up the phone that it will be someone reminding me of an overdue bill, or someone from the savings and loan saying to catch up on my mortgage or lose the house. My dad has helped out a lot, but he and Mother are overextended, too. I'm still paying for my kids' orthodontia. For Sherry's prom dress. For the dog's final illness. For the last plumbing disaster. For the new washing machine I had to buy when the last one quit.

"I feel like I'm sinking in quicksand, and here comes this nice man who falls in love with me and treats me like a princess. And it isn't one-sided, either. I've dated a lot of men, and Kevin is the first one I've been attracted to. Now, maybe that's not the once-in-a-lifetime stuff you read about in romantic novels, but when a woman is looking at her thirty-eighth birthday and is lonely and worried, it's pretty damned nice."

"Well said," Chad admitted, a heaviness falling over him. No, life wasn't like they wrote about it in books. If he were a book hero, he would be brash enough, or clever enough, or rich enough to make things turn out right. "I guess I understand," he said. "And lunch isn't necessary."

"No. I *want* to have lunch with you. I just don't want it to cause problems. Now, shut up and dance me over into the shadows by the hedge and hold me close for a minute."

He did as he was instructed. To the waning notes of the musical set, they stood swaying in the shadows, their bodies touching, his hands stroking the skin on her back. Soft skin. Smooth. Like the skin on the rest of her. On her thighs. On her breasts.

He could feel the swell of her breasts pushing against his chest. Her arms came around his neck. Still their bodies swayed. Vaguely he was aware that the music had stopped.

"Oh, Julie, baby," he murmured. "I'll never get over you."

And then he was kissing her—*really* kissing her. Deeply. "Soul kissing" they used to call it. Yes, he could feel it all the way to his soul.

SLEEP WAS IMPOSSIBLE. Chad got up and paced about his hotel room. He was still in love with her, damn it. Or in love with the dream of her, which felt like the same thing.

He tried reading a magazine. Finally a 1930's vintage movie on late-night television bored him into sleep.

But he was wide awake by five. The sun wasn't even up. He was so used to five o'clock sunrises that he found it somewhat amazing that the city outside his window was still clothed in darkness.

Finally, at seven, he dialed the number Betty Jean had given him. "Hey, it's seven o'clock in the morning," her sleepy voice said.

"I'm sorry," Chad apologized. "I guess I woke you up. I'm used to going to work at seven."

"Well, shift gears, sugar. At seven o'clock on Saturday morning in Houston, most people are still asleep."

"But I thought we were going shopping. Remember, the sport coat."

"Yeah, I remember. But the stores don't even open until ten. This is *civilization*. Why don't you just go back to sleep for a couple of hours? I'll come by for you 'round ten or so. The Holiday Inn on Katy Freeway. Right?"

"Yeah. Not for three hours?"

"You can't sleep, huh?"

"Something like that."

"How about in two hours, and we can have breakfast. That's the best I can do. It's against my religion to get up at this hour on a Saturday."

Chad got up and walked. For a couple of miles. He was standing in front of a barber shop in a strip shopping center when it opened at eight. Time for the beard to go.

He was waiting in the lobby when Betty Jean arrived. He had asked her to go shopping with him for a coat and tie. He didn't know what he'd do with them afterward, but he wanted to look like the others tonight. Beardless. Conservative haircut. Necktie. Proper. He supposed it was Betty Jean's remark about his refusing to rent a tux for the senior prom that propelled him into such drastic action. Of course, he hadn't had the money to rent a tux, and his pride wouldn't let Julie pick up the tab. But maybe he should have. Maybe he should have tried harder to fit into her world.

Betty Jean surveyed his beardless face. "I would have left your hair a little longer, but you look ten years younger without the beard. And I prefer clean-shaven. I don't know how Julie feels about it, but I always found it distracting to kiss a man with a beard."

"Who said Julie's going to kiss me?"

"It wasn't *that* dark over by the hedge. I had to take the lead out there on the dance floor to keep ol' Kevin's back to the action, and that man is not accustomed to a woman taking charge. It did look like a very nice kiss, however.''

"It was," Chad sighed. "Very nice."

After breakfast Betty Jean drove to the Galleria. The excesses of the huge multilevel shopping center stunned him. And Houston's economy was supposed to be in a slump. Someone must be buying all this stuff overflowing in store after store. Every Italian designer in the world seemed to have a boutique in the center, as did the best department stores: Bloomingdale's, Saks, Neiman's. Incredible. Simply incredible. Nicaragua's capital city, Managua, had a shopping center of sorts where one could buy clothing. The goods were utilitarian. Such expensive finery would seem inappropriate on most occasions in Managua, even if people could afford it.

Betty Jean led him into Bloomingdale's. When Chad saw the prices of even a modest sport coat, he blanched. They tried another store, then stopped for coffee at one of the many restaurants encircling the skating rink on the Galleria's lower level. The arched glass roof soaring four stories overhead was inspired by an architectural masterpiece in Milan, Italy, Betty Jean informed him. "I used to go with an architect," she explained. "Dating can be educational, but usually it's a real strain. I'm ready to give it up and settle down. You date much?"

Chad shook his head no. He didn't date. He didn't dress up. He worked with his hands. "Maybe this shopping trip isn't such a good idea," he said.

"Sugar, I doubt if they'll let you in the party tonight without a coat and tie. We're talking about a real snobby place. Jody made the arrangements, of course.

I thought we should use the high school gym and decorate it like prom night, but Jody wouldn't hear of it. We did talk her out of black tie, however. But I didn't realize how much a nice sport coat would cost. Look, minus a paunch, you're about the same size as my boyfriend. Why don't we just borrow a sport coat and tie from him?''

"You sure he wouldn't mind?" Chad asked.

"I'll get it while he's watching the baseball game this afternoon. He'll never notice. An earthquake couldn't shake him away from the front of a television set when the Astros are playing. I hope you don't mind a Western cut. I will try to find a necktie without little University of Texas longhorns all over it."

Chad decided to skip Saturday afternoon's family picnic. As he stretched out on his bed watching the same baseball game as Betty Jean's boyfriend, he considered not going to the banquet. But he wasn't that strong. He'd get to dance with Julie again. Tomorrow he would have lunch with her. And he was sure they'd kiss again. Maybe do even more than that. Then it'd be over, but he would have played the scene to the end. He was too much of a romantic not to. He'd go back home sadder but wiser.

And probably never see her again. Chad stared at the ceiling, tuning out the mindless dialogue of the baseball commentators. He'd lost track of American baseball. The teams he followed now had Nicaraguan names.

Never see her again. But what else was he supposed to do? Even if he moved to Houston, the best he could hope for was a low-level managerial job. He wouldn't make enough to pay her mortgage and send her kids to college. Mr. Diamond Rolex had bought her kids *cars*. New ones.

And he couldn't ask her to live in Nicaragua. Julie might have fallen on hard times, but by Nicaraguan standards he was certain that she lived like a queen. He thought of his house in San Juan del Sur. It had a spectacular view of San Juan Bay, but it was small and shabby by American standards, by Julie's father's standards.

Chad wished he was there now. He wished he hadn't come to Houston to reopen old wounds.

For no matter how fondly he remembered their time together, he and Julie hardly knew each other anymore. They were different people from the high school sweethearts who were so certain they would love forever, who refused to believe that the problems standing in the way of happily-ever-after were of any consequence.

After twenty years, the difference between them had accentuated. All that existed between them now were warm memories of an idyllic time in their lives.

Chapter Three

The restaurant was out of the way in a transitional area of the city where half the houses had been turned into antique shops or funky little restaurants. Ouise's was the sort of restaurant that had apparently opted for minimal decor and based its reputation solely on fine cuisine. But Julie hadn't chosen the restaurant for its food. It was across town from her usual haunts, and she wasn't likely to run into someone she knew here.

By the time she got to the restaurant, Julie was a nervous wreck. She hadn't been able to sleep last night but had overslept this morning. She'd had a terrible time deciding what to wear and hated the way her hair looked. She had forgotten to eat breakfast and had developed a terrible headache that a cup of coffee and two aspirins had not cured, which made her too trembly to do a good job with her eyeliner. Two lanes had been closed on the freeway, and the midday Sunday traffic was worse than usual.

She was too rattled to get her car into a parking slot that normally would have been a breeze. Finally she gave up and found another parking place a block away. And, of course, walking back to the restaurant, the breeze unsettled her already unsatisfactory hair.

Chad wasn't there yet, and Julie ducked into the ladies' room to assess the damage to her hair.

She stared at her flushed face in the dimly lit mirror of the restroom. *Julie, girl, we've got a real problem here. Either you've got a monumental case of guilty conscience from sneaking around like this to meet a man, or you're not as in love with Kevin McLaughlin as you'd like to believe.*

She smoothed her hair and patted some concealer on the bump that had chosen this morning of all mornings to erupt on her chin. Women her age weren't supposed to get pimples.

But, then, women her age were not supposed to be behaving like an adolescent airhead.

Adolescent. That's how she felt. As if she was eighteen again.

She closed her eyes, mixing memories of twenty years ago with last night.

When she was with Chad, she felt special. Alive. It had always been that way.

Last night they'd had just one dance, but, oh, lordy, how it made her feel!

When she got home she'd danced around her bedroom with a pillow for a partner, humming the tune of "I Want to Hold Your Hand." Chad had wanted her, *really* wanted her. Their dancing was more than dancing. It was messages being passed all up and down their bodies.

Julie hugged the pillow tighter and twirled around the bed. Then she saw Sherry standing at the bedroom door with a very knowing grin on her pretty face. "You and Kevin had a nice evening, I take it."

Julie blushed, and Sherry grinned even more broadly. "I've always said that cool, sophisticated-looking guys were the ones you had to look out for. You looked like Cinderella coming home from the ball.''

Julie hastily tossed the pillow on the bed. ''It was a nice evening,'' she said, busying herself with the catch on her dress. ''It was fun seeing all the old gang again. And the band played a lot of Beatles songs. Real nostalgia time. And during the banquet, there was a memorial service for your dad and Betty Jean's husband. They had slides made from old snapshots. One was of your dad in his Mustang convertible and one of Mitch in his Air Force uniform waving from a cockpit. And they even had an old home movie of Mitch and your dad and some other boys all dressed up like chorus girls attempting to do high kicks. Everybody laughed and cried a lot.''

''I'll bet Dad would have been the handsomest man there,'' Sherry said, flopping onto the bed.

''Without a doubt,'' Julie said, looking at her dead husband's picture in its silver frame on her dresser. Yes. Ross had been handsome. Always gregarious, he would have had a terrific time tonight. Of course, he probably would have had too much to drink, and she would have had to insist on driving home. How many fights did they have over that little problem? But maybe he would have gotten over his dependency by now. He'd gotten to the point where he was at least talking about the need to cut back and didn't get quite so irritated when she suggested he'd had enough.

''Hey, guess what!'' Julie said picking up a ribbon from the dresser. ''Your old mom won an award.'' Julie held up the blue ribbon printed with the words Sexy Bod. ''I got the award for the girl who'd done the best job of keeping her girlish figure.''

"All right!" Sherry said, clapping her hands. "Wait till I tell Steve. Living at the poverty level has had its good side, after all. Who else won awards?"

Julie joined her daughter on the bed and allowed herself a motherly caress of her daughter's wonderful blond hair. Ross's hair. And Sherry had Ross's eyes, Ross's smile. Steve, with his dark hair and green eyes, looked more like his mother, but not as much as Sherry looked like her daddy.

They leaned against the headboard, a customary place for mother-daughter visits. "Well, Betty Jean was voted the cutest," Julie answered. "Jody Zachery, of course, got the Best Dressed Woman award. Betty Jean thought she should have been voted the richest bitch, then she felt terrible when she found out it had been Jody's idea to have the memorial for your dad and Mitch. Troy Busby was the man who looked the most like he did in high school. I don't think you know any of the others. They gave an award for the man with the least hair. They recognized the person with the most kids—eight. And the most marriages—four. And the person who had come the farthest."

"Who was that?"

"A man who came from Nicaragua," Julie said, keeping her voice a careful neutral. "Now, tell me about your evening. Steve said you went to the rush party after all. How come? I thought we'd decided it was best to forgo the rush scene."

"Yeah. Please don't be mad. I know you'd rather I didn't get my heart set on pledging a sorority but Mom, *all* my friends were going to the party, and they all are going through rush this fall. Sorority life sounds like *so* much fun. Don't you think Kevin would pay for it?"

"Kevin and I are not married. We haven't even set a date. You know that. And he's already bought you kids cars. I really don't think we can expect him to start supporting this family when he's not even part of it."

"Well, why don't you two get married? After all, you're engaged. Grandma and I could help you plan something before school starts. That'd be fun, and then he'd be my stepdad by fall..."

"Sherry Ann Rhoades, *I am not* marrying Kevin for his money. I'm very uncomfortable with this notion you two seem to have that he's some sort of sugar daddy who's going to support us all in the old style."

"Well, wouldn't he? After all, he's rich enough. And he'd expect any wife of his to present a certain image. And I doubt if he'd expect her children to wait tables at college."

"Waiting tables would be character building," Julie insisted.

"Well, you've got a good character, and you didn't work at college," Sherry challenged. "Neither did Daddy. And besides, I've had my character built enough with all that baby-sitting. Do you have any idea how many hours of baby-sitting it takes to pay for one pair of Calvin Klein jeans?"

"Yes, dear. I'm well aware. I'm very proud of the way you kids have covered some of your own expenses." She started to add that at least Sherry got to spend the money she earned on new clothes, whereas her mother hadn't had a new outfit in years. But what would be the point? When she was Sherry's age, she never worked, never wanted for anything.

"Come on, Mom," Sherry said, scooting around on her knees so she could face her mother. "If you're going to marry Kevin anyway, why not go ahead and set a date? I heard you talking on the phone to that man at the bank about the mortgage payments. It sounds like you've got to do something pretty soon, or we'll be out on the street.''

''I'm well aware of my financial situation, young lady. But if you will just think very carefully about my position, surely you will see that I must be absolutely certain in my own mind that I am *not* marrying Kevin because of it. It would not be fair to him or to me.''

''What about what's fair to your kids?'' Sherry demanded. ''Women marry for security all the time. I read an article in the Sunday paper that said it's the number-one reason most women get and stay married—especially second marriages. I don't see that it would be so bad to marry a real nice man like Kevin *and* solve some of your problems in the process. It's not like you would be marrying some old creep. Kevin's real dreamy.''

''And when you get married, is that what you want your number-one reason to be? *Security?*''

''Well, it's different when you're young,'' Sherry insisted with a thrust of her chin. ''Like you and Daddy. That sort of falling in love probably only happens once to most people. After that, a woman usually has kids and responsibility and needs to be more practical. And besides, when I was watching you in the doorway, dancing around the room like that, you didn't look like a woman who was thinking about mortgage payments. You'd looked young and pretty—like maybe you were in love.''

Julie suddenly felt very tired. *In love.* Perhaps. But with whom?

She reached for her daughter's hand. ''I want you to go to bed now and think about what you have just said.

I love you very much, honey, but when you talk about me getting married so that you can join a sorority, I don't like you very much."

Sherry looked crestfallen. Wordlessly she slid from the bed and started for the bedroom door.

"But I still like you enough to need a hug," Julie said.

Sherry stopped in the doorway.

"Please," Julie said, holding out her arms.

Sherry obliged. "I'm sorry if I seem like a selfish brat," she said, her voice muffled in Julie's neck. "But it's hard not to want things."

"I know, honey. And it's hard for me too, to want things for you. And maybe you're right. Maybe it wouldn't be so bad to marry Kevin." She kissed her daughter's smooth head. "Okay, you're dismissed now. Make sure the front door's locked."

Julie closed her eyes, the euphoria completely gone. *Ross Rhoades, it's all your fault. Why'd you have to go and fall off that damned mountain?*

Or was it Chad's fault for pushing too hard for an answer nineteen years ago?

Or was it her own fault for letting Ross and her parents bully her into a marriage when all she wanted to do was not do anything. At least not then. She didn't want to marry, didn't want to commit to either man. If she had waited another year or two, she might have known herself better, known what was better for her. Nineteen is awfully young to be making decisions that alter the rest of one's life.

But her parents were so afraid Chad would spirit her away with him, and maybe their fear was justifiable. When she was around Chad, she would feel herself wavering. Maybe the Peace Corps wouldn't have been so bad. Then suddenly a wedding was being planned around her. Invitations being mailed. A dress being fitted. Julie felt like she was floating around in a dream, that she'd wake up soon and start over.

Chad showed up uninvited at the rehearsal dinner and demanded to have some time alone with Julie. Then he and Ross got into a fight. Her dad called the police. Her mother and Ross's mother got hysterical. It was awful. Absolutely awful. She had to beg her father not to file charges. What she should have done was put an end to the whole proceedings then and there—even at that late hour. What was the damned hurry? Everyone seemed to think that because Ross was going to Harvard for a year to get his M.B.A. that marriage was mandatory, but it could have waited a few years. She should have stayed in school and finished her degree. If she had a degree, she wouldn't now be working for slave wages at a bank. Of course, she had told herself at the time that she would finish her degree at the University of Houston when she and Ross came back from Boston. But a year later she was the mother of twins. And after that, finishing her education never seemed to matter. Ross was successful. She had had everything a woman could ever want.

Oddly enough, when sleep finally came, Julie had dreamed of a windmill, a lonely broken windmill out in a field, waiting for someone to come along and mend it. The water trough at its base was bone-dry, and she was in desperate need of a drink.

A drink of water was the first thing she'd thought of when she woke up. And it was almost nine o'clock. Damn! She should have set the alarm. She had promised herself a couple of hours working in the yard before she got ready for her luncheon date with Chad.

Weekend hours were the only time for so many things. She never appreciated how good she'd had it when her only job was that of homemaker.

By the time she'd made the traditional Sunday morning waffles for the kids, ironed the blouse she'd planned to wear, washed her hair, it was time to get dressed.

She hadn't liked the blouse. She'd ironed a cotton dress.

She had agonized over whether to wear hose and heels or sandals without hose. She'd opted for the sandals. But that had meant a hurried pedicure.

And now here she was in the ladies' room at the appointed restaurant, feeling ill, confused and hating her hair. Julie took one last look in the tiny mirror, took a deep breath and opened the door. Chad was waiting. Julie's heart jumped in her chest.

He was wearing another one of those Nicaraguan shirts. A dark blue one, like his eyes. His arms were tanned and sinewy, their hair bleached golden from the sun. She liked him better without a beard. He looked more like the boy she remembered.

If she hadn't been with Kevin last night, she would have gone back to Chad's hotel with him. She'd felt that weak. Wanted him that much.

"You're beautiful," he said, his lips brushing her cheek.

"So are you," she said, taking his hand.

The hostess led them to a corner table. When she was out of earshot, Chad asked, "Remember what I used to say about your lips?"

Julie laughed. "How could I forget you saying that I had the most kissable lips in the world?"

"It's true. And I've been all over the world now. I'm more of an authority. It made me crazy last night to be with you, to touch you, to want to keep on kissing you forever. Are you in love with Kevin McLaughlin?"

"We went through all this before."

"No, we didn't," he said, leaning across the table, his expression intense. "Not really. Just answer a simple question. If the answer is yes, I'll go back home with a clear heart."

"It's not simple."

"Yes, it is," he insisted. "Do you love him? And don't give me any of that 'care about him deeply' stuff."

Julie willed the tears not to come. "Damn you, Chad Morgan. You always made things so hard for me. You think everything is black and white, that you either love someone or you don't. Well, it isn't that easy. Everything gets all mixed up. Betty Jean said you told her how much you love your life in Nicaragua. Well, before Ross died and I ended up poor, I used to love my life here in Houston. I realize that by your lofty standards my lifestyle would have seemed very frivolous. I volunteered for several charities, but I didn't dedicate my entire life to doing good. I liked pretty clothes, and I liked being able to afford things for my children, to take wonderful vacations. My house was beautiful, my yard a joy. I enjoyed shopping with my mother, having lunch with my friends, going to parties and talking on the phone. While Ross was alive, I lived an almost perfect life. The only thing the matter with it was Ross himself. He had problems he hadn't dealt with yet, and I probably added to them. But anyway, it all ended rather abruptly with his death and bankruptcy of the company. It's been hard for me and hard for the kids. *Really* hard. And for my parents, Daddy, especially. He's wanted so desperately to bail me out but is struggling to keep himself and Mother afloat. So, my feelings for Kevin are not black and white. And that's hard enough for me to deal with without you coming along to muddy the water.''

"Does that mean you do or do not love him?"

Julie let out an exasperated sigh. "I love his courtliness, his generosity, his style. If you want me to say that I love you, that I've never loved anyone the way I loved you, then consider it said. But it doesn't change anything."

The waitress interrupted to ask if they were ready to order. They waved her away.

"Come back to Nicaragua with me," he said, leaning across the table to take her hand. His hands were rough, like a common laborer. Strong hands. Achingly beautiful. She wanted to kiss them.

"Come for a week," he said, his look so earnest. "For a month. For the rest of your life. Just come and see. I want you to know my life. I want you to see the view from my house. I want to show you the windmills. I want to walk with you on the beach and make love to you all night long."

"I thought you said I'd hate it there."

It was his turn to sigh. "Yeah, you probably would. But I have such a *need* to have you there. I can't function here in this world. I'd forgotten about traffic and noise and pollution. The windows at the hotel don't open. I feel like I'm suffocating without fresh air. And all you can hear at night are air conditioners. Yet, I know in Nicaragua, the damned roosters would keep you awake. We've got very talkative roosters who don't wait until dawn to do their crowing. But I miss them. I miss the sound of the waves. I'm an alien here."

"And I'd be an alien there."

"Yes. I know. Look, I'm not talking about anything except a trip. A vacation, if you will. Two old sweethearts taking time out for a romantic interlude. Just some time to sort all this out."

"You know I can't. I've got my job. My kids. Kevin. My parents. I'm caught in a web of responsibility."

"It's like before," he said, sitting back in his chair, folding his arms across his chest.

"Now look here, don't you put that guilt trip on me. You asked the impossible of me before. Now you're doing it again. Why don't you ask me something possible, like going to your hotel with you? That I might do. But I can't go chasing windmills in Nicaragua."

"I thought of that—asking you to make love at the Holiday Inn. But you'd have to lie to your kids and Kevin about where you were. You'd have to park your car in back so no one would see it from the street and recognize it. I can't make love to you on those terms, Julie. I love you too much. Does that make any sense?"

"All the sense in the world." She was crying now, tears spilling over onto the makeup she'd applied with such care. The waitress had started for the table a second time but discreetly backed away.

"Order me something," Julie said, retreating once again to the ladies' room. She repaired her makeup as best she could in the dim light.

It is all right, she told herself. He was leaving in the morning. Things would get back to normal, whatever that was. It was for the best. Maybe in another twenty years they could try again.

But that thought made her feel worse, and the tears welled up again. She looked at her reflection. *Okay, so what is it that you want? You can't straighten out your life* and *chase a dream. Which will it be?*

"Would you like to hear about my kids?" she asked as she reseated herself.

Chad nodded. He understood. It was time for safe topics.

Chad had ordered pasta salad for her, a Cajun shrimp stew for himself. Julie ate only because she knew she'd feel worse if she didn't. She supposed the salad was good, but she seemed to have lost her ability to taste. In between bites she told Chad about her children, more than he probably wanted to hear. But it calmed her to talk about Sherry and Steve. Her children had been the best part of her life. She told him so.

"Haven't you ever wanted to have children?" she asked.

"Sure. My wife and I tried. But I found out that I was sterile. I was devastated at first. We talked about adopting, but she wasn't sure. Finally we split up, and with each passing year, I worry less and less about having children. I take in foster kids from time to time, like my mother used to do. In my case, it's usually orphans with relatives who've emigrated to the U.S. or to some other Latin American country. The kids are waiting for the relatives to make arrangements to get them out. They come and go. I get attached, but when they leave, I'm happy for them."

"Isn't there any part of your life you live just for yourself?" Julie asked. "I feel like I'm in the presence of a saint."

"Did you feel like I was a saint when I was dancing with you last night?"

"Hardly. But you know what I mean. Almost every facet of your life seems to deal with the welfare of others. Don't you do anything for yourself?"

"I guess I do it all for myself. I'm the most selfish person I know. Everything I do makes me feel good. What could be more selfish than that?"

"A selfish saint," Julie said with a shrug.

"Are you a saint because you've been good to your kids?"

"Of course not. I'm good to them because I'm their mother, because I want to be."

"Well, One World tries to be a mother to people who need someone to be good to them. And I get paid for it. Not a lot, but I get by."

"I stand corrected, *Mother* Chad."

Julie pushed her half-eaten salad away. Chad continued eating for a time. Then they ordered coffee.

"What happened to your marriage?" Julie asked.

"She got tired of being poor and childless. We just kind of drifted apart. Every time she'd go to see her folks, she'd take a little longer to come back. And one day, she didn't."

"So you miss her?"

"Sure. Just like I'm sure you miss Ross. She was a part of my life."

The waitress refilled their cups. But finally there was no reason to stay any longer. The lunchtime customers had all left except for the two of them and one other couple.

He walked her to her car. And then it was time to say good-bye.

"What do you want me to say?" he asked.

"Nothing. Just kiss me."

"This is it, then?"

"I think so."

"Think?" he asked, his face hopeful. "But you're not absolutely sure?"

"No, I'm absolutely sure. Our time has passed, Chad. Maybe it never was."

Their kiss was mingled with tears. His and hers. Julie thought her heart would break.

"I love you," she whispered, clinging to him. "I guess I always have."

Chapter Four

"What do you think of dating services?" Betty Jean asked, moving her chair more deeply into the shade of Julie's covered patio.

"I don't think anything about them," Julie said, sitting back on her haunches in front of the bed she was weeding, and wiping the sweat from her brow. Weeds. She used to pay a man to pull them. More recently, she would coerce her kids into helping her. But they seemed to think that working at their summer jobs during the week gave them immunity from domestic chores on the weekends. Actually both Steve and Sherry had promised to help, but they and several friends left early this morning for an impromptu trip to the beach at Galveston. And tomorrow Julie was certain there would be some other *extremely* important reason for them to put off helping. To their way of thinking, the weeds would wait. Fun was more important. Julie vacillated between thinking her children were entitled to being young and carefree and resenting the disproportionate share of domestic chores that fell on her shoulders. She'd like some weekend leisure time herself.

Betty Jean had dropped by to keep Julie company and had even pulled weeds for a while. But she hated being in the sun. "It gives me freckles and wrinkles," she complained, heading for the shade and leaving Julie to her chore. Julie hoped the number thirty sunscreen she had applied would protect her own skin. How times did change. She and Betty Jean used to glory in deep tans; now they worried about premature aging.

"Would you ever date through a dating service?" Betty Jean persisted, adjusting the lawn chair so the lower half of her shorts-clad legs was in the sun.

"I've never thought about it," Julie said, tugging at a mystery weed that she hoped wasn't poison ivy.

"What if Kevin hadn't come along, and you were discouraged with the dating scene, and the service seemed very respectable, would you join up? Of course, you probably wouldn't need to. You've got long legs and sleek hair and always look so together, not short, frazzled and rounding like yours truly."

Julie laughed. "I've always wished I was shorter and had curly hair. As for being 'together,' you must be remembering the way I used to look before my wardrobe got dated and my pocketbook empty. But about joining a dating service, I suppose I'd consider it if I wanted to date and didn't have the opportunity to meet single men. Obviously *you've* been considering it. How come? Have you given up on Bobby?"

"Yeah, I blew up when we missed half the Diana Ross concert because he had to finish watching a sudden-death playoff on TV—after I'd gotten up at dawn and stood in line for hours to get those tickets. He knows she's my favorite. Lordy, I have tapes of every song the woman's ever sung. And I was still irritated about having to go alone to the reunion. You can't imagine how much I wanted him to go. I didn't want to be 'poor old Betty Jean,' the only woman there all by herself. He claimed he hadn't gone to his *own* high school reunion and had no intention of going to anyone else's, that he considered high school reunions to be narcissistic pranks perpetrated by the people who still looked good on those who didn't."

"Or perpetrated by silly women who want to see the old boyfriend again," Julie said.

"Whatever," Betty Jean said with an irritated shake of her head. "But just once in a while it seems like Bobby should be willing to do something *I* want. I told him so. I also told him it would be nice if he cooked for *me* once in a while, if he'd try to remember the names of my friends, if he'd ask me once in a while how *my* day went. I told him he needs to find a woman who not only understands a double reverse better than I do but who gives a damn. My sides are black and blue from him jabbing me with his elbow and saying 'Did you see that?' I've had enough! And I will never forgive him for not going to that reunion with me. Never."

Julie got up and moved over into the shade of the patio. She pulled a lawn chair over beside Betty Jean and stuck her own white legs into the sunshine. At least it was all right to get a tan on her legs. She'd never seen a wrinkled pair yet. "I'm sorry, honey," she said, reaching over to pat Betty Jean's arm. "Breaking up is always hard, even if it's for the best."

Betty Jean had her blond hair pulled back in a curly ponytail. Wearing little makeup and one of her son's T-shirts, she looked like a teenager herself—except for the network of tiny lines radiating out from her eyes when she smiled. She wasn't smiling now, however. In fact her lips were a bit quivery.

"Yeah, it's hard," she agreed. "I'm a basket case of doubts. Sometimes Bobby was kind of sweet. He'd work on my car for me and was always telling me that I'm one fine-looking woman. I loved the way he'd come up behind me and put his arm around my waist and nuzzle my neck. And I liked going to baseball games with him. But the man made a religion out of being a sports fan. He seemed to feel it was his moral obligation as a male of the species to sit there and watch every televised sporting event—football, basketball, bowling, wrestling, soccer, pole-climbing, horseshoes, anything! But I wonder if I shouldn't have been nicer to him, if he's the best thing out there, if I didn't know a good thing when I saw it. Maybe a male presence in front of the television set is better than no male presence at all.''

''Or maybe now you'll find someone who appreciates what a terrific person you are,'' Julie soothed. ''Like the new manager at your office. Didn't you say that he seemed very nice?''

''Yeah. But it turns out he's married with *four* kids. How come men can get by without wearing a wedding ring when it would be considered improper if a woman didn't? But I've decided to be calmer about men. If I don't find someone I *really* want to be with, I think I am now wise enough not to get involved in the first place,'' Betty Jean said, fanning herself with her hand. ''But I'm still going to look.''

''No harm in looking,'' Julie agreed.

Betty Jean glanced at her watch. ''I guess I'd better go do my Saturday errands. Can I get you anything at the grocery?''

''No. I need too much. I'll go myself later. Let's go inside and have a glass of tea before you leave. I want to hear more about this dating service.''

Over a tall glass of iced tea in the air-conditioned comfort of Julie's kitchen, Betty Jean said, "It's probably a stupid idea to spend money on a dating service, but when I think how long it took me to find ol' Bobby, I wonder if my next boyfriend won't be a fellow resident of the old folks' home."

"How do the services work?" Julie asked.

"The one I'm interested in does a personality profile of their clients and a videotaped interview. You can look through the profiles, then if you're interested, you ask to see the person's video. Then if you're still interested, you can request that the person look at your video. Then if both of you are interested, the dating service arranges for you to meet for drinks or dinner at a bar or restaurant. No last names, addresses or phone numbers are given out. Then when the two of you meet, it's up to you to proceed or run in the other direction."

"It sounds better than sitting around waiting for the phone to ring."

"Yeah, I suppose," Betty Jean said halfheartedly, "or prowling around singles bars."

"Have you thought about the singles class at the church?"

"I checked. It has five women for every man, and the men are either old and decrepit or so damned spoiled from having all those women fawning over them and inviting them over for home-cooked meals all the time that they're probably ruined for life. The church secretary said that when there's a new widower in the congregation, the poor man is inundated with casseroles and offers of comfort from single women. Can you imagine! I refuse to be that desperate."

"No. I'd hate for you to start reading the obituaries in search of new widowers. But maybe you should check the Sunday School class for yourself. I remember when we thought anyone over thirty-five was old and decrepit. *And* enroll in a dating service—after you've checked on it with the Better Business Bureau to make sure it's on the up-and-up. I don't see what it could hurt."

"Of course, the men who agree to go out with me will probably be seven feet tall and have lifetime passes to the Oiler games, a big-screen TV in every room of an otherwise sparsely furnished apartment and carry one of those little pocket televisions with them every place they go."

"Specify what sort of man you're looking for in your profile. 'Overly tall sports fans need not apply.'"

Betty Jean still looked unsure. "Kevin wouldn't approve," she said without looking at Julie.

"Of what? A dating service?"

"Yeah. He'd think it was real low class."

"Kevin's not as much of a stuffed shirt as you think he is. He doesn't talk about it much, but his dad was a struggling farmer over in east Texas. It's not as if Kevin was born with a silver spoon in his mouth. But if you're concerned about what people will think, don't tell anyone. Just do it."

"I don't care if he was dirt poor or a poor little rich boy. The way he is *now* makes me uncomfortable. When I'm around him I feel like I have to sit up straight and be careful of what I say. I know he doesn't approve of me, and I worry that after you and Kevin get married, he'll figure out ways to keep us from being friends. God, Julie, I don't know what I'd do without you."

"I know," Julie said, patting her friend's hand. She felt the same way. She and Betty Jean had always been best friends since grade school, and when they were both widowed young, the friendship became even stronger. "You're the sister I never had," Julie said. "We're friends for life."

"Promise?" Betty Jean said, her eyes growing moist.

"Cross my heart," Julie insisted. "But you're wrong about Kevin. He knows how much you mean to me."

"Have you heard from Chad?"

"Chad? What does he have to do with this conversation?" Julie got up and carried her empty glass to the sink.

"He likes me. Remember the great times we had—you and Chad, Mitch and me? Those were the days," she said with a sigh. "I wish they could have gone on forever."

"Me, too," Julie said, staring out the kitchen window.

"Well, have you heard from him?" Betty Jean persisted.

Julie turned and leaned against the counter. "No. And I won't. He asked me to come visit him. But I can't do that. I doubt if I'll ever see him again, and that makes me very sad, but it's for the best. Definitely for the best."

"Why can't you go to see him?"

"I can't believe you'd ask."

"Well, I did."

"Why can't I go? Money. Kevin. The kids. My job. And I guess I should put my parents on the list. They'd freak."

"I thought you had two weeks' vacation coming at the bank."

"I do, and I plan to do something with the kids before they're off to college. Mom and Daddy still have that old camper. I thought maybe the twins and I would borrow it and go to Padre Island. Why don't you and Donnie come along? The kids would have fun together. I'm sure Melissa will come, too. Steve seems incapable of going around the block without Melissa.''

"Three or four days' camping on the beach at Padre is all any adult human being can stand,'' Betty Jean insisted. "I mean, you end up with sand in your hair, in your food, in your bed, in your *everywhere*. That leaves plenty of time for a glamorous vacation in sunny, wartorn Nicaragua. You might start a new fad.''

"Don't be ridiculous!'' Julie said. "To use one of your favorite expressions, there's no point in beating a dead horse.''

"You told me several times that you'd wished you had insisted on some time to think things through before you married Ross. Don't make the same mistake again.''

Julie picked up a sponge and briskly started wiping off the counters. She could feel her blood pressure rising. Betty Jean might be her best friend, but she sure could be irritating at times. Julie sprinkled cleanser in the sink and rubbed away, feeling Betty Jean's gaze on the back of her neck.

The black marks in the sink wouldn't budge. Storebrand cleanser never worked as good as the more expensive kind. God, she was tired of always pinching pennies.

She threw down the sponge and whirled around. "So what am I supposed to tell Kevin, that I'm going to visit an old boyfriend? That'd go over *really* big!''

"Tell him you need some time to yourself to decide what you want to do with the rest of your life,'' Betty Jean said softly. "You're entitled, sugar.''

"But if I *don't* marry Kevin, what am I going to do about the kids' tuition, books, room and board? What if I lose my house? What if my car falls apart? God, I hate this. I blew up at Sherry the other night for suggesting that I hurry up and marry Kevin so she can pledge a sorority. I told her I would never marry a man for his money and that I had to be certain that I loved Kevin enough to marry him for himself. Before that damned reunion I had no trouble with that concept. I wasn't head over heels in love with him, but I *thought* I was sincere about my feelings. I *loved* being courted by him. Kevin was exciting and in charge, and I *loved* envisioning a wonderful, worry-free life with him. Now it seems that how I feel about him doesn't really matter. I *need* to marry him. And that makes me feel about three inches tall."

Betty Jean carried her glass to the sink, then picked up the abandoned sponge to wipe off the table. "Donnie's going to the University of Houston and live at home," she said. "He's always known that I wouldn't be able to send him away to school. And lots of people lose houses. There comes a point when you're throwing good money after bad, and you'd probably be better off without this white elephant anyway."

"White elephant!" Julie said, appalled. Her beautiful house. She looked around at her big, wonderful kitchen with its white oak paneling and quarry tile floor, at the formal dining room with its elegant crystal chandelier. Real crystal, imported from France. And the living room beyond with its matching white brocade sofas, its lighted breakfront full of antique Chinese porcelain. The draperies alone for those two rooms had cost thousands of dollars. Such a beautiful house. She and Ross had enjoyed planning it, enjoyed building it.

So much of her children's growing up was done here. Their last Christmas with their father was spent here just days before he died. She was sure that Steve and Sherry expected her to stay in this house forever, for her always to be here for holiday visits with spouses and grandchildren. She loved this house, and she didn't want to think of it as a white elephant.

"I have an equity of over one hundred thousand dollars tied up in this house," she said peevishly. "My daddy says I'd be an idiot to walk away from it, that real estate values are bound to come back. This house and a small insurance annuity are all I have. And I certainly can't spare the money for a plane ticket to Central America."

"Chad said it's only a four-hour flight from Houston—including three stopovers. It couldn't cost too much."

"Well, whatever it costs is an extravagance I can't afford. Now, I want you to stop talking about Chad. He's a part of my past, not my future. I'll always remember him fondly, but I can't go off chasing a dream of lost youth."

The back door opened and Sherry, Steve and Melissa came trooping in.

"Back so soon?" Julie said. "I wasn't expecting you guys until dark."

"We got hungry," Stephen explained, "and it's hard to buy much food on three dollars and ninety-two cents, which we discovered was our combined holdings. My rich girlfriend didn't even have her checkbook."

Melissa dutifully punched his shoulder. "I didn't even know we were going to Galveston until we were halfway there," she said. "Next time, you might consider planning ahead."

Steve headed for the refrigerator and looked inside, the girls peering over his shoulder. All three had cut-offs over their bathing suits, bare feet, long brown limbs, the picture of youth and health. Sherry and Melissa, with their matching silky blond hair, looked more like twins than Sherry and Steve did. "There's nothing to eat," Steve pointed out.

"Have some peanut butter and jelly," Julie suggested.

"Ugh. I thought you got paid yesterday. How come you didn't go to the grocery?"

"I will. I had no idea you'd be home so early," Julie said defensively. "In fact, now that you're home, why don't you guys go to the store, and I'll get back to my weeds. Any help on that front would be appreciated, too."

"Why are you always so worried about the yard?" Steve asked. "When you and Kevin get married, he'll probably have the whole thing redone, maybe put in a pool."

Sherry shot her brother a warning gaze. Obviously she had not warned him that Mom was in a funk and he shouldn't push about the marriage.

"If you'll make a list, Julie," Melissa chimed in, "Steve and I would be happy to go to the grocery, *wouldn't we, Steve?*"

"And I'll help with the weeds, I guess," Sherry said unenthusiastically.

"As much as I hate to leave the charming scene of domestic bliss, I'd better be on my way," Betty Jean announced. "I'll see you guys Tuesday evening," she said. "My turn to cook. Melissa, you be sure to come, too."

"Oh, honey, I forgot to tell you," Julie said hurriedly. "Kevin has tickets to the symphony. Could we have dinner another night?"

"How come he bought tickets for Tuesday night?" Betty Jean said. "He knows our families *always* have dinner together on Tuesday."

"He's having out-of-town guests he wants me to meet, a company executive from England and his wife. We're going to tour the company's facilities down on the shipping channel in the afternoon, then go out to dinner and to the symphony in the evening."

She didn't tell Betty Jean that the British couple would be in town for several days. Kevin had selected Tuesday night for Julie to meet them, claiming he forgot it was her evening with Betty Jean.

Julie hugged her friend good-bye. "I'm sorry, honey. How about Wednesday night?"

"Donnie has a ball game," she said.

"Well, we can all go to the game. Take a picnic. Maybe Kevin would like to come."

But Kevin had other plans. Julie asked him on the way to a movie that night. She was almost relieved when he said no. The evening would be more relaxing without him. Kevin wasn't the ball game and picnic type, she decided.

After the movie they stopped for a drink at the Houston Racquet Club, which was not only where Kevin played tennis but the center of his social life. Julie wished she had dressed up more. She was the only woman in the bar with low-heeled shoes.

After they left the club, Julie realized Kevin was not driving in the direction of her house. "How come?" she asked, but he just smiled mysteriously. Shortly he pulled up in front of a new, very elegant apartment building near Bayou Bend. The Towers, a brass marker by the front door announced.

"Who lives here?" she asked, checking her lipstick in the lighted mirror on the back of the sun visor.

"A surprise," he said with a devilish grin.

They rode the elevator to the top floor, and Kevin pulled a key from his pocket and reached inside the door to turn on the lights.

"Milady," he said, gesturing for her to enter the very large, very empty penthouse apartment.

The opposite wall was floor-to-ceiling windows and revealed a breathtaking view of the wooded area along Bayou Bend and the skyscrapers of downtown Houston beyond. Kevin opened the French doors and pulled her out onto a terrace. A lighted pool gleamed several floors below them, occupying the rooftop of the middle section of the building that joined the twin towers. Several people were enjoying a late-evening swim. Others were lounging poolside, refreshment glasses in their hands. Their laughter drifted up to the penthouse terrace.

"Come see the rest," Kevin said excitedly, taking her arm.

"What is this all about?" Julie asked, pulling back. "Whose apartment is this?"

"Mine. Ours. I just signed the lease this afternoon. It will be perfect for us. An excellent address. No worries about a yard. Plenty of room for entertaining. Look at the size of this living room. And this great wet bar. There's a study. Extra bedrooms for when the children visit. And wait until you see the master bedroom. It's enormous. The master bathroom has mirrors everywhere—even on the ceiling—and a sunken bathtub fit for a queen."

"Wait a minute, Kevin. I thought we were going to live in my house."

"You *assumed* we were going to live in your house. But the more I thought about it, the more I could see how unsuitable that was. I didn't want to live in a house some other man had built for you. I wanted us to start fresh in our own place—someplace more glamorous and exciting, someplace better than where you lived before. How about it, darling? Isn't it spectacular? I've lined up one of the best interior decorators in Houston to decorate it for us. We'll have all-new everything."

Slowly Julie walked into the space-age kitchen. It didn't have any windows. "I've never lived in an apartment," she said.

Kevin came up behind her and twirled her around to face him. He reached for her hands. "These hands need never pull another weed," he said earnestly.

"But you don't understand. I *like* my yard. I just don't have enough time to keep it up. But I'd miss not having a yard. You know how proud I am of my rose garden. My pecan trees will be old enough to bear this year. I thought the yard would be something we could enjoy together. Maybe put in a fountain. Add some shrubs along the driveway. Entertain on the patio."

"I thought you'd be pleased about the apartment," Kevin said, a frown creasing his brow.

"I wish you'd consulted with me before you decided I should give up my house—my home. And just what am I supposed to do with it?"

"We can probably rent it until the real estate market turns around, then we'll sell it. Hell, you can give it away if you want to. I can't believe your attitude—that you'd hesitate an instant over giving up that house for this," he said with a sweep of his hand. "This is the sort of place I'd always dreamed of living in, the sort of place that says a man has arrived.''

Julie put her hand on the kitchen counter for support. She was stunned. And Kevin was angry. But she couldn't bring herself to say she was sorry she'd disappointed him. Maybe he was right. Maybe it would be better to start fresh in a place of their own. But an *apartment*. Of course, it was the penthouse. And beautiful. Silk-covered walls. Marble fireplace. The plushest carpet she'd ever walked on. If only he had talked it over with her first. He'd already signed a lease!

Kevin was staring at her, his expression stern. ''I can't pretend I'm not disappointed at your reaction. Nor do I understand it. I've waited a long time to get my life to the place where I could have the kind of marriage and the kind of life-style I wanted. Then I waited for the right woman. I fell in love with you because you're sweet and lovely, yet mature enough to have a sense of style and an appreciation of the finer things in life. And your children are old enough not to be a part of your daily life. That was important, because *I* want to be the center of your life.

''My first marriage failed—at least in part—because I was too preoccupied with struggling for success and power. But now I'm at the pinnacle of my career. I don't have to struggle anymore, and I want a soft, lovely woman at my side to enjoy the good life with me. I will design a wonderful marriage for us—one full of travel and fascinating friends. I need a wife, my darling, who has her priorities straight. And surely digging in a garden isn't as important as living in an elegant penthouse.''

''By soft, you mean pliable, don't you?'' Julie asked. ''You like me because I let you set the tone of our relationship. I always let you say how we will spend the evening, where we will go, which of *your* friends we will be with. That was probably a mistake, maybe even a bit dishonest. I do have opinions, Kevin. I do have friends I will not give up. Some of my favorite places to eat are not elegant. And my favorite radio station is not the one that plays classical music. And one of the must luxurious things I can think of is enjoying a nice yard that *I* have created."

"Of course, you have opinions," Kevin said smoothly. "You make our relationship sound terribly one-sided, but you forget that I let you drag your feet on an engagement. I let you set the tone for the physical part of our relationship. I accepted your desire to get your children out of high school and on their way to college before you committed yourself to a new life. That's what I'm offering you, Julie. A new life. But I certainly won't force it on you. If you don't like the terms I set, then you must not care for me as much as I thought you did."

"Does caring for you mean I can't voice an opinion about where we live?"

"I came to realize that I would be unhappy living in another man's house," he said in a voice that indicated he was not open to negotiations. "I want you at least to try living here, and if—after a year or two—you haven't adjusted, perhaps we can buy a home. But I want you at least to try. I *am* paying the bills, and I feel I have the right to ask that of you."

Yes, Julie thought, he was paying the bills, and a man like Kevin equated money with power. Well, why shouldn't he? she thought ruefully. It certainly had given him power over her.

He touched her forehead. "Don't frown, pretty lady. No man could ever take better care of you than I can."

He turned her around and began to rub her shoulders. He was good at that. Strong hands. Julie didn't realize how tense she was until he began to knead the knots in her muscles. She murmured her appreciation.

"Feel better?" he asked.

"Yes. That feels wonderful. You could get a job rubbing backs."

"I'd like that, providing you're my only client."

Then he took her in his arms. Strong arms. They felt nice. He wanted to take care of her. Was that such a crime? How many times over the past six years had she longed for just that, to have someone take the burden from her shoulders and take care of her? Would she really mind not having to shuffle bills every month, to worry about income taxes and property taxes? And all that insurance—life, homeowner's, medical, car? She was tired of having every broken appliance, every automotive problem loom like a financial disaster. And it would be nice to have some new clothes, to buy things for her children.

But did she really love Kevin? She thought she was falling in love when he first began to court her. What a thrill it had been when the handsome, wealthy, charming Kevin McLaughlin started calling her, taking her to elegant restaurants, sending her flowers. She had been full of anticipation, her heart felt glad when she heard his voice on the phone. She felt appreciated, cherished. It was glorious. It felt like love.

And he was a kind man, kind to her and her children and her parents. Yes, she did love him, but she wasn't *in* love with him.

But that didn't make any sense.

Maybe she didn't love him as passionately as she would have liked, but his kisses were lovely and her feelings were sincere. Love would grow with time.

Relationships were like flower gardens. They took tending before they could turn into something beautiful.

Kevin opened the refrigerator where a bottle of champagne had been keeping a lonely vigil. In a cupboard were hidden two crystal champagne glasses. And a calendar.

Julie watched him pop the cork and pour two glasses. "To our new life," he said.

She stared at the calendar.

"It was your mother's idea," he explained. "She said, 'Don't you let another day go by without pinning that girl down to a date.'"

The calendar was turned to the month of August. They could get married in August, then she could send her children away to college and devote her time to Kevin—a pretty, sweet lady living in this high tower. There was a fairy tale like that. Rapunzel. She had long hair, and her secret love climbed up her hair to visit her in the tower. Julie remembered reading the story to the twins when they were little. "If her hair's that long, how come she doesn't cut it off and make a ladder out of it to climb down?" Sherry had asked. Both twins had agreed it was dumb for the lady to live in the tower if she didn't want to. They liked the adventures of "The Cat in the Hat" much better.

But they probably wouldn't object to their mother living in this tower. It would guarantee the college life they had always dreamed of. Her kids had been born knowing they wanted to go to the University of Texas.

"I want Betty Jean to be my matron of honor," Julie said.

"What about your friend Jody Zachery?"

"Betty Jean," Julie said firmly. "She's the best friend I've ever had. I don't even like Jody very well."

Their arms linked, Kevin escorted her through the rest of the apartment. There was à study, a sewing room, five bedrooms, including the spacious master bedroom with a pedestal for a king-sized bed, its own breathtaking view of the city and a set of French doors opening onto the terrace. The master bathroom looked like something out of a magazine. Skylights. Sauna. Gold fixtures. The sunken tub boasted a mosaic of a peacock—a work of art. And yes, mirrors everywhere.

They carried their champagne out onto the terrace and leaned against the railing. The pool area was deserted now, the now-dark water of the pool reflecting the moonlight. Overhead was a star-studded sky. And all around them were the lights of the city.

Kevin's kisses were tender. He had indeed let her set the physical boundaries of their relationship, never rushed her.

But why had she held back? Why had she felt so incredibly disappointed when she couldn't locate Chad?

She'd never forget looking up and seeing him come in the front door of the high school. Even with a beard, she'd recognized him instantly. Chad. Her first love.

Was it the man himself she had longed for or the feelings they had once shared? Such a sweet time it had been to be young and carefree and in love. But the carefree part had gone away and with it their chances of a life together.

CHAD SAT ROCKING in his combination living room-veranda and watched the sun sink below the horizon. Joe, his large yellow mutt, was dozing at his feet. He loved the way Nicaraguan houses merged with the out-of-doors. Most were left open onto a central courtyard with no walls, windows or doors separating the inside of the house from out-of-doors. His house was built on a high hillside, and the entire back of the house was open to the view.

Of course, a large percentage of Nicaraguans these days didn't have a real house but lived in shacks that provided little more than a roof over their heads. Managua, especially, had rampant poverty and sprawling shantytowns. But San Juan was more isolated—and insulated—from the troubles that plagued the rest of the country. The poverty here was not so acute.

He had finished his usual dinner of rice and beans and carried the dishes to the kitchen for his Nicaraguan maid to do in the morning. Carlos, the thirteen-year-old boy he was housing until arrangements could be made for him to join his aunt and uncle in Miami, was watching the evening soap opera from South America. Chad had lost interest in the ongoing, slapstick story of a dead saint named Rocque, who turned out to be neither dead nor a saint and threatened to ruin his town's lucrative tourist trade of pilgrims who came to kneel at the tomb of a saint and pray for a miracle.

He'd have to start paying attention again, Chad decided. *Everyone* in the country watched *Rocque*. It was the topic of conversation throughout the day. If any foreign power ever wanted to invade the country, it should do so at nine o'clock in the evening when the entire population was sitting in front of television sets.

Recently, however, Chad found television of any sort intrusive, preferring instead to be alone with his dog and his reverie, finding solace in the sound of the eternal waves and the reflections of the moonlight on the waters of the bay. And the stars. Brilliant stars. Millions of stars. In Houston the smog hid the stars. People there had forgotten how a nighttime sky could look.

But the beauty made him sad. Could it be that after years of wandering, it was time to go home?

Home. What meaning did that word hold for him? America, certainly. The thought of his native land still brought a swelling of patriotic feeling in his breast. Last Fourth of July, he'd had a fish fry for all the misplaced Americans in this corner of Nicaragua. After dark, they'd built a fire on the beach and drank too much rum. Then they started singing every patriotic song they'd ever learned as youngsters. At first Chad was embarrassed by his tears, but then he realized that every set of eyes was glowing damply in the firelight.

But while he would forever be American, Chad had no city, certainly no dwelling, in the United States to call home. The house where his mother had raised him had long since been torn down. And he was no longer a city person. He'd discovered that fact on his trip to the reunion. Houston made him crazy. God, all that traffic and hustle. It took longer to drive across the huge city than it did to walk to the next town down here.

And he couldn't imagine living and working in a place where people didn't know each other. Yes, he definitely preferred life in small towns.

So was San Juan del Sur his home?

It could be, he supposed, if he had someone to share it with. All that had been accomplished by his returning to Houston was that he was more lonely than before.

Carlos called to him, insisting he come to watch. Rocque was about to confront the woman who had claimed to be his widow during the years he was supposedly dead. He was hiding in her closet. When the woman opened the door and gasped, Carlos clapped his hands with delight. Chad envied him his pleasure.

Lighten up, old man, he told himself. *I don't like this tragic figure bit.*

Chad got himself a beer and moved his rocking chair over to watch the rest of tonight's episode. The pretend wife was in a panic. As the widow of a dead saint, she'd enjoyed much prestige and wealth in the community. She must prevent anyone from finding out that Rocque wasn't really dead. But could she convince him to stay in hiding? To disguise himself? The town fathers came to scheme with her. Rocque spied on them from another closet.

It was silly but fun, Chad had to admit. It kept the country from dwelling on its troubles for at least an hour every evening. Local governments often found it necessary to turn off the electricity for a period each day in order to conserve, but they knew better than to turn it off between nine and ten in the evening.

By the end of the episode, Chad was laughing with Carlos.

Chapter Five

Opening night of the symphony season was a glittering affair with the audience attired in evening clothes and a guest appearance by an internationally renown pianist.

Julie's sequined gown was ten years old, and this was the first time she had worn it in at least eight years. But its lines were timeless, and it still fit her perfectly. All she needed to update the dress was to add shoulder pads to the jacket. At dinner, she planned to take off the jacket and bare her shoulders. She enjoyed dressing up once in a while. During the years of her widowhood, she'd missed that. Life had been so very serious and routine. Kevin had brought a sense of anticipation to her life. Usually she enjoyed his flair and the way he turned their dates into occasions.

Even this afternoon's tour of company offices, warehouses and one of its huge tankers anchored in the Turning Basin had been made more special by Kevin's imaginative planning and preparation. They picked up the Sullivans at their hotel in a limousine stocked with Brent Sullivan's favorite Scotch and Sarah Sullivan's favorite brand of sherry. And there was a regular British high tea waiting for them on the decks of the tanker with a damask-covered table bearing an ornate silver tea service and delicate china dishes and an impressive sampling of pastries and finger sandwiches arranged on a footed silver tray. The mirrored facades of the city's downtown skyscrapers reflected each other in the distance. While they enjoyed their tea, Kevin entertained them with stories about the colorful history of the city, which had survived yellow fever epidemics and a devastating fire to become the fourth largest city in the country—and one of the fastest growing, due in part to its manmade shipping channel that had turned the inland city into one of the world's busiest seaports. "The port handles over a hundred million tons of cargo a year. Only New Orleans and New York handle more," Kevin explained to his guests.

Tomorrow he planned to take the Sullivans on a tour of the Johnson Space Center and was irritated with Julie's refusal to join them. But she had had to trade next Saturday morning to get off for this Tuesday afternoon excursion. And it wasn't fair to her co-workers to expect them to cover her unscheduled days off. "How can your working a half day at the bank possibly be more important than helping me host an important colleague and his wife?" Kevin demanded.

"I take my responsibilities just as seriously as you do," Julie had defended.

Brent Sullivan, Kevin's counterpart in the company's London office, was jovial and full of stories about his days as a merchant marine. Like Kevin, he was proud that he'd worked his way up through the ranks to his present position of prestige and power. His wife, Sarah, listened graciously, although Julie was certain the woman had heard the stories dozens of times before. Then she turned the tables and told a few family anecdotes herself, with her husband guffawing as though he'd never heard any of them before. Julie had found the couple charming and devoted. They were wealthy but had not lost the common touch.

And now both couples were enjoying the evening together, first at the concert and then a late supper to follow.

The Sullivans were impressed by Houston's wonderful Jones Hall for the Performing Arts, by the quality of the orchestra, by the elegance of the crowd. It was their first trip to Texas, and Julie suspected they had expected to find dirt streets and cowboys on horseback instead of a glittering modern city with futuristic architecture and formally clad symphony patrons.

The orchestra played selections from Mozart. The music was moving, and Julie found herself feeling happy and melancholy at the same time. She was happy with herself, with the man at her side, but there was an emptiness inside of her that the music spoke to and brought tears to her eyes.

Kevin took her hand. "Yes," he whispered, "it's *that* beautiful."

They had a late dinner at the Ritz Carlton, where the Sullivans were staying. Julie turned a few heads when she walked into the dining room in her beautiful bare-shouldered dress with her handsome escort. The hotel prided itself on being Houston's most continental, and the cuisine was exquisite, the service perfect.

The Sullivans insisted that Kevin and Julie come to visit them in London. "Or better yet, we have an eighteenth-century cottage in Suffolk with a genuine thatched roof," Sarah suggested. "I have to get out of the city in the summer to garden—we Brits are avid gardeners. If you want a quieter sort of holiday, Suffolk would be the place to come.''

Some Americans were avid gardeners, too, Julie thought. At the penthouse apartment, any gardening would have to be done in pots. But she didn't say anything. There was no point in bringing tension to their evening.

Kevin was proud of her. She could see it in his eyes. And he was feeling amorous. She could tell that in the way he was continually touching her. He couldn't keep his eyes and hands off of her.

He was getting impatient for some intimacy in their relationship, and Julie felt a bit foolish putting him off. After all, his ring was on her finger. A date had now been circled on the calendar. And it wasn't as though she were a young, inexperienced girl. Her reluctance was starting to cause problems.

She let him think it was for romantic reasons that she wanted their wedding night to be special. Which she did—if they were to have one.

But just weeks before she had been willing to make love to Chad without a wedding license in the drawer, or even the promise of one to come. But it was just as well Chad had said no. The memory would have just added to her confusion.

Today Kevin had sent a deposit to UT for her children's dormitory rooms. If she wasn't going to marry the man, she had to put a stop to things *now*. But she already felt like she had crossed some irrevocable line. She felt obligated. It would be indecent to back out. Unfair. Ungrateful. Embarrassing. Stupid.

And she'd miss Kevin, miss the excitement he brought to her life. She had enjoyed the afternoon and evening immensely. She would enjoy going to England someday with Kevin and visiting the Sullivans in the cottage with the thatched roof—and garden. Kevin would be a marvelous traveling companion, she was sure. He would be a fine husband. She was a lucky woman to have him.

She returned a squeeze of his hand.

"You're beautiful," he whispered. "You were born to be dressed like that."

She smiled. "Thanks. It is fun, once in a while. But don't forget, I like blue jeans, too. I'm basically a pretty informal person."

Kevin had no comment. Julie realized she had never seen him in a pair of jeans. How incredible—a Texan who never wore jeans. She wondered if she could tease him into a pair.

It was almost two when the driver stopped the limousine in front of Julie's house. "Such a wonderful evening," she said sincerely as Kevin walked her to the door. "But is this poor working girl ever going to have a hard time getting up in the morning!"

"It's time for you to quit your job," Kevin announced.

"Quit! Kevin, we are not married yet. I can't afford to pay my bills without a paycheck. And no, I don't want you to pay them for me. Besides, I may want to continue working part-time after we are married, just to have some money and a niche of my own. For someone who never worked at a paying job a day in her life until she was past thirty, I must admit I enjoy having a job and wonder how I'd fill my days if I didn't." Especially without a yard to care for, she wanted to add but did not.

"No," Kevin said firmly as he pulled her into his arms and began planting tiny kisses across her forehead. "Suit yourself about the next two months, but after we're married, I won't have you working. I want you available for trips and entertaining. And you'll need to take up tennis so I can have the most beautiful doubles partner at the club. I don't want to share you with a job or anything else. Now, come here, you ravishing lady. I at least deserve a special kiss after an evening like that."

Julie submitted to his kiss. She listened while he whispered how he was counting the days until she was his wife, that she was a devil to make him wait, but he'd come to realize how exciting waiting could be. "You're driving me crazy, and I love it. Do you think about it, too, dear? Our wedding night?"

"Yes. I think about it a lot."

JULIE TOSSED AND TURNED during what was left of the night. Her sequined gown hung on the back of her closet door like a glittering ghost. She had bought the dress to wear to the party Texas Central held to celebrate the opening of its new building in downtown Houston. A special evening. Ross had been as smitten with her in that dress as Kevin had been tonight. She remembered how, after paying the baby-sitter, they had checked on the children—two formally clad parents, arm-in-arm, glowing as they looked down at their beautiful sleeping children. And then they had gone to their own bedroom, to undress each other and make love. In this very bed.

Before she married Kevin, she had planned to get rid of this bed and move into the one from Kevin's apartment, along with his antique armoire and his signed Audubon bird prints. And she'd paint the walls. Change things around to make the room feel different. But now instead of redecorating, she'd be leaving this room, this house, behind. The memories would follow her, however. She'd always miss Ross. There would continue to be times of unbearable sadness, like when the twins graduated from high school and Ross wasn't there with her to watch their rite of passage, to hear Sherry perform the solo part when the choir sang "Climb Every Mountain," to see how delighted their beautiful children had looked in caps and gowns.

But life does go on.

How sick she'd gotten of that awful cliché, which she'd heard so often from well-meaning friends in the months following Ross's death. But it was true. And after she'd gotten over her initial grieving and accepted the fact that while Ross's death had unalterably changed her life, there would still be joy and laughter and love, her thoughts had turned to Chad. Was he married? Was he still the hotheaded idealist? Did he think of her still? She'd used her memories of a past love to make her strong, to help her understand that life is lived in phases, to help her through those times of self-pity when she kept thinking *why me?* Widowhood and all its accompanying problems sometimes overwhelmed her. Remembering Chad had helped keep her sane.

Then finally, after years of struggle, there had been Kevin to make her feel desirable, to make life easier for her. He'd seemed like her knight in shining armor. He *was* her knight in shining armor.

But maybe she didn't want a knight. Maybe she wanted a more ordinary man who wouldn't expect her to be his princess in the tower.

Julie was beginning to understand the high price she would pay for being Kevin's wife. She would give up her independence and her life-style. Already she felt the very essence of herself slipping away.

She got up and opened the window, hoping some fresh air would clear her head. But the night air was still and heavy. She took a couple of aspirin and crawled back onto her mussed bed.

Sleep, damn it, she ordered her uncooperative mind and body. *You're going to be worthless in the morning if you don't quit this nonsense and go to sleep!*

And eventually she floated down into a soft comfortable place where sleep waited. She started to crawl back out when she realized a dreamtime Chad was there to hold her while she slept, but she didn't. His imagined arms felt nice. She curled her body into them.

During her break the next morning, she called Betty Jean. "Can you talk?" she asked.

"Only a second. But I'm so glad you called. I've been dying to talk to you. Guess what! The dating service came through. I've got a date tomorrow night with a doctor, the medical variety. And unless he lied about his age on his profile, he's not old and decrepit. I'm meeting him in the bar at the Ritz. Oh, Julie, I'm so nervous. What if he's a nerd? What if he's a lush? What if he's Jack the Ripper?"

"Just have a drink and talk to him. If he doesn't appeal to you, don't tell him your last name or your telephone number."

"Geez, how embarrassing. What am I supposed to say? 'Sorry, Jack, but I can't reveal my true identity because I don't like you'?"

"Hell, Betty Jean, I don't know what you should say. Tell him you're thinking of entering a religious order. Tell him you're a journalist on assignment writing about dating services. Tell him you're really seventy-five years old but have had a lot of plastic surgery."

"Do I detect a note of irritation? Hey, why'd you call anyway? You down about something?"

"No, I'm on top of the world," Julie said, rubbing her temples. "I need to get back to work. Are we still doing the picnic tonight?"

"Sure, unless *Kevin* has decided you have to go someplace with him. And we certainly never say no to Kevin, do we?"

"Look, I'm awfully tired. If we're going to be nasty to each other, I'd just as soon call off the evening and go to bed early."

"Hey, I'm sorry. You *are* down. I made potato salad and baked a cake. Let's have the picnic, but you don't have to stay for Donnie's game if you're feeling beat."

"Okay. I'll peel a few carrots and buy some fried chicken."

Of course, she had wanted to talk about something, Julie thought as she hung up the phone and hurried back to her window. She wanted Betty Jean to remind her again that she should not rush into a marriage of which she was unsure. She wanted to be lectured to, to be told that she owed it to herself to take more time to think things over.

Over the picnic dinner, Sherry, Steve and Melissa rattled on and on about their college plans. "Oh, Donnie, you should try to get a baseball scholarship and come to UT," Sherry said. "We'll be experienced sophomores by then and can show you the ropes. I'm so excited about going I can hardly stand it. It's going to be so much fun with the football games and parties. Did you know that when a girl gets pinned to a boy, his whole fraternity comes over to serenade her? Isn't that just darling?"

Donnie's freckled face creased in a frown as he put down the chicken leg he'd been attacking. "Even if I had a scholarship," he said, "I wouldn't have the money to join a fraternity. Or for the prerequisite wardrobe and car."

"Well, not every guy joins a frat," Sherry said, patting Donnie's arm. "I'm sorry. I didn't mean to sound like a snob."

"No problem," Donnie assured Sherry. "I wouldn't be comfortable in a frat. I'll be working part-time and studying a lot. I need to make good grades so I can get into law school. I think I'll fit in better at the University of Houston. It's more of a commuter school."

Dear Donnie, Julie thought, with his red hair and shy smile. *Such a sweet, earnest boy.*

"I guess Steve and Melissa and I sound pretty spoiled, don't we?" Sherry asked.

"Naw. You're just lucky that you get to do what you want."

"What you need is for a rich man to sweep your mom off her feet," Steve said with a wink.

Melissa jabbed Steve in the ribs with her elbow, her brown eyes shooting a warning.

"Steve!" Julie said, horrified. "I can't believe you said that. It would serve you and Sherry right if I call off my engagement right this minute. I can't believe my children are so money-grubbing."

"Mom, you're not serious," Sherry wailed. "Please say you're not."

"I don't know. I'm very uncomfortable with this whole state of affairs. Kevin was buying you kids cars and promising to pay your tuition before I really knew what I wanted to do. And now everything seems more muddled than ever."

"You took his ring," Steve accused. "That implies that you had made up your mind."

"An engagement ring is not tantamount to marriage," Julie said, putting her left hand with its intimidating ring in her lap. "It only shows intent. At the time I accepted it, I had every intention of marrying the man... well, almost every intention. I wanted to spend time with him, get to know him better, understand how he would fit into our lives and us into his."

"Well, I think he'll fit just great," Sherry said. "I *like* him."

Steven nodded enthusiastically. "Yeah, Mom. Kevin's a great guy. And he's crazy about you. Grandma and Grandpa are so relieved that you've got a swell man like Kevin to marry. I don't understand why you're uncertain all of a sudden. You sound like you wish he were *poor*. I mean, all things being equal, I'd think a woman would rather marry a wealthy guy instead of a poor one."

"And you kids don't mind giving up the house?" Julie asked.

"That's a tough one," Sherry admitted. "It will be sad to move out of our home, but the Towers is such a posh place. Everything is a trade-off, like when I didn't get elected cheerleader so I joined the chorus and found out I could sing."

"Wow, my sister the philosopher," Steve teased, pulling on Sherry's blond ponytail. "This conversation is getting a little heavy for me. Let's go toss the ball around for a while and get Donnie warmed up. Is this team you're playing any good, Donnie?"

Julie and Betty Jean packed up the remainder of the picnic, then joined the kids for a round of catch. It felt good to throw a ball again, Julie thought. She and Betty

Jean had played church-league softball for a few years back when the kids were little. Ross had ridden herd on the twins and Donnie in the stands and told them to cheer for the mommies. It would be fun to play again sometime. Julie had enjoyed being on a team, enjoyed the camaraderie with the other women. But somehow she couldn't see Kevin sitting in the stands watching his wife play softball.

AFTER THE REALTOR had toured the house, measuring every room, checking every closet, even climbing the pull-down-steps in the hall to peer into the attic, Julie led her to the living room. "Could I get you a cup of coffee or a glass of tea?"

"Tea would be nice," the woman said. Mary Crawford was her name. One of Julie's colleagues at the bank had recommended her.

Julie poured two glasses of iced tea and carried them to the living room.

"Well, what do you think, Mary?" she asked as she seated herself across from the woman.

"It's a lovely house, and Tanglewood is a great area, but I won't kid you, Julie. Houston is full of lovely houses for sale. Savings and loans are trying to unload houses they've gotten back on defaulted loans. The same with government-lending agencies. You can bid a house at government auction and usually get it at a steal. Of course, we're hoping things will turn around in a couple of years, but right now your best bet would be to rent the house or stay put."

"My two children will be starting college this fall, and I need the money now for their expenses. If I was willing to take a substantial loss, do you think I could sell it?"

"You've got such a large equity, that even at a loss, the house would probably have to be refinanced, and quite frankly, with real estate valuation so depressed right now, I think you'd be shocked at how little you'd realize from the sale. But if you're willing to be patient, maybe someone will come along who wants this particular house in this neighborhood and has some money to invest in an equity. We can list it and give it a try."

"Patient? For how long. Weeks or months?"

"Years maybe," Mary admitted. "It's hard to say. Maybe your kids could get student loans."

"It's too late to apply for next fall. I checked. Applications should have been in by March first."

Julie signed the papers giving the realtor permission to show and sell her house. A quick sale of the house would alleviate her situation, but it seemed the possibility of that happening was someplace between remote and impossible. She would feel much better if she could pay Kevin back for the kids' cars and dorm down payment and face the prospect of marriage to him with a clean slate. If she had some money in the bank, she could make a decision about marriage based on nothing but her feelings for the man. But apparently that was a luxury she was not to be allowed.

And the weeks were ticking by. Already it was the end of June. Her wedding date was only six weeks away.

As she said good-bye to the realtor, Steve, Melissa and Donnie arrived, driving Julie's car with her parents' camping trailer in tow.

"Where's that worthless twin of mine?" Steve called. "We've got a lot of work to do if we're going to make this old relic habitable. And you were right, Mom, there was a tent in their attic. Gramps said he used to take it on fishing trips. Us guys can sleep in the tent. There's room for the four females to sleep inside the trailer. And Melissa got the refrigerator to work. Amazing, isn't it? There's a brain in that pretty little head.''

Melissa leaped on Steve's back, and they fell tumbling to the ground. ''Pig,'' she called, pounding on his back. ''Male chauvinist pig.''

Julie stepped inside the camper. It did indeed need cleaning, and it was smaller than she remembered, but the whole idea of camping a few days on the beach had sparked a sense of adventure in the kids, and she looked forward to getting away.

Kevin was in New York on business, and she hadn't yet told him that she and the kids would be gone to Padre when he got back. She'd tell him this evening during his nightly call. She wondered what his reaction would be. The nightly calls had been a bit cool; Kevin thought she should have gone to New York with him.

Kevin was staying at the Plaza. He *always* stayed at the Plaza. Two hundred and fifty dollars a night. It seemed obscene. Julie wondered if he'd ever been camping. Maybe she'd soften the news of the proposed camping adventure with an invitation for him to join them when he returned. He could fly Southwest Airlines into Port Isabel and spend a night or two on the beach.

She stepped to the doorway of the camper. ''Do you think Kevin would like to camp with us?''

Three faces turned to stare at her. Melissa giggled.

''I don't think Kevin's the type,'' Steve said.

''It might be good for him,'' Julie said.

''I guess he could sleep in the tent, too. It seemed to be a pretty good size. But . . .'' Steve hesitated.

''But what?'' Julie pushed.

"Well, it wouldn't be as much fun with him there. I doubt if he eats hot dogs. And we're going to take the guitars and harmonicas for sing-alongs. Rent dune buggies and take you and Betty Jean for jaunts up the beach. Tell ghost stories around the camp fire. You know, dumb stuff like that."

"Stuff a *cool* guy like Kevin wouldn't enjoy?" Julie asked with a touch of sarcasm.

"Well, he is a bit proper," Steve admitted sheepishly.

"But you like him a lot? Right? Not just his checkbook? You want him for a stepfather?"

"Come on, Mom," Steve admonished. "You've made your point. Kevin's not your basic all-around guy. But he's a nice man, and he's been good to us all. And so what if he's not the camping type? I hardly think you were planning on a camping trip for your honeymoon. Is he still keeping the honeymoon destination a surprise? Sherry thinks it will be Paris. I say Rome."

Julie realized Steve was deliberately changing the subject. That was all right, though. She'd taken the conversation as far she wanted to.

When Kevin called that night, she told him of the upcoming trip to Padre and invited him to fly down and join them when he returned from his trip.

"But Saturday is your birthday," he protested.

"Yes, I'm aware of that. My folks are driving down and spending the night in a hotel on the island. I think my children are planning a celebratory wiener roast and sing-along. We'd love to have you."

"I have made special plans for your birthday."

"That's very sweet of you, but I had no idea. Can't your plans wait until another time?"

"Julie, I've planned what was supposed to be a surprise dinner party in your honor. I mailed out printed invitations to forty people and have arranged for a caterer, flowers and a pianist. You will have to be there, of course." His voice was very stern.

"*Forty* people? Who?"

"You've met some of them at the racquet club," he said. "They are people whose friendships I most value."

"I've always spent my birthday with my parents, my children, Betty Jean and Donnie," Julie said, trying to keep her voice calm.

"Are you telling me that you won't be at the party?" Kevin asked. "Do you have any idea how embarrassing that will be for me?"

"But what made you think I wouldn't have plans for my birthday?"

"I *assumed* you'd want to spend your birthday with me," he said indignantly.

"*And* your forty best friends, *some* of whom I've met," Julie added just as indignantly. "What about my best friends? What about my family?"

"I want these people to be your friends, too."

"Then why don't you postpone the gathering and change it from a birthday party to an informal meet-my-fiancée gathering? Your secretary can call everyone and explain the change. And then you can drive down to Padre with my parents for the wienie roast."

"I detest wieners and all processed meat," he said, making no attempt to disguise his irritation, "especially when they are served with sand."

"Then we'll cook hamburgers to serve with sand," Julie said. "Try to be a good sport, okay. I know my family and friends don't measure up to your high social standards, but we rather like ourselves this way. Just let my parents know if you plan to come down, otherwise I'll see you at the end of next week. And don't bother to call tomorrow evening. I'm sure we'll be busy packing up the trailer.''

And she hung up. Just like that, without waiting for him to say good-bye.

Her heart racing with anger, Julie sat staring at the phone for a long time trying to decide how she felt about the conversation that had just transpired. How horrible for him to have to call off the surprise party. But damn him for expecting her to spend her birthday with a bunch of strangers instead of those who had always been nearest and dearest to her heart!

SENTIMENTAL SLOB that she was, Julie got tears in her eyes as she watched her children, Melissa, her parents, Betty Jean and Donnie sing "Happy Birthday" to her. She loved them all so much.

They were sitting around a small fire, the litter from their shish kabab à la hot dog dinner stashed in a plastic trashbag. They'd driven up the beach to this isolated place between two sand dunes where they were protected from the night breezes. Julie's parents sat in lawn chairs; the rest of them were sitting cross-legged on blankets.

The air smelled of salt and smoke, the sky was clear and star-filled. She was surrounded by dear people. If she had to be a year older, this was the best way to celebrate it.

They should come to Padre more often, she thought. There was something inspiring about the ocean. And renewing.

Donnie took pictures with his Instamatic while Julie blew out the candles on the cake her mother had brought. And while Betty Jean cut slices for everyone, Julie opened her presents by the light of the fire.

Her parents gave her the usual hundred dollars, a gift that seemed far more generous now than formerly. Melissa and Steve gave Julie a bottle of her favorite cologne. Sherry presented her with a beautiful photograph album. "For your wedding pictures," Sherry said. "Look, I've even had your names and the date stamped in gold."

Julie stared down at the empty album and tried to imagine it filled with pictures of the happy bride and groom.

Then Betty Jean handed her an envelope. "I love you, sugar," she said. "This is from Donnie and me to help you take care of a little unfinished business."

Inside the envelope was a round-trip airplane ticket to Managua, Nicaragua.

Julie was stunned. "You can't afford this," she said.

"It wasn't so much," Betty Jean said with a shrug. "After all, you're looking at a woman who spent fifteen hundred dollars on a new bustline. If I decide something needs to be done, I can usually scrape together the money, and I just couldn't stand by doing nothing while my dearest friend was so unhappy."

"What do you mean, unhappy?" Angela challenged. "Julie isn't unhappy." Angela turned to her daughter. "Tell her you're not unhappy."

"Where is the ticket for?" Steve asked.

Taylor Harper leaned over his daughter's shoulder and took the airplane ticket from her hand, adjusted his glasses lower on his nose and examined it. "Nicaragua!" he said increduously.

"I thought you had more sense than that," Angela said, shooting an angry look in Betty Jean's direction.

"Julie cannot go off and visit an old boyfriend when she's engaged to another man."

"Would someone please tell us kids what this is all about?" Steve said. "Why in the world would anyone want to go to Nicaragua? I'm not sure it's even safe there. And what old boyfriend? How could Mom have an old boyfriend in Nicaragua?"

"It's safe," Donnie chimed in. "Mom and I checked with the State Department. Americans go down there all the time. Julie doesn't even need a visa, just a current passport."

"Didn't you say someone came to your class reunion from Nicaragua?" Sherry asked, her tone suspicious.

"Your mother dated a boy in high school who went off chasing rainbows and ended up down there," Taylor explained from his lawn chair, with a shake of his white head to show his disapproval of the person in question.

"But I thought you dated dad in high school," Sherry said, staring at her mother. "You never told us about some other guy."

"I can't imagine what in the hell you were thinking about, Betty Jean," Taylor said, actually shaking his finger at her. "Julie's mother and I have finally been able to rest easy now that she's about to get her life straightened out. You can't imagine how we've worried about her, and I for one don't appreciate your meddling."

Betty Jean looked at Julie, her blue eyes reflecting the light of the fire. "How about it? What do you think of my meddling?"

Julie scrambled across the blanket and hugged her friend. "I love you for it. I'm not sure I'll go, but I know you did this because you care about me. Thanks."

"If you don't go, I can cash the ticket in. I didn't buy one of those nonrefundable kind even though they cost less because I didn't have that much faith you'd really go. I tried to think of something for a backup gift, but I couldn't think of a thing to buy a woman who's about to have everything."

"Well, did you date someone else in high school?" Sherry demanded of her mother. She was sitting on her haunches now, hands on her hips.

"I don't understand," Steve whined. "If she's engaged to Kevin, why would she even want to go see some other guy? And what do you mean, chasing rainbows? Is this fellow some kind of nut?"

"Shut up, Steve," Melissa said.

"Julie, tell us you're not seriously thinking about going," her mother insisted. She was sitting up very straight. "Betty Jean can get her money back."

"Mom, don't go messing up our lives," Sherry begged.

"Stop!" Betty Jean said in a loud voice as she scrambled to her feet. "Okay, folks, Mother Betty Jean is about to deliver a lecture. I may step on a few toes, but I've had enough of this nonsense. Steve, Sherry, Angela, Taylor—the four of you are so intent on marrying Julie off to Kevin McLaughlin that you refuse to admit she is having second thoughts. Do you hear me? *Second thoughts!* She is not sure! Now, Angela and Taylor, I understand that you both would like to see Julie in a more secure position financially, but do you really want her to enter into a marriage without being absolutely certain that is what she wants to do? As for Steve and Sherry, if you kids weren't so big, I'd spank you both—just like I did when you were three years old and poured all my perfume down the toilet. You kids are trying to sell your mother to the highest bidder just so you can have a really neat time in college. Well, I can understand wanting to have the ultimate college experience with all the amenities, but do you really want your mother to marry Mr. Rich Guy when she doesn't want to? Back off! I think that Julie needs to get away from all of you and have some time to figure out what's best for *her*."

"Then why didn't you buy her a ticket to New Orleans or Acapulco?" Sherry demanded. "She doesn't have to figure things out in *Nicaragua*!"

Julie got up and put her arms around Betty Jean's shoulders. "She bought me a ticket to Nicaragua because she knows I need to see Chad again before I can make up my mind about Kevin."

"That boy doesn't have a thing to offer you," Taylor scoffed.

"He has his heart," Betty Jean said.

"Well, I think she should go," Melissa said.

"That's easy for you to say," Sherry said, her voice quivering. "Your parents can afford to send you to college."

"Okay, then," Melissa said with a toss of her blond hair. "How's this instead? I think your mom should marry some guy she may or may not be in love with because the most important thing is for you and me to pledge the same sorority at UT."

Sherry glanced at Melissa then scrambled to her feet and went racing off between the dunes.

"Go after her, Steve," Julie said. "She shouldn't be out there alone after dark."

Chapter Six

"I'd like to place a person-to-person call to Mr. Chad Morgan, in San Juan, Nicaragua," Julie told the international operator from the pay phone outside the campground headquarters.

"What number, please?" he asked.

"I don't have the number. You'll have to get it from information."

"One moment, please."

The operator put her on hold. Julie waited for an interminable time, wondering if she'd been cut off. Then the man's voice came back on the line.

"I'm sorry, ma'am. There are no lines into Nicaragua at this time."

"When should I try again?"

"The best time to call that country is between two and four a.m. Sometimes it's possible to get a line then."

"You mean in the middle of the night?"

"Yes, ma'am. It used to be easier, but they lost a lot of service during that bad hurricane."

"But that was a couple of years ago."

"Yes, ma'am."

"The middle of the night?"

"Yes, ma'am."

She hurried back to the camper where Betty Jean and her parents had unloaded the picnic paraphernalia from the car. Taylor and Angela were waiting to say goodnight and go to their hotel for the night. "Won't you have a cup of coffee first?" Julie asked.

"No. I need to get to bed. I have a terrible headache," Angela said, putting a hand to her forehead for emphasis.

"Your mother's very upset," Taylor told his daughter, his tone an indictment. "I'd think you'd want to reassure her that you are not going to follow up on this harebrained scheme Betty Jean has dreamed up."

"Daddy, I know you still think of me as your little girl. But I just turned thirty-eight, and I'm old enough to make my own decisions without getting bawled out by my parents. I'll see you both in the morning. The kids are in charge of breakfast."

In the cramped quarters of her camper berth, Julie would doze a bit then stare at the clock on the shelf over the stove. She wasn't really going to get up and go make a phone call in the middle of the night. But if she was going to use the second week of her vacation for a trip to Nicaragua, she needed to find out if Chad still wanted her to come. Maybe this would not be a good time for him. Maybe he wasn't even in San Juan del Sur. He had mentioned having to travel around the country.

But through the doubts came the dream of seeing him again. Her beloved Chad. Just the two of them with no apprehension about Kevin's watching eyes. She could escape for a time from the monstrous problems that faced her. Her mind wandered off into thoughts of Chad's arms around her, his kisses. Oh, God, yes. Lots of kisses.

She imagined their bodies pressed together, hands touching, lips searching. They would make love, and Julie had no doubt that it would be wondrous. Soul-searing. Passionate beyond belief. And she wanted that with him. No matter what came after, she wanted to have a time of love with Chad.

And what would come after? Would it be easier to make a decision after seeing him again? Maybe it would be harder. For even if she didn't marry Kevin, she wasn't sure she could manage a life with Chad. She had instinctively known, even as a nineteen-year-old girl, love does not conquer all. She couldn't imagine living the kind of life he lived any more than he could be happy with an eight-to-five desk job in Houston, Texas.

All she knew was the thought of seeing him filled her with such longing. Her body ached with it. Her mind focused on images of what could be.

By the time the phosphorescent hands of the clock had finally crept around to two o'clock, Julie acknowledged to herself that she would try again to place a call.

She pulled on her shorts and touched Betty Jean's arm. "I'm going to try to call him again," she whispered.

"Wait. I'll come with you."

The campgrounds were dark but for the circles of illumination formed by pole lights posted at intervals along the asphalt roadway. On either side of them were an incredible variety of camping outfits ranging from sleek self-contained motor homes as big as buses to tiny pup tents.

The phone booth stood like a lonely sentry by the dark headquarters building. Julie left the booth door open, and Betty Jean hovered outside.

This time the international operator was a woman. After several attempts, the operator got a line into the Central American country, and Julie could hear her speaking Spanish to another woman who sounded very far away.

"There's only one telephone in San Juan del Sur," the operator reported back. "Would you like me to ring it?"

"Whose phone is it?"

"Some sort of municipal exchange, apparently."

"Would the operator there speak English?"

"I don't know, Ma'am. Would you like me to try?"

"Yes, please. But please stay on the line. I don't speak Spanish."

Julie listened, while the line rang and rang. "Apparently the exchange closes at night," the operator suggested.

"But I couldn't get a call to go through earlier."

"It's really difficult with some countries," the operator sympathized. "Would you like me to give you the number? You can try dialing it directly in the morning. If you just keep trying, you'll eventually get through."

Julie had nothing to write with. She made the woman repeat the number, saying it after her. By then Betty Jean had found a scrap pencil in her pocket and had fished a piece of paper out of a trashcan chained to a lamp pole. Julie quickly wrote the number before she forgot it.

"What if I can't contact him?" she whispered into the quiet of the night as she and Betty Jean linked arms and started back down the asphalt road. "I can't just go down there unannounced. I suppose I could write him a letter and wait for a reply, but I remember him saying the country's mail service is unreliable. And if I'm going to go, I should go right away, while I'm still on vacation."

"You could call him when you arrive in Managua," Betty Jean suggested.

"What if the phones don't work any better inside the country than they do internationally?"

"Surprise him. Take the bus or the train to that town. God, I'd love to see his face as he opens his front door and sees you standing there."

"Surely once I got to San Juan del Sur, there would be someone who could tell me where Chad lives. I don't think it's a very large town."

"What will you tell Kevin?" Betty Jean asked.

"The truth, I suppose," Julie said with a sigh. "I'll tell him that I need to find out how I feel about Chad before I go any further with our wedding plans."

"He won't accept that, Julie. If you tell him the truth, I suspect it's all over with you and Kevin."

"Isn't that what you want, or do I detect a note of doubt?"

"Well, maybe a bit," Betty Jean admitted. "It seemed like such a great idea to play matchmaker and get you and Chad together again, but maybe your dad is right. Chad apparently doesn't have anything to offer you in the way of financial security. And Sherry was so upset. Poor kid. She really has her heart set on going to UT and being a sorority girl. And who am I to say that's not important? I got to do all those frivolous things when I was young. I adored my times at the Chi Omega house. You made me so mad when you married Ross at the end of our freshman year. You never even lived in the house."

"You only lived there a year before you and Mitch got married. We both ended up marrying awfully young."

"I was in love. What's your excuse?"

"I had to hurry up and get married to protect myself from Chad. I know you blame my folks for my hasty marriage, but it was as much me as them. I was afraid I'd weaken and go to the Philippines with Chad, and I was so furious at him for joining the Peace Corps and saying that if I really loved him, I'd join, too, and go with him—just like Kevin's trying to force me to give up my home and live in a penthouse when he knows I'm not cut out for high-rise living. Chad knew that I wasn't the type for outdoor latrines or beating clothes clean on a river bank. It makes me mad all over again just to think about it. Damn him, anyway. I'm still not the type. It's one thing to camp for four days and use the showers in the bathhouse, but you were right. A few days of this is sufficient. And I'm beginning to wonder in just what sort of place it is that Chad lives. No phones. No mail. God knows what else there isn't."

"Maybe you could ask him to come back to Houston to live."

"Then I'd be doing the same thing to him that he tried to do to me," Julie said, "the same thing that Kevin's trying to do to me nineteen years later. I'd be asking Chad to change his entire life for me, to give up who he is for my convenience."

It was Betty Jean's turn to sigh. They had arrived back at their campsite, but by unspoken agreement, they climbed over a sand dune and headed toward the moonlit beach. "Nothing is ever easy, is it?" Betty Jean said. "My mother used to say that I never knew when to leave well enough alone. You said after the reunion that Chad's place in your life was that of a fond memory. I thought you were just rationalizing, but maybe you were right."

"We seem to have reversed roles here," Julie said as they sat on a piece of driftwood. "You're trying to talk me out of following the road to Chad and seeing what happens. And now I want to go."

"Are you sure? What if you throw away your chance with Kevin for an impossible dream?"

"Then I'll be sadder but wiser. We don't always know going in how things will turn out."

"Amen to that," Betty Jean said.

They were silent awhile, listening to the waves. Two old friends with no answers.

"You got any more dates coming up?" Julie asked.

"Yeah. The dating service called. Number three is next week."

"The doctor never called back, I take it."

"No, but the health nut did. He wanted to take me to his health club. He said he'd put me on a weight-lifting regimen that would improve muscle tone and flexibility. He kept quizzing me about my diet, too. He's big on fish and legumes. I'm not even sure what a legume is."

"Are you going out with him again?

"I don't think so. I don't think he really liked me. He just saw me as a challenge. He wants to tone me up and convert me to tofu."

The ocean was mysteriously beautiful at night. Chad lived by the ocean. On a hill. Not on the gulf side, however. His ocean was the Pacific. He had wanted her to walk with him on his Pacific beach. She wondered if he still did.

Fearful that someone who spoke only Spanish would answer, Julie tried the number in Nicaragua before her parents arrived in the morning for breakfast and again after they had left for their drive back to Houston. Both times she got a recording. "Your call cannot go through at this time in the country you are calling."

When she did get through, she'd just have to ask for Chad and hope for the best. Maybe he lived close by.

One telephone for an entire town. Unbelievable.

Julie took along a loaf of bread as the group marched down to the beach for their morning swim. They all delighted in throwing pieces of bread in the air for the sea gulls to catch midflight.

The water was cold and invigorating. The kids shared their paddle boards with Betty Jean and Julie until the two women decided to abandon the water and applied a heavy layer of sunscreen before stretching on their beach towels.

At noon they drove into Port Isabel for hamburgers and fries. "No, I couldn't ever date a fitness freak," Betty Jean said, reaching for another French fry. "Not if it meant giving up French fries and nachos and all the things I love."

After lunch they climbed the town's old lighthouse for a look at the beautiful view. The kids took turns snapping pictures with Donnie's camera.

They roamed though a couple of gift shops and bought shrimp to boil for dinner. Back at the campground, Julie tried the San Juan number again. Then she and Betty Jean napped while the four young people spent the afternoon on the beach with their portable radio and a cooler of Cokes. And Julie tried to call several times before dinner. Once she got a busy signal; other times there was only the recording.

Betty Jean boiled the shrimp in her own special concoction of beer and spices. Everyone agreed they tasted fantastic. They rounded out their meal with leftovers from the tiny refrigerator and the remainder of the birthday cake. In the morning they would head home.

Finally, about ten o'clock that evening, the distant phone in San Juan del Sur actually rang, but no one answered. When Julie arrived back in Houston the next day, she called Western Union. "I'd like to send a telegram to Nicaragua."

"What name and address please."

"Chad Morgan, San Juan del Sur, Nicaragua."

"Street address, please."

"I don't know it."

"Telephone number?"

"Apparently he doesn't have one."

"I'm sorry, ma'am. I need more information than the name of a city."

If she went to see Chad, she would have to go unannounced. Julie called Tan Sahsa Airline to confirm her reservation for the next day on the flight to Managua. Then she called Kevin.

"I hope you find what you are looking for," he said, his voice more sad than angry. "I've felt you slipping away from me. You don't like the life I'm offering, do you?"

"I know that's hard for you to understand," Julie tried to explain. "I'm used to working, to being busy, to being my own person. It would be hard for me to sit around that penthouse all day, isolated from the world, waiting for you to come home. If I were to marry you, we would have to negotiate some changes."

"If you make this trip, the engagement is off."

"Yes, I understand that. Do you want me to call when I get back?"

"Only if you have come to your senses. And I'm not sure how I'll feel even then."

"Take care of yourself, Kevin. You're very special to me. I'm sorry I didn't turn out to be the woman you thought I was."

The next morning, Melissa and Steve agreed to drive Julie to the airport. Sherry refused to come.

"What would you have me do, honey?" Julie asked her daughter.

"I don't know. I guess you shouldn't marry Kevin if you don't want to, but what happens to Steve and me now? I feel like I've had my whole future pulled out from under me just so my mom can go off and have an affair with some guy she knew back in high school."

"I want a week off from worrying about the future," Julie said. "We'll deal with things when I get back. Now, can I at least have a hug?"

Sherry's hug was less than enthusiastic. She went into her room and shut the door.

"She'll come around," Melissa promised, slipping a comforting arm around Julie's waist. "I told her I'd go to the University of Houston, too, if she and Steve have to go there."

"Oh, honey, you shouldn't promise that. I know you've looked forward to UT just as much as they have."

"I want to go to college where Steve and Sherry go. And besides, I can still live on campus. Sherry can come spend the night with me a lot. Living at home won't be the end of the world for her."

Steve was quiet on the way to the airport, but when they said their good-byes, he hugged her and told her to have a good time. "This guy must really be something

if you're willing to go to all this trouble to see him
again.''

"Maybe I'm just using his re-entry into my life to
extract myself from my engagement to Kevin.''

"Yeah, I'd thought of that. Sherry and I, we pushed
on you too hard about marrying Kevin. Melissa kept
telling us we were. She said from the very first that you
weren't really in love with him. I'm sorry about that,
Mom. I don't want you to marry anyone just so Sherry
and I can live well. Sherry doesn't, either, not really.
She's just having a hard time sifting through things.''

Julie gave a warm hug to Melissa. "I never realized
what a wise young woman you were," she said.

"Have a glorious time. You deserve it," Melissa said,
returning her hug.

Steve engulfed his mother in a bear hug. "Just don't
go down there and make other promises you need to
extract yourself from.''

"No, darlin', I won't. Be nice to your sister.''

Julie passed through airport security, then turned to
wave.

That Melissa, she thought as she rode on the people
mover through the long corridor. *What a gem.*

And poor Sherry. Julie felt her daughter's pain and
was assailed once again with doubts.

TAN SAHSA flight 515 was an hour late in arriving and
almost two hours late in departing. While she waited,
Julie tried to read, but she was too excited to concentrate. She couldn't believe that she was really doing this.
Safe, sane Julie who had always been the good daughter, the good wife, the good mother, had put herself first
for once and was going off on a whim. Melissa had said

she deserved it. Maybe she did; maybe she didn't. But either way, she was going.

She studied the eclectic assortment of waiting passengers, who included mangy young people with backpacks, aging hippie-types—also mangy—with backpacks, Hispanic families, Hispanic men traveling alone, a German rock-and-roll band, a priest, half a dozen nuns and one overdressed woman in a hat and gloves.

Finally the flight was called. Julie put away her unread book and boarded.

The interior of the plane was a bit shabby. She hoped the shabbiness didn't reflect the state of its engines. She sat next to a handsome white-haired man from Houston on his way to visit his lady friend in the tiny Central American country of Belize. "She lives on an island off Belize City," her seatmate told Julie. "Such a lovely little place. Only two thousand people on the whole island, and forty-five automobiles. It's hell at rush hour," he said with a wink. "Belize is wonderful for a change, but after a while I get bored with fishing and beachcombing and head on back to the hustle and bustle of our overgrown city. And she usually comes to see me about once a year and finds the hustle and bustle a delightful change until she gets homesick for her little smog-free world."

"How did you meet her?" Julie asked over their meal trays.

"We were sweethearts in college, but we broke up— I can't even remember why—and she married my best friend. I've been widowed for years, and five years ago when I heard that old Geoffrey had died, I tracked her down. She and Geoffrey had moved to Belize years ago.

I'd read a story about them in our college alumni magazine. They raised sugar cane.''

Julie had to smile. She explained that she was going to visit an old sweetheart herself, but when she gave him a call, it didn't go through.

"I wouldn't worry too much about showing up unexpected. I suspect he'll be happy to see you," the man said with a knowing nod of his head. "Isn't it funny how we never quite get over the one we didn't marry?"

An announcement in Spanish came over the public address system and was then repeated in thickly accented English. They would soon be arriving at Belize International Airport, and passengers were advised to finish their drinks and buckle up. When the plane was on the ground, Julie looked out the window at the small one-story building and asked, "Is *that* the international airport?"

Her companion laughed. "Everything is small in Belize. Only about one hundred and sixty thousand people live in the whole country. The skyscrapers have three floors. Well, goodbye now, and good luck with your adventure," he said, shaking her hand. "I always say 'nothing ventured, nothing gained.' I admire your courage."

Courage. Julie was beginning to feel like she had left it in Houston. She thought of her father's description of this trip. *Harebrained.*

The plane landed again in San Pablo, Honduras, and again in Tegucigalpa, the capital city of Honduras, where Julie changed planes, hiking with other passengers across the runway, which was built on the side of a cliff. She hoped no pilots ever overshot the runway. It would be a disaster if they did.

The plane was delayed taking off from Tegucigalpa, and darkness had long since fallen when it landed in Managua. The modern terminal building there was larger than those at the previous stops. The passengers were directed first through a passport check, then to a counter where foreigners were required to buy sixty dollars in Nicaraguan currency. Julie was startled to see that her sixty American dollars had bought thirty-six thousand cordobas, the Nicaraguan currency! She'd need a calculator to figure out how much things cost.

Next stop was the customs lounge. When Julie's turn came with a customs official, he motioned for her to open her bag, and she watched him paw unceremoniously through the contents. Apparently satisfied, he motioned her on.

As Julie exited into the airport lobby, she felt a bit jealous at the happy reunions taking place all around her. Everyone seemed to have someone meeting them except her.

She approached a uniformed guard. "Telephone," she said, putting her hand to her ear.

He pointed to an office. The woman in the office did not speak English, but Julie made her understand that she needed to make a call and showed her the San Juan del Sur phone number.

The woman tried several times, but the number never answered.

In dismay, Julie returned to the lobby and looked around for someone to help her. But the small gift shop was closed. The only official-looking person was the guard. She carried her suitcase outside.

There was no bus parked out front, but there were taxis.

"¿Habla usted inglés?" Julie asked several men leaning against the building.

"Sí, señora," one of the men answered. "I speak English."

"I need to take a bus or train to San Juan del Sur."

"To San Juan. Tonight?"

"Yes."

"No train," the round little man informed her.

"A bus?"

"Maybe. Tomorrow. Or the next day."

"Nothing tonight?"

The man shrugged and addressed his companions in Spanish. Everyone seemed to have an opinion. Finally the man turned back to Julie. "No regular bus," he said. "But maybe private one."

"Would you please help me get a taxi to the bus station?"

The ticket windows were closed at the bus station, but outside there were several assorted vehicles—vans and trucks—loading up passengers.

Julie walked down the line saying "San Juan del Sur" in a hopeful voice. A man with a battered panel truck nodded. By writing a figure on a piece of paper, Julie understood that he expected to be paid almost all the cordobas she had just purchased at the airport. She wondered if that was a "special" price for the American lady, but she paid it gratefully and crawled in the back of his truck with five other people. By the time the van departed, however, the number of passengers had increased to ten—seven men and three women, all sitting on the floor with assorted sacks, boxes and Julie's suitcase.

The shocks of the ancient vehicle had long since worn out. Julie bounced around for a while on the metal floor then tried sitting on her suitcase. That helped a little, but she kept sliding off and into the man next to her every time the driver put on his brakes.

The inside of the panel truck was hot and airless. As they jogged along in the darkness, Julie felt as if she had jumped out of reality. Was she really riding on the floor of a truck, bumping across the Nicaraguan country-side? Her sense of adventure had completely left her. She felt like a total fool.

She had been dozing when the van finally stopped. "San Juan?" she asked when the driver opened the door.

"No. Rivas," he said, motioning for her to stay in the truck. "No San Juan."

They were parked by a square in front of a large church. The town was quiet, dark. Julie tried to see what time it was but couldn't read her watch in the darkness.

Very shortly, they were on their way again. And again, in spite of her extreme discomfort, Julie dozed. She'd wake abruptly when a bump bounced her head against the side of the truck but would doze off again, exhausted.

When the vehicle stopped again, the first light of dawn was coming in the front window. Very shortly, the door swung opened. "San Juan," the driver told her. Julie, pulling her suitcase behind her, crawled ungrace-fully out of her prison, her body one big cramp. A man followed her out, the others remained inside. Appar-ently the truck had not yet finished its journey.

Julie looked around as she carefully attempted to stretch out the muscles of her poor abused body. On one side of the street, the beach stretched down to the ocean, the sound of waves filling the air, and the sleeping town crawled up a steep hillside on the other. Chad was up there in one of those houses. She hoped.

With a wave, the driver got back in the truck and drove away. The truck had no taillights.

She turned to the young man who had gotten out of the van with her. "Chad Morgan?" she queried.

He shook his head. He didn't understand.

"Chad Morgan," Julie repeated.

"No hablo inglés," the man explained, then tossed a military-style duffel bag over his shoulder and started up the hill.

Across the street was a two-story building that said "hotel" on its front.

The lobby was open. No door. No windows. Just open. There was no one at the desk. The room was empty except for a hen roosting on the back of one of the many rocking chairs scattered about the room. Julie sank into one of them. She had never been so hungry and tired in her life. Her body ached. Her head hurt. Her feet were swollen painfully in her shoes. She longed for a drink of water. And she wondered what in the hell she was supposed to do next. A rooster crowed from behind the hotel. A rooster further up the hill responded noisily. And soon another and another. Dozens of roosters seemed to be arguing with each other.

The hen pulled her head out from under her wing, fluttered down from the chair back and ambled out to the street.

Julie leaned her head against the high back of the chair, closed her eyes and waited.

When she opened them, the sun was up, and a wizened old man was sitting in one of the other rocking chairs. He offered a snaggle-toothed smile. *"Buenos días,"* he said.

"Buenos días," Julie said, returning his greeting. *"¿Habla usted inglés?"*

He shook his head no.

"Chad Morgan," Julie said. *"La casa de Chad Morgan?"*

The old man nodded and pointed up the hill.

Julie used both her hands to gesture at herself. "Me. Please. *La casa de Chad Morgan.*"

He smiled and nodded. Julie waited, watching him expectantly. He took a couple more rocks in his chair, then shuffled over and picked up her suitcase.

"No," Julie protested. "I can."

But the old man started out the doorless opening, and Julie followed, feeling rather ridiculous that a man half her size and twice her age was carrying her suitcase.

The unpaved road up the hill was very narrow and steep and so rutted, Julie doubted if a car could pass. She was grateful for her flat shoes. The houses opened directly onto the street.

They met two skinny pigs and a couple of chickens coming down the hill. Very quickly Julie was out of breath, but the old man was having no problem in spite of the heavy suitcase.

Already the town was stirring around them. Brown-skinned children stood in the doorways of houses, curious brown eyes watching her pass. Through the open doors, Julie caught glimpses of dark interiors with courtyards beyond.

A woman scattering feed in a side yard for a cluster of clucking hens called out a greeting. The old man waved.

Finally he turned onto an even narrower street. And they walked at least another half mile past primitive houses. More people were coming out of the houses.

Adults on their way to work, barefoot children playing in the yards. Julie looked at her watch. Only a quarter of seven.

More curious eyes followed her. Julie didn't even have the energy to smile.

The houses were getting further apart. Where was the man taking her?

"Chad Morgan?" she asked again.

The old man smiled.

They stepped aside to let an ox cart loaded with logs go by them. Julie's companion called out a greeting to the driver.

The road cut across the hillside, sloping slightly downward, with the ocean to the right below them—a small bay really, with the ocean beyond, a beautiful gem of a bay rimmed by green hills, ships anchored at its mouth. Dozens of barks and other crafts were scattered at anchor in the bay's interior. The sun was so bright on the water, it hurt her eyes.

The road curved onto a small plateau. Ahead was one last house built on the edge of a drop-off with a large shedlike building directly across the road from it. *Please,* Julie thought. If that wasn't Chad's house, the old man was going to have to go bring Chad to her. She really couldn't go any further.

She breathed a sigh of relief when they stopped in front of the small windowless dwelling, and the old man knocked on the wooden door. "Chad Morgan," he told her, nodding his head. "Chad Morgan," he repeated.

Gratefully Julie managed a weak smile.

And very shortly the door was opened by a breathtakingly beautiful young woman.

Chapter Seven

The young woman had the most beautiful skin Julie had ever seen. Smooth, brown, absolutely flawless. She smiled sweetly at her early-morning callers. Her teeth were perfect, too.

Julie felt physically ill. She had come all this way only to find Chad had someone else.

Well, what did she expect? That Chad was living like a monk? After all, she had given him no encouragement. Absolutely none.

And this girl was so lovely. . . .

Julie put her hand out to steady herself against the doorframe. She was light-headed from hunger and sick at heart with disappointment. She knew she had to sit down or she was going to collapse.

The old man was saying something to the girl. Julie recognized Chad's name. And he pointed in her direction.

He was probably explaining how he found this foreign woman sleeping in the hotel lobby, how she asked for Chad. The mystery woman who appeared from no place.

Julie leaned against the side of the house. She was fading fast. Whether she liked it or not, she had to get some food and water from someone. And this beautiful young creature seemed to be the only one around who could supply them.

The girl was looking at Julie with concerned eyes. Huge, richly brown eyes. Thick, long lashes.

Julie tipped her thumb to her mouth, motioning that she wanted something to drink. "Water." Then she remembered the Spanish word. *"Agua."*

The old man nodded at Julie sympathetically and, leaving the suitcase sitting by the dusty road, offered a wave and shuffled off back toward town.

The girl picked up the suitcase and, taking a firm hold on Julie's arm, led her into the house. A strange house. There was furniture, pictures on the wall, a television but no back wall—only a wooden railing opening onto the steep hillside and a panoramic view of the bay.

The girl led Julie to one of the rocking chairs grouped in front of the television set and brought her a drink of water.

"Gracias," Julie said. She drank half the glass in one gulp, then fished around in her purse for some aspirin to take with the rest.

"Now, I need food," she told the girl, making motions of feeding herself. For the first time, she wished that she had paid more attention in her high school Spanish class.

But the girl seemed to understand. She nodded and went into a kitchen whose walls were nothing but screening. Julie watched her for a minute as she bustled about, then with great effort, pulled herself out of the chair and headed toward a door she hoped was to the bathroom. It was.

The bathroom was a stark affair with a dim, bare light bulb overhead, bare concrete floors and a tiny cracked mirror over an ancient chipped lavatory that must have been removed from another, much older building. Several impressive spiders were crawling around in the shower stall, and an overgrown cricket sat on the back of the toilet. Julie splashed water on her face and attempted to comb her hair. She was beyond caring about her makeup.

When she returned to the open living room, a plate of beans and brown rice was waiting for her on the formal-looking dining table surrounded by six ornately carved high-backed chairs. Julie sat in one of them and ate gratefully. She knew that hysteria was lurking very close at hand, but she couldn't deal with the mess she had gotten herself into until she had nourished herself. Maybe then she'd have the strength to face it.

The food tasted good. God, she was hungry. Julie all but inhaled several bites, but then she forced herself to eat more slowly. She didn't need indigestion on top of all of her other problems.

Almost immediately she began feeling less light-headed, but as her thoughts cleared, a misery of another sort replaced her extreme hunger. She was sitting in a house in a remote area of a strange country with her ex-boyfriend's girlfriend and hadn't the faintest idea how she was going to get herself out of here and back home again. She wondered if the driver who had brought her to San Juan made regular runs between the town and Managua.

She felt the girl's eyes on her. "Your name?" Julie asked. She knew that "What is your name?" was the second phrase learned in high school Spanish—right after *¿Cómo está usted?*—but Julie couldn't remember it. She pointed at herself. "I am Julie. Julie. You are...?" she asked, pointing at the girl.

The girl flashed another of her brilliant smiles. "Lola," she said.

"You and Chad...here?" Julie asked, waving her arm to indicate the house.

Lola nodded enthusiastically.

So, Julie thought, here she was with Lola, who was apparently Chad's live-in. Or wife. She glanced at the girl's hand. No ring. But Julie wasn't sure if Latin American wedding customs included a wedding band.

What was she supposed to do now?

Never in her whole life had she felt so utterly stupid. To have come all this way for nothing was more than she could bear. She'd give anything to get out of here before Chad materialized. But she'd need someone who spoke English to help her exchange money and arrange transportation for her back to Managua. And she'd need her airplane reservation changed to an earlier departure.

She wondered where Chad had gone so early in the morning. Or maybe he was off on one of his trips checking on other do-gooders stationed about the impoverished country.

"Chad?" she questioned. "Where is Chad?"

The girl shook her head. She didn't understand. So young, Julie thought. Lola couldn't be more than twenty. Maybe less. Her body was slim under her loose-fitting, faded dress. She was too young for Chad. He should be ashamed.

Suddenly Julie couldn't stand to be here in Lola's presence another minute. She had no choice, however, except to call upon Lola's hospitality one more time. Julie put her hands together and rested her face against them in the universal gesture for sleeping. "Sleep," she said. "Bed."

Lola picked up the suitcase and led the way from the living area down the open veranda past several shuttered windows and a closed door to a second closed door.

Inside the dark room was a bed. Lola placed the suitcase inside the door and left her there.

Julie pulled off her shoes, belt and earrings and curled up on the bed—actually a wooden platform with a couple of pallets piled on top and covered with threadbare, patched sheets—and cried into a hard, lumpy pillow until exhaustion took over and she felt herself falling asleep.

She was aware of sounds throughout the day. A radio playing. Lola singing. Doors opening and closing. Noisy plumbing. Julie stumbled back to the bathroom once, nodding to Lola, who was working in the screened kitchen. When Julie turned on the bathroom light, a giant roach scurried across the concrete floor and disappeared behind the toilet. In spite of the spiders still occupying the shower stall, Julie took a hasty shower in water that refused to get warm, then put her clothes back on and returned to the bedroom more out of having no place else to go than wanting to sleep anymore. But she was overcome with lethargy. Sleep was an escape. A drug. If she slept, she didn't have to cry.

When Chad came back, she'd have to face him. And ask him to help her go home. She had no choice. But in the meantime, she would hide under a blanket of sleep.

SHE AWOKE to the sound of Chad's voice calling to someone named Joe. Then suddenly the bedroom door swung open and his lean form was silhouetted against the pallet of a vivid sunset.

"What the hell?" his voice exploded.

He took several steps into the room, approaching the bed tentatively. "Julie? My God, Julie, is that you?"

A large dog came bursting into the room after him.

Julie pulled herself to a sitting position. "Hello, Chad," she said meekly.

He stood by the bed looking down at her, the dog at his side, tail wagging. "What the hell are you doing here? I can't believe this. I open the door to my bedroom, and there's a woman in my bed. And the woman turns out to be you."

"Didn't Lola tell you I was here?"

"Lola? No, she's gone. She usually only works in the morning."

"Works? You mean she just works here?" Julie felt sweet hope surging in her breast.

"Yeah," he said, sitting on the bed beside her, taking her hand. The dog seemed unimpressed by Julie's presence and ambled out of the room. "You thought something else, huh?" Chad asked.

"Yes, I thought something else. Damn it, Chad, I'm going to start crying . . . again."

"I'm not sure what this is all about, but I damned near had a heart attack when I opened the door and saw you in here."

"I came to see you," she sobbed. "Betty Jean gave me a plane ticket for my birthday, but this was the worst trip I've ever taken in my life, bouncing all night on the floor of a truck until every muscle in my body was on fire. And when I got here, the most beautiful girl in the entire world opened your front door, and I didn't know how to turn around and go back, but I'm glad now that I didn't, and I wouldn't have blamed you if you lived with Lola. You probably should. I didn't give you one bit of encouragement, and you came all the way back to

Houston to see me. Oh, Chad, I haven't been able to get you out of my mind. I keep thinking about how good it was to see you, to be with you. I wanted..."

He hushed her with a kiss, a very salty kiss. Julie clung to him like the drowning cling to life preservers and followed his kiss with one of her own. Suddenly the horrors of her journey were forgotten. She was here in Chad's arms, in Chad's bed.

Yes, his bed. "Make love to me," she said.

"Oh, Julie," he groaned, burying his face against her hair.

She fumbled with the buttons on his shirt. "Yes. I want you to make love to me. I think I'll just wither up and die if you don't. It's the very least you can do after all the horrors I have endured getting here."

And suddenly they were in a frenzy to extricate themselves from clothing. Except they kept having to stop and kiss—incredible soulful kisses that went deep and long, kisses that spoke more eloquently than any words of twenty years' worth of longing.

"You're really here?" he asked. "You're real, and I'm not dreaming."

"I'm real," she said as she pulled him down onto the pillow.

"No, you're a dream," he said. "I'm living in my dream. But I hope it lasts forever. For the rest of my life."

Julie wasn't sure if she was celebrating the sweet memories of an old love or if she was truly in love with the present-day version of Chad Morgan, but she would find that out later. Right now, all that mattered was the celebration itself. She wasn't going to deny herself something she had dreamed of countless times in varying degrees of intensity over the years. She prayed that she could love Chad for the rest of her life, but if that was not to be, she would at least have these sweet memories to sustain her.

They would have a few days, then she would have to go back and face her future. But right now, regardless of what that future held, she wanted to make love to Chad.

He was so solid and manly, and his heart was pounding in his bare chest. She clutched at his shoulders and back, wanting him closer, wanting to crawl inside of him and be one with him.

At last they had to give each other up long enough to remove the remainder of their clothing. The last rays of the setting sun flooded through the open door and made their bodies golden. His midsection was still as flat as a boy's, his hips as slim. But his shoulders and arms were larger and stronger than those of the boy she remembered.

Julie put her face against his smooth chest and inhaled the warm, moist, male scent of him. She wanted him so much it was almost painful.

And he wanted her. Julie gloried in the physical evidence of his desire.

"I'll never forget this night," Chad whispered against her hair. "I've never wanted anyone as much as I want you at this moment."

Without clothing, they could glory in the feel of flesh against flesh. Eagerly they explored each other's bodies with their hands and mouths. Julie relished the feel of his firm, muscular body. The maleness of him was intoxicating. She couldn't decide what she liked more, the touching or being touched.

He was groaning, and his body grew ever more tense and ready. So hard he was, bursting with his desire for her.

"Make love to me," she said.

His body was over her, hovering. Her legs came around his back, making herself open to him.

Chad looked down into her eyes. "I love you, Julie. God, how I love you."

She answered by reaching around his back and pulling him down into her. It was as though she had waited her entire life for this one moment. Nothing had ever felt so perfect, so right, so meant to be as Chad making love to her.

Her darling Chad. Most precious man. Beloved dreamer.

She knew their first time would be fast. They were too full of their need for it to be otherwise. They rose very quickly on a wave of white, hot passion, higher, ever higher. He kept saying her name over and over.

When she reached the crest of the wave, she felt him exploding inside of her.

"Yes," she cried out. "Oh, yes, my darling!"

They hovered for a time, floating above the earth like two exhausted birds who had reached the pinnacle of their flight, and were drifting earthward, slowly returning to the house, the room, the bed.

And then there was peace. They clung together while their breathing quieted and their bodies calmed.

"I knew it would be like that," Julie said. "I just knew it would."

"I never dreamed..." Chad began, then stopped, words failing him.

"You never dreamed about making love to me," Julie teased.

"I never dreamed anything could be that wonderful."

Julie felt a smug smile tugging at her lips. She wanted to be that special to him.

They caressed each other, prattling in the silly language of satisfied lovers about how it had felt, what they had been thinking, how they had been born to make love to each other. How they loved each other's skin, eyes, lips, thighs, sighs, everything.

"How long can you stay?" he asked. "Forever, I hope?"

"A week. A day of which is already gone."

"No. I won't let you go," he said, clutching her to his chest. "I don't think I can bear to have you like this then lose you again. What about Kevin? Does he know you're here?"

"Yes."

"What did you tell him?"

"That I couldn't marry him without figuring out how I felt about you."

Chad grabbed her left hand. "No ring?"

"No ring. I gave it back."

"And your kids' tuition?"

"I don't know. But let's not spoil the mood by talking about my financial problems. Right now, my sweet darling, I think you'd better feed me before my poor stomach growls its way right out of my belly."

"Your stomach? I thought it was mine. I hope you like beans and rice."

"As a matter of fact, I acquired a taste for them only this morning."

Chad rolled out of bed and groped for the string to pull on the light. He tried two or three times, but the room remained in darkness.

"Is the light bulb burned out?" Julie asked.

"I doubt it. We have a shortage of everything here, including electricity. Sometimes the government interrupts services as a conservation measure; other times a transformer malfunctions."

He opened the wooden shutters to let in more moonlight and pulled on his jeans while she dug in her suitcase for a robe. Then she padded behind him to his open-air kitchen, where he turned on a battery-operated lamp. The yellow dog ambled over from the corner of the room, and Chad introduced Julie. "Joe, this is Julie. We love her."

Joe wagged his tail and moved closer so Julie could pat his head. She and the dog hovered about the kitchen while Chad warmed the beans and rice left on the two-burner stove by the departed Lola. And he sliced bread, tore greens for salad and warmed some already fried plantains, a bananalike fruit that Julie had sometimes seen in the grocery store but never tasted.

Chad found a candle for the table and poured fresh pineapple juice and rum into two glasses. They sat at the handsome table on the edge of the veranda overlooking the moonlit bay. The sound of waves carried quite clearly to their high perch, and the roosters from nearby farms occasionally woke to offer noisy challenges to roosters in the town.

And the star-studded sky was spectacular beyond belief. The electricity was indeed off everywhere. The town that hugged the bay was clothed in darkness. With no smog to dim them, no electric lights anyplace to compete with him, the stars were more numerous and more brilliant than Julie thought possible. The sky was completely covered with stars of every intensity.

"I didn't know the night could look like that. It's more beautiful than a cathedral, more spiritual," she told Chad.

"Yeah, I think so, too," he agreed. "Only I must confess that it's never been more beautiful than it is sitting here with you."

"I know what you mean. The night is special because we're together. It even makes the food taste fantastic. This is absolutely the best food I've ever tasted in my life," Julie insisted as she helped herself to seconds. "The beans and rice tasted good this morning. Tonight, they taste like ambrosia."

He laughed. "I'm glad you think so. You'll be seeing this particular delicacy again, I'm sure."

"You eat beans and rice a lot, I take it."

"Almost every meal. Sometimes accompanied by other things. Sometimes not. Tomorrow night, I'll take you out for a wonderful seafood dinner. What do you think of the plantains? There's no sugar added. The natural sugar in them caramelizes like that."

"They're better than Banadas Foster. And *fresh* pineapple juice. I've never had such a luxury."

Joe decided to stretch out by Julie's feet, and she obligingly rubbed the dog's back with a bare foot. Chad explained that Joe had come to his door one day and never left. "He was little more than a skeleton and hardly had the strength to walk across the room, but he could still wag his tail," Chad said affectionately. "He's been my buddy ever since."

The rum in the pineapple juice was making Julie pleasantly light-headed, and any part of her body that had previously forgotten to relax was now in the process. She felt deliciously languid, thoroughly happy, completely in love.

And through all this smug contentment, she felt a sense of anticipation. They would sit here, talking, drinking, enjoying each other's company and the beauty of the evening until they returned to the mussed bed in the room at the end of the veranda.

Chad quizzed her about her trip and moaned over her difficulties.

"Next time, I'll meet you in Managua and bring you here myself."

Next time. Julie liked the sound of that. She wanted a next time. She wanted Chad always to be a part of her life, but she didn't see how that would be possible given the widely divergent paths they had taken with their lives. For the duration of her visit, however, she was going to do something rare for her. She would live for the moment, taking what pleasure there was with no thought of what came after.

And maybe nothing was impossible. After years of being alone, maybe Chad would realize he was ready to return to his native land, to live in a house with four walls and be a good husband to an ordinary American woman.

"How can you talk about next time after the difficulty I've had with this trip?" she demanded. "With no reliable means of communication, how are people traveling to Nicaragua ever supposed to let anyone know when they're arriving?"

"A friend of mine has set up an electronic mail service. It's how I communicate with the home office in Chicago when I can't get a call through. And we're starting to get an electronic network in place connecting all the One World workers here in the country. Maybe you and I can stay in touch that way. And sometimes telephone calls do go through. You just can't count on it.''

Julie started to say that next time he could come to visit her, but she couldn't honestly say there would be a next time. Instead she asked, "Will you stay here forever?''

"Probably not," he said, refilling her glass. "But for the time being, this is home. It's where my work is. And I'm sorry you've gotten such a horrible introduction to Nicaragua. The country has a lot to recommend it. Fantastic beaches. Lovely people. No pollution. No traffic jams. A saner pace of life. In spite of incredible problems and hardships, I swear the people smile more here. And everyone helps everyone else. Hitchhiking is a way of life. And sharing.''

"Are all the houses open like this?" she asked.

"Most are open to a center courtyard, but I wanted to take advantage of the view.''

"What about cold weather? And doesn't it rain in?''

"It never gets cold, and it generally rains straight down. I built this house myself," he said, taking a proud look around the room. "It may not be like much by U.S.A. standards, but considering the difficulty I had getting wood, roofing, concrete, pipes, plumbing fixtures and even nails, I feel like I accomplished a minor miracle. That's the problem I have with the windmills—getting parts, materials. There's been an embargo from the U.S. because of the political situation and not much support from other countries. We don't have medicine, schoolbooks, building supplies, parts to fix our rusty old cars. I'm looking for a mule or horse as a hedge against my truck breaking down or the next gas shortage, but I can't even find a mule to buy. Everyone else has the same idea. People are hitching their cows up to carts, and I even saw a man riding one the other day.''

"Don't you get tired of all the shortages and hardships?'' she asked.

"Sure. But I get paid in American dollars, and by Nicaraguan standards I'm a wealthy man. And I feel good about myself and about what I do. It's nice knowing that long after I'm dead and gone, some of these windmills I'm putting together will be pumping water and helping farmers eke out a living from their land. So for me, the inconveniences are worth it. Besides, I'm used to them. And sometimes there's a trade-off. When there are no electric lights, the night sky is more brilliant. And when you live in a poor country, you learn what things are really important. Materialism isn't a problem here. Of course, I'll admit that I haven't figured out the trade-off for substandard education and health care. Those are the things that bother me the most. But as the economy improves, everything else will in time.''

"And now that we've had this second reunion, will it bother you to be here without me?''

He reached for her hand. "Being without you has been a problem in my life since you told me you were going to marry Ross.''

"You forced me into that, you know.''

"Yeah, I suppose,'' he admitted. "Your dad never thought much of me, but as long as I was the basketball star, he tolerated me. I wasn't a good student. The only things I was good at were things I could do with my hands. Then when I got hurt and had to face the rest of my life without basketball, he panicked. So did I.''

"But you and I had it all worked out. You were going to major in vocational education, become a shop teacher in a high school."

"Julie, I'll never forget the look on your father's face when you explained that to him. Taylor Harper couldn't abide the idea of *his* daughter marrying a shop teacher. I felt that if I didn't get you away from your parents, I'd lose you. Then one afternoon I wandered into a Peace Corps recruitment meeting and immediately decided that I'd just have to get you far enough away from them so I'd feel secure. But in doing that, I scared you away."

"Oh, it wasn't the far away that bothered me as much as your deciding I should drop out of school and join the Peace Corps without ever talking it over with me. You made it an ultimatum. 'Come with me or else...Them or me.' You never gave us a chance to find a middle ground, something we could both live with."

"If I stayed in Houston, would you have married me?"

"Yes. Maybe not till we finished school," Julie said. "But you made your ultimatum, and I didn't know what to do. My parents were freaking, and Ross gallantly stepped forward with what they considered the perfect solution. Suddenly I found myself in the middle of wedding-dress fittings and bridal showers. Then just as suddenly I was married and pregnant and living in Boston. There was no time for regret. And if Ross hadn't died, I would be married to him still. We had our problems, but we were working on them. And the twins were a joy. What about your marriage? Do you still miss her?"

"No, not really. Maybe it would be different if we had kids, but we just drifted apart. The divorce was just a formality."

Julie helped him clear the table and watched as he made coffee. As a bachelor of many years' standing, he was quite at home in the kitchen.

He pulled two rocking chairs over to the railing, and they sat there under the canopy of stars, rocking and sipping very strong coffee. After sleeping all day and drinking this stiff brew, Julie doubted if she'd sleep much tonight. But she didn't care. She would almost rather stay awake and listen to Chad breathing, watch his sleeping face, feel him next to her. "I'm glad that I came," she told him.

"I'm ecstatic that you came," Chad said with a catch in his voice. "Nothing in my life has ever pleased me more."

"It took a lot of courage," she reminded him.

"I know. Like when I went back to that reunion. I want you to like it here, Julie. I'll try to show you the best of Nicaragua, but there will be things that distress you. Just remember, however, that there are distressing things in Houston, too. You're just more accustomed to them, and they've lost their shock value."

"Don't put pressure on me," Julie said. "Just let me be here with you. I want to enjoy being with you whether or not I ever come back again."

They finished their coffee, then Julie slipped on her shoes and, still in her robe, followed Chad down a steep path to the beach. They held hands and walked, the only people in the world, two shipwrecked lovers who had only themselves to please.

They took off their clothes and waded out into the surf. It was cold at first but not for long. They paddled out to calmer water beyond the incoming waves and, treading water, they embraced, relishing the erotic feel of each other's wet bodies.

"Come now," he said. "I want to show you some magic."

They swam back to the beach. "Look at us," Chad instructed when they emerged from the water. The phosphorus from the water clung to their bodies, and their skin glowed in the darkness.

Julie clapped her hands and laughed with delight. "Oh, we are *so* beautiful. Our skin looks like the sky— all dusted with stars. You're right, Chad. It's magic. But I know some magic, too," she said as she slipped her arms around his neck.

She felt him grow hard against her bare belly. Yes, magic. Like warm honey, it poured through her veins.

In her mind's eye she soared above them, memorizing an image of two naked lovers embracing in the moonlight on the deserted beach. She knew that for the rest of her life, she would remember that image and treasure it.

As one, they sank to the warm, silvery sand and made love. Sweet, tender love that made her cry.

Chapter Eight

Julie awoke to the strange feeling of a lumpy, cotton-filled pallet rather than her accustomed innerspring mattress. Immediately she felt a smile tugging at her lips. She wasn't at home. She was in Nicaragua, in Chad's bed. Without opening her eyes she reached for him.

But he was gone.

His pillow was empty and the shutters open to the morning. She rolled over and groped for her watch on the shelf beside the bed. Only five-thirty and already so light. She groaned and closed her eyes.

Water was running in the bathroom. But why in the world was Chad taking a shower so early? If he turned out to be one of those awful morning people who bound out of bed at the crack of dawn disgustingly cheerful and ready for the day, she'd never forgive him. Surely she hadn't been fantasizing all these years about a *morning person*.

She stretched a bit to test the state of her muscles and decided that she was either still suffering the effects of her uncomfortable journey the night before last, or her body was protesting the lack of a proper mattress.

Of course, human beings slept on the ground for millions of years before beds were invented, and tens of thousands more years went by before the advent of innerspring mattresses. But her back was definitely unhappy with the current arrangement. Julie decided she wouldn't have made a very good cave woman.

With another groan, she slipped on her robe and headed for the kitchen to make coffee, but a pot of freshly made coffee was already sitting on the stove. Julie found a pitcher of milk in the tiny, dented refrigerator that looked like a legacy from the 1940s and added some to a cup of coffee. She carried the cup to a rocking chair and was half finished when Chad emerged from the bathroom with a towel around his middle. His hair was mussed and damp. His bare arms and chest were tanned and smooth. And his good-morning smile was feisty. He looked so darling, she almost forgave him for getting up so early. In fact, he looked more than darling. He looked downright sexy.

"Next?" he asked, bending over to nibble her earlobe.

"Later. It's nice sitting here. These rocking chairs are seductive. I wonder if anyone has investigated them as a cure for high blood pressure."

"They are soothing," he said, leaning against the railing, the bay and morning sky forming a backdrop behind him, "but only if one takes the time to sit in them. People in the States hurry around too much to benefit from a rocking chair's therapeutic value."

"Seems to me you're the one hurrying around. Why did you get up so early?" Julie asked. "I wanted you there beside me when I woke up."

"Nicaraguans go to bed early and get up early. It's the sun, I suppose. It rises early and sets early here. We usually go to bed after our soap opera. Last night was an exception," he said with a wink.

"Why couldn't this morning be an exception?" she said with a deliberate pout. "I hate getting up early. I live for the weekends and vacations when I can sleep past six a.m. And I'm on vacation now."

"My mother used to tell me I could sleep late when I was dead or old, whichever came first. You go take your shower and get dressed. I'm going to put you to work."

"Can't you take some time off this week?" she asked, feeling a bit out of sorts. After all, she hadn't come all this way to work or watch him work.

"Sure. But today, I've got promises to keep. Tomorrow, I'll take you to the most beautiful beach on the face of the earth."

"I thought that's where we were last night," Julie said.

He grinned. The man was older than the boy she had once loved, but his grin was the same. Julie's heart melted. "It just seemed that way," he said. "The best is yet to come. Now, go, I'll fix us some breakfast."

"Let me guess," Julie said over her shoulder as she headed for the bathroom. "Rice and beans, right?"

"My, you are a clever woman. You can have them heated or unheated. With or without sour cream."

"Warm with a bit of sour cream. Not much, though. It's fattening."

Julie would have preferred to lure him back to bed, but he seemed intent on going to work, so she dutifully showered and shampooed her hair—there was still no hot water—and put on a pair of jeans and a red cotton shirt with a navy bandanna at her neck. Grateful that she had brought a cosmetic mirror, she used the light from the window in the bedroom to put on her makeup and comb her hair. Did one still call it a window when it was just an opening? she wondered. Such a strange way of life—open to the elements. She felt like she was camping out.

"Next time, I get to shower first," Julie said as she joined Chad in the kitchen. "You used up all the hot water."

"There was none to use up. I don't have a hot water tank. Such a contraption is virtually unheard of in this country. If you want hot water, you've got to boil it."

"You mean people always bathe in cold water?"

"You get used to it," he assured her.

"But what about hot water for washing machines? I'm sure the clothes don't come out very clean without hot water."

Chad pulled an old-fashioned scrub board from under the galvanized kitchen sink. "This is a Nicaraguan washing machine," he said. "Works pretty good with a bar of lye soap, but it takes a lot of elbow grease."

"But it makes no sense for people to have television and no washing machines or hot water tanks."

Chad laughed. "But television is a necessity. Without television, we couldn't watch our baseball games and soap operas. It gives us something to think about besides embargos, shortages, the economy, the international political scene and whether or not the war is really over."

Julie tried to decide which she'd miss more, her television or her automatic washer and dryer. The television lost, provided, of course, there were lots of good books readily available.

Chad had set the table and cut up a cantaloupe. Julie ate several slices, and her rice and beans. The veranda was as lovely a place to eat breakfast as it was to have dinner. Last night they had dined under the stars. This morning a bright new day surrounded them, the bay a lovely blue-green, the hills on either side a rich emerald green. Already several barges were scurrying back and forth unloading ships anchored offshore.

The town of San Juan was to the right and below Chad's house. The buildings in the town were mostly white, many with tin roofs, many with television antennae. The streets seemed to take no particular pattern. A church belfry towered over the lower part of the town, but most of the houses were built up the steep hillside and looked down on the church tower. At this distance, the town looked picturesque, but Julie remembered the rutted streets and shabby houses she had seen yesterday morning. She realized Chad's house was probably as nice as any.

"I like your interior decorator," Julie said, indicating the view.

"Yeah, old mother nature paints a pretty nice picture."

Julie wouldn't have minded lingering with him over another cup of coffee, but she could tell he was anxious to be off.

Joe came loping around the corner of the house and followed them across the dusty road to the shed.

Two men, one middle-aged and the other quite elderly, were already working inside. Large doors at both ends of the building had been pushed open, and a pleasant breeze was blowing through. The younger man was working at a table saw, cutting windmill blades. The older man was assembling a set of blades onto a unit. Shelving alongside the building was filled with gears in assorted sizes, coils of cable and motors in various states of assemblage.

In fluent Spanish, Chad introduced the men, Manuel and Pablo. They offered shy smiles and accepted her handshake.

"Who did you tell them I was?" Julie asked.

"I said when I went home last night, I found you in my bed, that I'd never seen you before in my life."

"No, really. What did you tell them?"

"You'll just have to learn Spanish and ask them," he teased. "Actually that's not a bad idea, learning Spanish. How much do you remember from high school?"

"*¿Cómo está usted?* and a few other words. Not much, I'm afraid."

While he helped the men, Chad told Julie the names of things they could see either in the building or outside. "Bird—*pájaro*. Door—*puerta*. Hammer—*martillor*. Man—*hombre*. Dog—*perro*.

He put her to work cleaning old, grease-encrusted gears. She started to protest that it would ruin her manicure but decided to be a good sport. With a stiff metal-bristled brush and gasoline, she scrubbed away the thick, greasy residue, trying to keep the gasoline from splattering on her blouse.

Here goes my manicure, she thought. *Some vacation.*

But then she remembered last night and decided she couldn't really complain. And it was a pleasure for her to watch Chad work with the two men. He was definitely the boss, but also the teacher. She couldn't understand their conversation, but she could tell by his tone, his gestures, that he was instructing the men in the ancient art of windmill making.

Obviously the men only partially assembled the units here in the shed. The towers would have to be built on site. Chad explained that the machines were used both to pump water and to generate electricity, and the far end of the shed had the look of an electrical shop with wiring, batteries, gauges and other electrical gear scattered around wooden benches.

Julie thought of her tour of Kevin's shipping company with its vast warehouses, fleet of ocean-going freighters and tankers, hundreds of employees and luxurious corporate offices. Chad's tiny operation seemed pitifully simple by comparison.

Although Chad supplied a vital service to farmers in this area of Nicaragua, it was an out-of-the-way part of the world with such a small impact on the world's economy that it made Chad's work seem inconsequential. But obviously he was not the sort of man who aspired to be rich and powerful. Julie wasn't sure if that was an admirable quality or not. In her world, the most admired men were the ones with wealth and power. Her parents, her children, Jody Zachery and most of the people Julie knew would find Chad's life and work unimpressive, even foolish. In fact, the Nicaraguans themselves apparently thought the foreigners who came to help out were somewhat foolish. Chad had said foreigners like himself were referred to as "useful fools."

She understood, however, that Chad felt more important here than he would back in the States, more needed. Here he could take pride in his work and in the simple house he had built with his own hands out of recycled materials. In America, such a house would have been an embarrassment. And men who worked with their hands often did not command much respect.

Julie wondered if her own father wasn't part of the reason Chad had sought a life far away from a world where success was measured by the size of one's house and the make and number of cars in one's circle driveway. Years ago, Taylor Harper had made Chad feel inadequate. By her father's standards, a man who wanted to work with his hands would never be successful, would never amount to anything. The irony of it was that her father had lost most of what he had spent his life acquiring. His brash cleverness had done him no more good in the end than Chad's more humble talents. Yet, just as her father's opinions had filled her with misgivings when she was a vulnerable young woman, Julie still found herself judging Chad by traditional standards, which said a man must be able to offer a woman security and a standard of living that was at least equal to what she was accustomed to. Chad couldn't do that as a twenty-year-old. He couldn't do it now as a man approaching forty.

If she and Chad returned to Houston and got married, Julie wondered if she wouldn't always be slightly embarrassed by her less-than-successful husband. He had only one semester of college and would feel out of place in an office. But here in his windmill shed, he was obviously respected. Julie suspected that he was valued elsewhere in this tiny, needful country. Fool or not, Chad had a nobleness about him that simple people could see. She feared her more sophisticated parents, children and friends would look right past it.

Only Betty Jean would understand. Julie felt a stab of loneliness for her friend and wished she could call her. Betty Jean would reassure her. Betty Jean would say love was more important than anything else.

And Julie wished she could call Steve and Sherry. At the back of her mind, a mother's anxiety nagged at her. For the first time ever, she was completely unavailable for her children. If there was an emergency back home, they would have to manage on their own.

Midmorning, she and Chad washed the grease from their hands and climbed into his truck to make what he called his "house calls." Joe rode in the back.

The traffic along the country road was sparse, and what vehicles there were would have been relegated to the junkyard years ago in America. She saw vehicles without bumpers, headlights, windows, fenders and even doors. Some of the cars were so worn and rusty, it was difficult to tell what their original color had been. That they ran at all seemed a miracle. Julie was beginning to realize that there was little new in Nicaragua. Like the sheets on the bed, Chad's jeans and shirt were patched. His truck was at least fifteen years old and had mismatched fenders. Even the plumbing fixtures in his house had been recycled.

At the first farm, Chad went with the farmer into the pasture to see what it would take to get his ancient windmill working once again. Joe followed along, something he was apparently accustomed to doing.

Julie stayed in the shade of the family home—just a shack really, with no walls and two small pigs wandering in and out at will. But the dirt floor was freshly swept, and the primitive kitchen was quite clean. Freshly washed clothes were hanging from tree branches and over a fence. A scrawny milk cow was tied to a tree, and a half-full bucket of milk sat on the table. There was no refrigerator. No television. No electricity.

The three young children were barefoot and dressed in little more than rags, but such beautiful children with handsome features and bright dark eyes that regarded Julie shyly. The mother had probably once been beautiful herself, but now she was painfully thin, and her teeth had begun to rot. The sight of her made Julie sad.

Such a hard life with no better prospects for her children.

Julie dug a package of gum from her purse and passed it out among the children. And showed them a picture of Steve and Sherry with accompanying gestures to explain the boy and girl were her babies.

When Chad finally returned, he was covered with dirt and grease. He cleaned his hands and arms using a rag and gasoline from a can in the back of the truck.

And they were off again. Soon Chad turned off the road onto little more than a cow path, and they bounced along for miles, twice having to pull over for ox carts. To Julie, the road seemed impassable, but Chad kept going and she held on for dear life. Sometimes the bumps were so severe, she hit her head on the top of the truck.

On either side of the road were occasional dwellings even more humble than the one they had just visited. More pretty little children came running toward them to wave and call out.

Chad stopped in front of what had once been a surprisingly large and grand house but was now a study in decay. The second floor of the building had caved in on the ground floor. Chad explained that the house had once been the home of a wealthy landowner under the old Samoza regime, and the smaller dwellings up and down the road had been occupied by the landowner's tenement farmers. But the man had died many years ago, and the land had passed to relatives who lived elsewhere. Then the new government had instigated land reforms and decreed that no one could own land on which they didn't live and work. The former tenement farmers were now on their own but didn't have the resources to take advantage of the situation.

The cellar of the collapsed house was occupied by two brothers and their families. Julie watched while Chad and the brothers spent the next hour trying to get a balky generator to work. Soon she was surrounded by children. This time she had no gum, but Joe sat patiently and allowed the children to pet him and examine his floppy ears and impressive teeth. Like his owner, Joe was a dear.

By the time they arrived back at Chad's house, it was almost one o'clock. Julie felt as if she'd already put in a day and was absolutely starving. The smiling Lola opened the door for them. Julie didn't find the girl's beauty quite so intimidating today. In fact she could smile back with an easy heart. Lola just worked for Chad. The girl was only sixteen, he said, the daughter of Manuel.

Lola had fixed a lunch that not only included the inevitable beans and rice but offered cheese omelets and a heaping plate of fresh, sliced tomatoes. This time the freshly made juice was grapefruit.

While they ate, a heavy rain fell, a daily occurrence during the summer months, Chad explained. The rain did indeed come straight down.

"Are we still eating out tonight?" Julie asked as she helped herself to a second glass of juice.

"Oh, yes. But first we'll make some social calls. I need to show you off to my friends. I'm sure the word has gotten around, and people will be curious to meet you."

"Is the siesta a custom here as it is in Mexico?" Julie asked after she had cleaned her plate. "I'm sure we'd enjoy our evening more if we took a little rest."

"A siesta is not unheard of. Are you sleepy?" he asked.

Julie stretched and offered him a teasing smile. "Yes, that and other things. The rain has stopped. Don't you think it's time for Lola to go home?"

JULIE PUT ON a bright cotton sundress and white sandals for their night out. Chad wore a freshly ironed Nicaraguan-style shirt with a pair of blue cotton trousers. He looked cool and clean and so delicious that Julie had to nibble his neck.

The visiting took hours. First they drove to the town of Rivas to visit the man who handled the electronic mail service for this region. Michel was a charming Frenchman with a Nicaraguan wife and two babies. The largest room of his house had been taken over by a maze of computers with electrical cords looping from the ceiling, over doors and windows, on top of filing cabinets. To support his computer habit, Michel worked as a barber, and Chad helped him apply for grants from U.S. foundations interested in Third World projects. With Chad translating, Michel explained in Spanish about his mail operation and gave Julie his computer "address" so she could send messages to Chad through his system.

Next they went to see the parish priest in San Juan. The padre was a robust man of indeterminate middle years who spoke a little English. Chad explained that he and the padre played chess several nights a week.

"You make big surprise," the man told Julie. "We all have big surprise when a North American lady come see our Chad. You stay long time?"

"Only a few days," Julie said.

The priest looked profoundly relieved. Apparently there weren't too many chess players in San Juan.

From the rectory, they climbed a hill to the home of Ricardo and Maria. He was the town mayor, casket-maker and undertaker. She was the local midwife. "She brings people into the world, and he takes them out," Chad explained. "They are, without a doubt, the town's leading citizens."

Maria kissed Julie on both cheeks and beamed her approval. Two freshly made wooden caskets were stacked beside the television. Maria proudly served them brandy in crystal glasses, and Ricardo offered Chad a cigar.

Next, they went to Manuel's house, where Lola and her mother served coffee in cracked cups. Lola was the oldest of seven children, and their home seemed far too small for so large a family but was luxurious compared to the dwellings Julia had visited this morning. Lola's house had electricity and running water. There were pictures on the walls and flowers in a vase.

By the time they reached the restaurant, Julie was once again famished.

But she was disappointed to find that the restaurant was a primitive affair with a plank floor and rough wooden tables and benches. Julie could see fire burning in an open grill in the kitchen. And chickens and pigs wandered in and out at will.

"Aren't there rules against animals in restaurants?" Julie asked indignantly.

"No rules. We live very close to our animals around here."

"It seems very unsanitary," Julie said, shooing away a scrawny little pig. She wasn't sure she could eat a meal in such a place.

Chad shrugged and gave their order to the waiting boy, who immediately brought back two bottles of Nicaraguan beer, followed shortly by a large platter of black mussels, which smelled heavenly. Julie scowled at the pig, then tentatively picked up one of the mussels and used her fork to extract the meat from the shell. It tasted as good as it smelled. She tried another and soon was greedily devouring the delicacy. The animals were a disgrace, but the mussels weren't.

Next came a delicious seafood stew. But the pièce de résistance of the meal was the most wonderful lobster Julie had ever tasted. "Why does the seafood taste better here?" she asked.

"For one thing, it was all caught today. And I think the flavor has something to do with the fact that our waters are not polluted. The food chain has not been interrupted, and the ocean is still fertile and healthy. I'm glad to see that you are managing to choke down the lobster despite the unsanitary surroundings."

"I still don't approve of the animals," she insisted, taking another heavenly bite. "The Department of Health in Houston would never allow such a thing. And they would insist on screens for the windows and doors. The fire department wouldn't put up with those bare light bulbs and an open fire in a kitchen with such a low ceiling."

"And my truck would never pass a Texas motor vehicle safety inspection. My house wouldn't pass Houston's building codes. Most of the buildings in this town would be condemned by U.S. standards, including the schoolhouse and local medical clinic. But we do the best we can," Chad said.

"I didn't mean to sound so critical. It's just that everything is different here. I don't understand how you've managed to adjust so completely."

"Maybe it's because I didn't come from much in the first place," Chad said. "Nicaragua wasn't that much of a comedown from the neighborhood where I grew up. In fact, it's cleaner. Even in the shantytowns in Managua, people pick up the trash and plant flowers. But sure I miss hamburgers, apple pie, hot-fudge sundaes, movies, nice cars, my native language, basketball, the sports section from the Houston *Post*, telephones that work, mail that arrives, hot water, lots of things. Yeah, I miss them. But I've learned to do without. I wouldn't expect anyone else to, though. I'm weird. You always knew that. Your dad was right."

"No, you're not weird. Just different. You're a good person—better than I am. I'm too selfish to give up all that you have. I think that even after ten years I'd miss hot water when I take a bath. But I'm also too selfish to give you up, so I have a real dilemma, don't I?"

"You'd like me to come back to Houston, wouldn't you?"

"I've thought about it. A lot. But I worry that you'd be as unhappy in Houston as I'd be down here for the long term. But won't you want to come back someday? Or are you planning on living your entire adult life as an expatriate?"

"I don't plan ahead much," he admitted. "It's a luxury you are allowed when you only have yourself to worry about."

"And you have only yourself? There's no one else that matters?" Julie was fishing. Blatantly. But she needed to hear him say that he viewed life differently now that she was a factor.

"You matter. You know that. What would you have me do, Julie?"

"I don't know," she admitted. "In fact, I haven't the faintest idea. All I know is that I love you. And I love my two children. For the time being, I have to put them first. Now, if you don't mind, I'd like another of those beers. I guess I really don't want to decide about the rest of my life tonight."

When they returned to Chad's house, he put recordings of their old high school favorites in his tape-player. They danced under the stars on his veranda, the ocean waves blending with the music.

It felt so right to be in his arms, to be dancing with him. How could she be so in love with a man so unsuitable for her? Julie asked herself. But she was. She loved the feel of him, the smell of his skin, his breath against her cheek. She loved the sound of his voice, his boyish grin, his kind heart. And she loved being loved by him.

For the first time in her life, she actually wished she were older. If Sherry and Steve were out of college and on their own in the world, she could give life here a try. As it was, she didn't have the right even to think about such a thing.

And the hours were ticking by. Her time here would be up before she knew it.

No, don't think about that, Julie told herself. *Think only of tonight.*

They drank their nightcap of rum and orange juice leaning against the railing with their elbows touching.

"Oh, look," Julie said, pointing at the sky. "A shooting star."

"Did you make a wish?" Chad asked.

"Oh, yes. I wished that you would always be a part of my life, that you would always love me."

"Always, my love," he said, putting an arm around her waist and pulling her close. *"Siempre, mi amor."*

TRUE TO HIS WORD, Chad took the rest of the week off. The next morning they packed a picnic basket and headed for his "most beautiful beach in the world."

Once again, they left the main road onto what was little more than a cart trail. Finally, after many bumpy miles that took them deep into the forest, the trail disappeared altogether and they abandoned the truck. With Joe running ahead, they walked the rest of the way, carrying their food and blankets with them.

Julie heard the waves before they walked out of the woods onto the deserted beach with its unbelievable white sand—pristine, unblemished sand that surrounded a perfect little cove of brilliant, aqua-colored water. Along the sides of the cove were impressive dark outcroppings of rock that contrasted dramatically with the white of the sand.

They spread their blankets in the shade of some trees at the edge of the beach, kicked off their shoes and raced across the warm sand to the water. Such clean water. Julie could even see the bottom, which was as clean and clear as the beach. Joe barked at them from the shore and finally plunged in after them. He paddled around for a while, then left them to their devices while he hurried off to explore the rocks.

Chad gave her lessons in body surfing. They would wait for just the right wave, then, with their backs to it, Julie would wait for Chad to say "now" and she would plunge forward, arching her body and allowing the wave to take her. She felt like a mermaid.

Again and again, they rode the waves. It was glorious fun.

Finally, exhausted, they trudged up the beach and stretched out on their blankets. They dozed for a time and, upon waking, enjoyed their lunch of bread, cheese and fruit.

"We have company," Chad said as he nibbled on a banana.

"Where?" Julie said, looking around. The beach was still deserted, but in among the trees, children peered out at them. Julie motioned to them, and after a minute, a tiny little girl came out, and the others followed. The children here were browner than the children in the village, either from the sun or from more Indian blood. Brown eyes regarded her with frank curiosity.

"They've never seen anyone so white," Chad explained. "Hold out your arm so they can touch you."

Julie obliged and several of the children came up to touch her white skin.

"Do they go to school?" she asked.

Chad talked to one of the older boys for a time. "The road has gotten too rough for the school bus to pass," Chad translated. "His father can't take them because he has no money to buy gas for his truck. And the ox-cart takes hours. Most of the children around here don't go anymore. This boy says he went for two years and is not sure if he remembers anything."

"What does he want to be when he grows up?" Julie asked.

"He wants to be a truck driver," Chad translated.

Julie passed out the remainder of their food for the children, then she and Chad went off to explore the rock outcroppings.

"Look behind you," Chad instructed as they walked down the beach.

The band of ragamuffin children was following them. Feeling like a mother duck with her ducklings in tow, Julie and Chad clambered over the rocks with Joe, stopping to look at the amazing variety of sea life that scurried in and out of the pools of trapped water. From a vantage point on the highest rock, Julie surveyed the tiny bay and its pristine beach outlined by a wall of forest. Yes, it was the most beautiful beach in the world.

And Chad was the most beautiful man.

She truly loved him, yet she had no doubt that in three more days she would get on a plane in Managua and leave him. Her duty to her children took precedence over her love for Chad.

But she ached already with the pain of leaving him.

Chapter Nine

Chad decided that Julie should see something of Nicaragua other than San Juan del Sur. On Thursday morning they packed their clothes and loaded up the truck. Julie took one last foray into the bedroom and bathroom to make sure she hadn't left anything, then hugged Lola and gave her a tortoise-shell bracelet as a parting gift. *"Muchas gracias,"* Julie told her.

The girl's eyes glistened with delight, and she offered some rapid-fire Spanish for Chad to translate.

"She says the bracelet is the most beautiful thing she has ever owned, and she will treasure it forever."

Julie felt a bit guilty over the girl's affluent thanks. The bracelet was nothing special. She had found it on a sale table at Foley's, an impulse purchase that had cost no more than four or five dollars, the sort of inexpensive costume jewelry that filled her jewelry box back home. Yet Julie was certain Lola's words were sincere. The cheap bracelet would indeed be the girl's most prized possession.

Julie thought of how her own daughter considered herself underprivileged because her wardrobe had not been as expensive as many of her high school classmates. Still, Sherry had drawers full of costume jewelry, a closet full of clothes, dozens of pairs of shoes.

Steve, too, had a closet full of clothes. The price of his Nikes would be a month's wages in Nicaragua.

My children and I have so much, Julie thought, *that we don't appreciate what we have.*

And suddenly Julie realized she had a reason other than Chad for wanting to return to San Juan. She'd like to bring lovely Lola back a suitcaseful of bracelets and clothes and all manner of trinkets to make a young girl smile.

And she'd like to come back someday to sit on this open veranda and drink rum and orange juice with Chad while they watched the sun sink below the horizon. And pet old Joe. She knelt to hug the dog's neck. "You take good care of Chad," she said.

She stood and took a last look. Chad's home. A haven of peace and beauty. After only a few days, it seemed a little bit hers in spite of the roaches and terrible plumbing, in spite of the neighboring roosters who annoyed her in the night.

Would she ever come back?

Julie honestly didn't know. A few short weeks ago she had known exactly where her future lay, but now she had absolutely no vision of what was ahead for her and her children, and the fact frightened her.

Julie hurried past Chad, her eyes filling with tears, and climbed into the truck.

Love made life so damned confusing, she thought as they bumped along the highway. She was much happier when she just thought that she was in love. Since Chad had re-entered her life, she'd been in a constant state of confusion.

Chad drove first to the shore of Lago de Nicaragua, a lake so vast it was impossible to see across it. And rising from a distant island in the lake's center was the majestic volcano Concepción.

"I've climbed up there," Chad bragged, shading his eyes as he stared at the distant peak. "Some crazy friends of mine go around climbing the country's volcanoes, and sometimes I go with them. We actually go down into the craters. It's quite exciting."

"You have lots of friends, it seems," Julie observed.

"Yeah, both Nicaraguan and other international misfits. I'm a rich man when it comes to friends."

They drove northward along the lake to the beautiful city of Granada, where the influences of Spanish colonization could still be seen in the architecture and in the people, who tended to be fairer-skinned than other Nicaraguans, with an occasional blond head standing out among the dark ones.

They had a wonderful picnic lunch in a vast public park by the lake, then explored a decaying film set that had been designed to portray Granada in the last century. The set had been used a couple of years before during the making of an American film about a band of American adventurers who invaded Nicaragua in the 1850s. Julie took a picture of Chad standing in front of what looked like a hotel but was really just a facade propped up along a street with dozens of other facades.

And then Chad showed her the Nicaraguan version of Shangri-la. A long-ago volcano eruption had left hundreds of tiny islands scattered across this end of the lake. Exquisite little islands green as jade. Some had a house or two; others were too tiny even for houses. Like a scene from a Japanese watercolor, each island had graceful trees that dipped their branches to the water.

Julie sat on a rock and marveled at the beauty. She tried taking a few photographs of the islands but was sure her camera would in no way do the scene justice.

Julie would have liked to explore Granada at greater length, but Chad hurried her along. "I don't like to drive into Managua after dark," he explained.

"Why? Is it dangerous?" Julie asked, thinking immediately of bandits or military roadblocks.

"Yeah. Half the cars on the road don't have headlights or taillights, and none of the ox carts do. It's best to get into the city before dark."

The traffic became heavier the closer they got to Managua, often backing up behind the oxcarts and behind buses packed so full of people that they barely had enough power to make their way up hills. And all along the highway were hitchhikers. "Public transportation is a real problem," Chad admitted. "Country people who work in the city have a hard time getting home at night."

As they drove into the outskirts of Managua, Chad pointed out the many pickups-turned-taxi. Their enterprising owners had put railings around the bed of their trunks to hold their standing-room-only passengers. Sometimes there were so many people loaded in the back of the trucks that the front wheels did not touch the ground as the vehicles made their way through rush-hour traffic.

They passed huge shantytowns with acres and acres covered with tiny dwellings made out of every material imaginable. But there was no trash, and the dirt around the houses was generally swept clean, and many dwellings had flowers and vegetables planted in front. Julie couldn't begin to imagine what it would be like to live in such a place without electricity, plumbing or privacy.

It was almost six when they checked into a small, shabby hotel. While the owner greeted Chad like a long-lost friend, Julie looked warily around the sparsely furnished lobby. At least it seemed clean. She hoped the rooms were. In the courtyard, she was startled to see a two-foot-long lizard sunning itself on the wall.

"An iguana," Chad told her. "They bite."

"Well, I wasn't planning on petting it," she said, wondering what would keep the creature from coming into the open room like the pigs in San Juan.

The owner's wife came swooping out the back to embrace Señor Chad and to beam at Julie. Chad introduced the aging couple as Consuelo and Luis Hernando. "This hotel is where I stayed my very first night in Nicaragua," he explained. "The Hernandos have been my good friends ever since."

A teenage boy took their suitcases up the stairs, and Consuelo and Luis, both talking at once, herded Julie and Chad around the front desk and into their apartment.

Julie accepted a glass of fruit juice and kept looking pointedly at her watch for Chad's benefit. It was getting late, and she wanted to bathe and change for dinner. She planned to dress up in a low-cut white faille dress she had borrowed from Betty Jean. Julie envisioned a lovely, lingering, candlelight dinner in a *real* restaurant—one with four walls, white-clad waiters and no wandering animals underfoot. She wanted wine instead of beer or rum. She wanted to dance to soft music and return to their hotel room full of desire.

"Luis wants me to look at the motor on his old washing machine," Chad announced. "We'll be back in a minute."

The "minute" dragged on to fifteen and then to thirty. With dismay, Julie realized Consuelo was setting the table for four. She hoped the two extra places weren't for her and Chad.

After an hour, when Chad and Luis finally returned, Julie kept her voice pleasant and a smile carefully fixed on her face while she explained to Chad that she was irritated and that she didn't want to have dinner with these people.

"Come on, Julie. Consuelo has everything prepared. Consuelo would be hurt if we didn't stay."

Already the woman was bringing food to the table. Julie sucked back her disappointment and allowed herself to be seated. The beans were cooked with potatoes. How novel. Consuelo must be a Nicaraguan gourmet. Julie picked at her food. She'd wanted something special, and here she was eating beans again. Chad had entered into an animated conversation with Luis and Consuelo. Julie didn't even try to listen for familiar words. She didn't care what they were talking about. All she wanted to do was leave. She certainly didn't want to share Chad with these people. She was hurt that he was willing to sit there chatting away while their evening was ruined.

Luis glanced at his watch and hurried over to turn on the television set. "The nightly soap opera," Chad informed her and made no move to go.

Julie watched the program for a while in utter boredom. Chad explained that it was about a man named Rocque, who was supposed to be a dead saint but turned out to be a live sinner. Finally, Julie pulled on

Chad's sleeve. "Can you get me a key to our room? I want to go upstairs."

Chad took a reading of her face and offered quick words of farewell to Luis and Consuelo. But Consuelo insisted they stay long enough for a nightcap and hurried into her tiny kitchen to pour four glasses of rum.

Julie didn't trust herself to speak until they were finally in their room with the door closed. "I can't believe you did that to me," she blurted out.

"Julie, those people are my friends. They charge me next to nothing when I stay here. Consuelo has fed me countless meals. They would have been hurt if we hadn't accepted their hospitality."

"But we've wasted one whole precious evening with them," Julie said, marching to the stuffy room's one window and opening it as high as it would go. It didn't help. The air outside was as heavy and still as that in the room. "What made you think I'd like sitting there with people I'd probably never see again, not understanding a word that was being said—or a word of that ridiculous soap opera? I couldn't believe it when you abandoned me for a whole hour while you went off to fix some dumb old washing machine when you could have waited until after I was gone. And I thought you said everyone used scrub boards and lye soap."

"Not everyone. That washing machine is very important to the Hernandos," Chad said, his tone defensive. "They do all the linens for the hotel in it and would be hard-pressed to manage without it."

"Well, it was certainly nice of you to fix it for them. But what about me? I wanted us to go someplace intimate and romantic this evening. Couldn't you see that I wanted you to myself!"

"We could still go over to the bar at the Interconti-nental," he offered, but his voice sounded unsure. "I don't know how intimate and romantic it is, but we could give it a try."

"Is there music?"

"I don't know, Julie. I've never been there. When I come to town, I always stay here or at the home of friends, and I usually spend my free time in the eve-ning visiting other friends. I don't hang around bars very much. We go to the baseball games a lot, and oc-casionally there's a concert or an art show, but life is pretty simple even in a city as large as Managua."

"Oh, never mind. I'm sure they've rolled up the streets by now." She sank onto the bed, feeling cooped up in the small, airless room after the openness of Chad's house. In Houston, she would have turned on the air-conditioning. In Houston, there would have been plenty to do—dinner theater, dancing, concerts, art ex-hibits, shopping malls, rodeos, all manner of sporting events, cozy bars. In Houston, television programs were in English.

Chad sat down beside her. "I'll ask around tomor-row. Maybe there's something we can do tomorrow evening to make your last night special."

Julie took a deep breath to relieve the tightness that was building in her chest and realized she was going to cry. Maybe she was acting like a spoiled brat, but she couldn't help it. She was angry and felt absolutely mis-erable.

"Don't say that, damn it!"

"What?" Chad asked, puzzled.

"That tomorrow is my last night."

"But it is."

"I know it is," she said peevishly. "But I don't want you to say that it is."

"What do you want me to say?" He reached for her hand but she pulled it away.

"I don't know. I just wanted to have a wonderful evening tonight because I know tomorrow night will be too sad to bear."

"I'm sorry, Julie. I guess I'haven't been very sensitive."

"No, you certainly have not," she said with a sniffle and wiped at her cheek with the back of her hand. "Apparently you'd just as soon be with Luis and Consuelo as spend time with me. Maybe you should go back down there and watch the rest of your precious television show with them. Or maybe you can go find something else that needs fixing. You're just too damned noble for me, Chad. I want a man who will put me first and not always be putting Band-Aids on the world."

Chad jumped up from the bed and glared down at her. "Talk about the pot calling the kettle black. What about a woman who would sacrifice herself to a loveless marriage so her spoiled children can have new cars and a great social life at college?"

"How dare you say that!" Julie said, raring back her shoulders. "My children are not spoiled, and right now, Kevin McLaughlin seems a whole lot more lovable than you do. He's never yelled at me or made me cry."

"I am not yelling at you. But sometimes the truth hurts." Chad turned and walked to the window, his shoulders rigid.

Julie stared at his back, the silence hanging thick and angry in the small, hot room.

"I'm sorry," he said finally, still facing the window. "I shouldn't have said that about your children."

"Don't say anything else," she said. "Just come hold me."

When he put his arms around her, the dam broke. She sobbed so long and hard, her chest began to hurt.

At last, when exhaustion began to quiet her, Chad gently laid her back on the bed and pulled off her shoes. He brought a damp towel from the bathroom to bathe her swollen eyes.

Then he helped her ease out of her clothes.

In the darkness he cuddled her like a child, caressing her back and hair, telling her he loved her above all else, that he would make things right for her somehow.

Finally she felt herself drifting off, sleep claiming her aching body.

She didn't know how long she slept, but when she awoke, Chad was still holding her. The moonlight through the open window bathed their bodies in silvery light. Julie touched Chad's mouth. His beautiful mouth. And then she kissed it with all the yearning in her soul.

They made love very carefully, willing it to last forever, whispering continually of their adoration, their love.

And finally the awesome heat of desire began to take her body. She clutched at his back and buried her mouth against his throat. She wanted to be a part of him, to blend with him. Her body arched upward in her need, and sweet, liquid warmth coursed through her veins. Behind her closed eyelids, there was white light. A magnificent white light, pure and beautiful and perfect. She soared upward toward the light, closer, ever closer until finally she exploded with such exquisite sensation she wondered if she could die of it.

Gradually she became aware once again of the room around them, of Chad's breathing, of the their hot, damp flesh. She wondered if she could still speak but was too spent to try. And what could she say? No words could describe the emotion she was feeling.

Neither one of them moved until she realized his breathing had changed. She touched his cheek. Tears.

"Oh, Chad, my darling Chad," she cried out as she gathered him to her. Oh, dear God, how she loved him. How could she ever bear to leave him?

THE NEXT DAY, by unspoken agreement, both seemed determined to make the day a festive one. Julie had awakened to the aroma of coffee as Chad brought her breakfast in bed. Along with the coffee, there were sliced oranges, bread and soft cheese for spreading.

Then they had set off to tour Managua. Chad took her first to what had once been the downtown of the nation's capital city but was now empty fields crisscrossed by unused, broken streets. Only a few large concrete buildings and bare foundations remained. "It was all destroyed in 1972 by an earthquake," Chad explained. "Over five thousand people were killed."

He drove through the emptiness and parked in front of what remained of the city's cathedral. The roof was gone, and weeds now grew where people had once worshiped. Faded murals were still visible on the walls.

"It must have been majestic," Julie said, standing in the center of the derelict building. "It's humbling to think a building that had stood for centuries can be destroyed in a matter of minutes."

"Yes, everything is temporary," Chad said. "I read a poem once about celebrating the temporary and decided that was good advice. We shouldn't wait until tomorrow to start enjoying life.''

As they drove around, Chad explained that the commerce of the city was now conducted in outlying centers that had sprung up since the earthquake. The city's shopping center was a large prefabricated structure with dozens of sparsely stocked shops and few shoppers.

The two open-air public markets, on the other hand, were teeming with people. The first market was a vast maze of booths where farmers sold their produce. Vegetables and fruits were displayed on benches. Animal carcasses hung from hooks. Large vats contained cream and butter. Julie kept hearing a strange slapping sound above the buzz of animated shoppers, but she didn't realize what it was until they came upon the open-air tortilla factory, where dozens of women were vigorously patting dough into tortillas and cooking them on huge griddles.

At the second market, as they wandered up and down the alleys lined with small stalls, Julie saw all manner of handcrafted items for sale—pottery, wooden bowls, leather goods, furniture.

They stopped at one stall where rocking chairs were sold, and Chad immediately fell into a heated conversation with the proprietor. They seemed to be arguing, and Julie wondered what over. Finally, Chad peeled off numerous bills from the roll of cardobas in his pocket and watched as the man bundled up an unassembled rocker in a burlap bag. ''Another rocker?'' Julie questioned. ''Four aren't enough?''

''This one's for you to take back with you. You can rock in the evenings and feel a little bit Nicaraguan. Maybe it will help you remember your time here.''

"As if I could forget," Julie admonished. "Thank you, my darling. I can't think of any souvenir I'd rather have more."

She bought iguana billfolds for her father, Steve and Donnie. For her mother, Sherry, Betty Jean and Melissa she found handsome iguana belts.

Then they bought an assortment of food from vendors for their lunch and sat on the tailgate of Chad's truck to eat it until the afternoon rain shower forced them into the cab of the truck.

In the afternoon Chad drove up the winding road to Momotombo volcano, and Julie had the thrill of looking down inside an active, smoking volcano.

"When did it last erupt?" she asked.

"In 1982, right before I came," Chad said.

Poor Nicaragua, Julie thought. The country seemed to get far more than its share of troubles—earthquakes, volcanic eruptions, hurricanes, war.

Back at the hotel, Julie washed her hair and fussed at length with her makeup. The white faille dress showed off her figure to its full advantage, and the look of admiration on Chad's face made her grin with delight. "Not bad for an old broad," she said, assessing herself one last time in the mirror.

They had dinner in the restaurant on the top floor of the Intercontinental Hotel, an unusual pyramidlike structure that was one of the city's few first-class hotels. But Julie decided the food was not worth the high prices listed on the menu, and the view of the city's devastated center was a sad reminder of a national tragedy.

"I'd rather be in your house at San Juan," Julie admitted.

After dinner they went to the first-floor bar to dance, but the bouncy Latin rhythms did not match their mood. Chad stopped on the way back to their hotel for some cold beer.

They said little as they sat in the hotel courtyard drinking beer and rocking in the moonlight. Julie felt strangely shy. Early tomorrow morning she would be leaving Chad, and it seemed as if significant words needed to be spoken. They should discuss what her coming here had accomplished. They should decide what the future held, where they fit into each other's lives, when they would see each other again, if ever.

But she didn't know where to begin.

"Are you glad you came?" he asked finally.

"Yes. I wouldn't have missed it for the world. But what does it all mean?"

"That love can endure over the years. And I've discovered I can't live without you. Give me a year to get things in order down here and train Manuel to take over the windmill operation, and I'll come back to Houston. I do want to put you first in my life."

"But what will you do?"

"Get a job. Finish my college degree at night. Be with you, if you'll have me."

"Oh, Chad, down here you're important and happy. It wouldn't be fair for me to let you give up the life you've made for yourself."

"And it wouldn't be fair of me to ask you to live down here with me."

Julie wanted to say that in a few years, she might do just that. But what sort of life would she live in the isolated little town of San Juan del Sur, Nicaragua? Who would be her Betty Jean? How often would she see her children? Her parents? The words would not come.

She reached for a second beer. This wasn't how it was supposed to be. People in love should have clear sailing not turbulent waters.

There was no good solution. Their decision was that, for now, they would do nothing. They would go back to their respective lives and see how they felt about things after time had put Julie's visit in perspective.

The beer bottles empty, they climbed arm-in-arm up the stairs and walked softly down the deserted hallway. Once in bed, they embraced in silence. Julie put her head against his shoulder and drifted in and out of sleep, waking from strange dreams of windmills and volcanoes. It wasn't until the small hours of the morning that they made love, kissing and clutching at each other as though it would be the last time for a lifetime.

And suddenly it was five o'clock in the morning. Time to dress and head for the airport.

A week. Six days, really. In some ways, it seemed like a very short time. In other ways, she felt as if she'd been here with him forever.

An airport security guard would not allow Chad into the departure area. There was time only for a hurried kiss, a whispered "I love you," and suddenly she was alone again.

Julie sat in a window seat on the flight home and made no attempt to visit with her seatmate. She was too heavy of heart for small talk.

THE SIGHT OF HER CHILDREN and Melissa waiting in the arrival area of Houston International cheered her. She was pushing a cart loaded with her suitcase and the rocking chair from the customs lounge.

All three were waving and grinning broadly. Sherry fell into her mother's arms. Steve wrapped his arms around them both. Melissa hovered in the background until Julie managed to pull her into their embrace.

Julie could swear Steve and Sherry had both grown while she'd been gone. They were big and beautiful and no longer her babies.

"Gosh, Mom, it seems like you've been gone forever," Sherry said. "I'm glad you're back."

"Did you have a good time?" Steve asked.

"Betty Jean says to call her the minute you get home," Sherry interrupted.

"What's in the burlap bag?" Steve asked, hefting the bag from the cart.

"A rocking chair," Julie answered.

"Did you miss us?" Sherry asked, picking up the suitcase.

"I was only gone a week," Julie said. "I worried about being out of pocket more than I missed you guys."

"Ah, you don't need to worry about us," Steve said. "We're grown up and responsible. What should we tell her about first, Sis? The fire or the wreck?"

"Don't forget about the flood," Melissa said with a wink.

"Or the summons," Sherry added.

"Okay, guys. Seriously now, how are things on the home front?"

"Well," Sherry began, "Kevin's called twice to find out if we'd heard from you. He said 'it was very irresponsible of you to run off to a place where your own children couldn't even find you,' and he's not sure if he'll call you back. The real-estate lady brought some people to look at the house—real creeps who said it would cost a fortune to 'restore' the house. Grandma and Grandpa are still in a state. They also think 'it was very irresponsible of you to run off to a place where your own children can't even find you.' And they seem to be of the opinion that you should be declared incompetent for taking up with 'that man' again and should be immediately admitted to a home for willful daughters. Steve and I went to talk to the people in the admissions office at the University of Houston, who indicated they accepted mediocre students at their fine institution. And Betty Jean's in love."

"What can we have for dinner?" Steve asked. "I'm starving."

Julie's head was spinning. She stopped in the middle of the corridor. "Do you kids think I'm irresponsible?" she asked.

"We've talked about that a lot this week," Steve admitted, tugging at her arm to get her started again.

"And?" Julie asked.

"We're not sure, but we love you anyway," Sherry said.

Julie stopped again. "Do you kids think that you're spoiled?"

"Sure," Steve said, giving her arm another tug.

"Absolutely," Sherry said. "But you love us anyway. Mothers are like that."

HER SUITCASE was still unpacked in the corner of the room and the dinner dishes still waited in the kitchen, but Julie got out the toolbox and assembled the rocking chair. It was made of beautifully carved mahogany with a wicker seat and back. She dragged the boudoir chair that had for years occupied a corner in her bedroom to the spare room and replaced it with her wonderful new rocking chair.

Julie switched off the television on her bureau and sat down to rock. The house seemed very quiet, with only the hum of the air conditioner.

She closed her eyes and leaned her head against the chair's high back. She felt like a deep-sea diver in a decompression chamber, trying to get her body acclimated to a different world. Home.

For dinner, Sherry and Melissa had made a salad while Steve cooked hamburgers on the grill. Thinking of Chad's veranda in San Juan, Julie set the table on the patio, even though the kids insisted it was too hot to eat outside. They had been right. Everyone ended up carrying their plates back inside.

After dinner Julie had presented Steve with his billfold and Sherry and Melissa with their belts. "They're made of iguana," Julie explained. "Iguanas are big and green. I don't know how they make brown leather out of a green lizard. One was sitting on top of the courtyard wall of the hotel in Managua. Almost every building has a courtyard." The young people had tolerated her stories of life in Nicaragua for longer than Julie would have thought before they offered one last "really glad you're home" and raced off to spend the rest of the evening at a swimming party with their friends.

They hadn't asked her about Chad. And she hadn't mentioned him. Anyone listening to their conversation would have thought Julie toured Nicaragua alone.

She had tried repeatedly to call Betty Jean but only the answering machine was at home.

"I'm back," Julie said at the beep. "I hear you're in love. Who with? Call tonight if it's not too late."

She had had a dutiful, stiff conversation with her parents on their respective extensions. They allowed as how they were glad she was safely home from that "godforsaken place" and did not ask her anything about her trip. Angela did ask, however, if she'd talked to Kevin.

"No, Mother. I haven't."

"Call him, young lady," her father had ordered in a stern voice Julie remembered well from her childhood. "If you let him know you've come to your senses, he might consider a reconciliation."

"Don't tell me what to do, Dad. And don't use that tone of voice. I didn't like it when I was ten, and I don't like it now."

Her mother started crying.

Welcome home, Julie told herself as she rocked back and forth. She probably should go to the grocery. There wasn't any milk or juice. She needed to unpack, clean up the mess in the kitchen, start a load of laundry. She really should look through that stack of bills to make sure no one was going to cut off the water or repossess the refrigerator. But all she had been able to motivate herself to do was put together her rocking chair.

And now all she wanted to do was rock.

Chapter Ten

The ringing was not her alarm clock, Julie realized as she rolled over and stared at the digital dial. Only 6:00 a.m. She had set it for six-thirty.

And it wasn't the telephone. But there it was again, and she realized the ringing was from the doorbell.

"What in the world...?" she muttered as she grabbed a robe from the closet.

She hadn't heard any ringing for a whole week, Julie realized as she padded down the hall to the front door. No intrusive doorbells, telephone, alarm clocks. Of course, there had been the roosters.

After a check through the peek hole, Julie opened the door to Betty Jean in a jogging suit, holding a white paper bag.

"Do you know what time it is?" Julie asked. "And where's your car?"

"I rode over on Donnie's bike. Here's breakfast," she said, handing Julie the sack.

"Rode over on a bike. You? All the way from your house?" Julie looked past Betty Jean. Yes, there it was, leaning against a porch railing. A boy's bicycle.

"It's only a couple of miles," Betty Jean said disdainfully. "I'm in training. Kit and I are going to bicycle across France next spring with a Houston group. Now, give your best friend a hug and start talking. Are you in or out of love?''

"In, I guess," Julie said with a melancholy sigh. "Come on, I'll make coffee."

"Then why the long face, sugar?" Betty Jean asked, following her to the kitchen. "Why aren't you floating?"

"Because I'm here and he's there, and I suspect that's the way we'll stay." Julie stood in the middle of her own kitchen, trying to remember. Coffee. The cupboard over the stove. After only a week in another world, she still felt out of touch with this one. "He offered to move back," she said as she measured the water, "but I couldn't do that to him. He belongs down there, at least at this point in his life. He'd be a misfit here, and I'm not even sure he could get a decent job. Then he'd lose his self-esteem and resent me for letting him ruin his life, and he wouldn't love me anymore. I couldn't bear that—for Chad not to love me."

"Oh, my," Betty Jean said. "Maybe I didn't do you any favor, buying you that ticket."

"No, please don't think that," Julie insisted. "Even if I never marry him or never see him again, I'll always love Chad. He's the sweetest, kindest, dearest, most unselfish, most passionate human being I've ever known, and I'll thank you until my dying day for giving me the most memorable week of my life—and memorable in other ways, too, besides being with Chad.

"I saw so much and learned so much. Nicaragua's a sad little country full of people who refuse to be sad. Being there makes you stop and think what it means to be an American, about how much we have, how convenient life is here, how privileged we are. But more of that later. We don't have time now for me to get philosophical. And I gather you had a pretty memorable week yourself.

"*Kit*. Wasn't that the name of the health nut you went out with week before last—the guy who was horrified when you ordered nachos and Mexican beer and couldn't believe the last time you exercised was in junior high gym class?"

Betty Jean nodded eagerly. "Yeah, Christopher Carson. He goes by Kit. Isn't that cute? Kit Carson. He's really something. I can hardly wait for you to meet him. He's a nutritional biochemist at Baylor Medical Center. He has a weekly television program on cable called *Your Body and You* and knows everything there is to know about food and health and exercise. And don't make coffee for me unless it's decaf."

"Decaf—for the original caffeine kid. How come?"

"I'm weaning myself," Betty Jean said, searching the cupboard for coffee other than the can of regular that Julie was holding in her hand. "Kit says caffeine's bad for the blood pressure. Those are oat-bran muffins in the sack. Kit says oat bran's great for keeping your cholesterol down."

"But what about your morning doughnut?" Julie demanded. "You've started the day with coffee and a doughnut your entire adult life."

"No more doughnuts," Betty Jean said firmly as she located a can of decaffeinated coffee on the top shelf. "Kit says doughnuts and other pastries have zero nutritional value, and they're full of saturated fats. I have also given up nachos, French fries, fried everything, soda pop, candy bars. You're looking at a changed woman. Hallelujah, I've seen the light! I love my body, and we must take care of that which we love."

"Sounds to me like yours isn't the only body you're in love with," Julie said with a bit of sarcasm. "I can't believe that this dramatic change in life-style happened in only one short week. This Kit Carson must be some sort of a wizard."

"Well, he's pretty magic," Betty Jean said with a shy smile.

"What does Donnie think of him?" Julie asked.

"Well, Donnie got irritated when Kit started lecturing him about the evils of hot dogs and soda pop. But you know how kids are. They don't want anyone to tell them anything. Kit's going to teach him to play handball, though, and get him started weight lifting. Me, too."

The idea of Betty Jean lifting weights was too much. Julie sank into a chair, leaving the coffee-making to Betty Jean. She opened the sack and took out one of the muffins, which had the look and specific gravity of a rock. Tentatively, Julie took a nibble. It tasted rather like ground-up cardboard with raisins.

"Aren't they delicious?" Betty Jean asked as she used the electric opener on the coffee can. "Kit makes them. His own recipe. He won first place with them at the health food fair. They have one hundred and twenty calories, six grams of oat bran, two grams of nutritional fiber and only three grams of fat. I think he should make them commercially, what with everyone wanting to lower cholesterol."

Julie tried another nibble. Brown, cinnamon-flavored cardboard. Maybe it would taste better with a little butter. But she had a feeling Kit Carson would say butter was a no-no. "So you've really fallen for the guy," she said, not sure she wanted to hear the answer.

With the coffee scoop in midair, Betty Jean paused, her eyes going soft, her face relaxing into a smile. "Yeah. He makes me feel like I'm important, like it matters how I eat and live. It's kind of like having a bossy mother who's bossy because she cares about you. And just think how perilously close I came to settling for a couch potato because I was afraid no one better would come along."

Julie decided that maybe the muffin wasn't *that* bad if the guy who made it was making her best friend happy. But she'd finish eating the thing later. Right now she had to hug Betty Jean.

"I'm so happy for you, honey. You look like a girl...no, you look like a woman in love."

"Well, we haven't talked about anything permanent yet. You know, we're still just finding out about each other—slowly—sort of tiptoeing into a relationship. I think we're both afraid we'll find out something terrible about the other one, like maybe our politics or religion or music are totally incompatible. I couldn't possibly love a man who didn't like Diana Ross. Or Willie Nelson. Of course, he was appalled when he found out what I ate and that I didn't exercise, but I've been saying I was going to straighten up and fly right for years. Haven't I? I always intended to start eating better and go to aerobics with you, but I just couldn't bring myself to make a commitment. Kit was just the impetus I needed. Imagine finding a man who is good for my health! And even if Kit isn't the long-term relationship I've been wanting, just being with him this past week has given me faith that it is possible to find love the second time around. I'd honestly begun to wonder if I'd ever feel deeply about any man again."

"Enjoy it," Julie said with a second hug. "God knows, you deserve a good man to love you and fuss over you."

"But what about you?" Betty Jean said. The two women leaned against the counter, their shoulders touching. "Sounds like being in love hasn't brought you much joy."

"Oh, but it has. But Chad and I are so different. Our lives just don't blend, and I can't figure out anything to do about it. I wish that working things out for us was as simple as taking up exercise and giving up nachos."

"Where there's a will, there's a way. Seems to me the first thing you have to do is get those kids of yours situated. Then maybe you can do some serious thinking about yourself."

Julie nodded. "I've been thinking about having an auction."

"Gee, isn't that kind of drastic? And I'd be the first to agree that Sherry and Steve are cute kids, but I'm not sure there's much demand for eighteen-year-old twins."

Julie ignored Betty Jean's humor. She was dead serious about her idea. "I can auction all the living and dining room furniture and all the furniture from the guest room," she explained. "I can clear out the attic and the garage. Ross's gun collections. All those silver bowls we got as wedding presents and never used. Outgrown kids' clothes. Toys. My grandmother's dishes. Ross's mother's dishes. All that ski equipment we haven't used since Ross died and will never use again. Books. Tons of stuff. And my parents can weed out, too. Remember that auction over in Rosenburg that we went to a couple of years ago, and people bid on a *push* lawnmower and appliances that didn't work!"

"How could I forget? They also bought water-damaged paintings, warped records and cracked dishes. Your stuff may be too good. No one would want it. And besides, what will you use for living room furniture?"

"I won't have room for all that stuff in a smaller house, and I can't afford to live here anymore. I'm going to call that realtor today and tell her to sell the house for whatever she can get. Maybe the kids can go to UT after all."

"What about supporting yourself in your old age? I can hear your dad reminding you in his most paternalistic voice that 'this house is all you have, Julie, and you must be patient until the market comes around.'"

"Right now I need to live for the present rather than worry about my old age. I've been such a cautious person all my life and always done what other people thought was best for me. Going to Nicaragua was just about the first imprudent thing I've ever done, and I wouldn't have done that if you hadn't forced my hand. I can be old when I'm old. Right now I want to be young and alive and glow like you do."

"All right!" Betty Jean said, laughing and giving her a high five.

There was only time for a hurried cup of decaf before the two women had to get on with their day. Julie watched out the front door as Betty Jean went riding off on Donnie's bike. She tried to remember the last time she'd seen her friend on a bicycle. Sixth grade, she decided. They were earning their cycling merit badge for Girl Scouts.

Julie closed the door and paused to walk through her elegant living room before getting ready for work. She ran her fingers over the rich brocade of the sofa, over the fine wood of the mahogany credenza, the smooth marble of the mantel. She admired the brass and crystal scones that hung over the mantel, setting off a handsome oil painting of the sea wall at Galveston by a well-known Texas artist. The painting would be out of place being auctioned with her hodgepodge of household and personal items. She'd need to take it to an art gallery and sell it on consignment. Actually she would be a bit relieved to get rid of it. She had long since let the insurance rider on the painting drop, unable to afford the high premium, and she continually worried about something happening to the valuable work of art.

Julie thought of the special days her family had celebrated in this wonderful room. The Christmas tree always stood in the bay window. Wearing their caps and gowns, the twins had stood in front of the mantel to be toasted on the occasion of their high school graduation. She'd had a surprise party for her parents' fortieth wedding anniversary here.

Julie wandered into the dining room, remembering birthday and holiday dinners with Ross at the head of the table carving the roast or turkey. She'd sell the dining room furniture, too. From now on the more utilitarian table and chairs in the kitchen would suffice.

She would cry when she sold it. In fact she could already feel the tears stinging her eyes now at the thought of giving up so much. She loved her house, her possessions and the memories they represented. But perhaps ultimately it would be for the best, a symbolic way of putting the past behind and starting anew. A new home—just for her. Maybe a smaller house wouldn't seem quite so empty with her children gone.

The future. It was time to start dealing with it, and an auction would be the first step. Just the idea that she would be *doing something* instead of sitting around worrying about what to do made Julie feel better.

A glance at the kitchen clock sent Julie scurrying down the hall to get ready for work. The water was running in the kids' bathroom. That would be Steve. He had to report for his job at McDonald's by eight. She and Sherry didn't have to be at their respective jobs until nine.

Julie stepped out of her robe and gown and into her shower. The steady stream of hot water seemed like an incredible luxury. She let it pour over her body—a body that did not ache from sleeping all night on a hard, cotton pallet. Chad had admitted that he missed the certain amenities that life in the United States had to offer, such as hot showers, good beds, and telephones that worked. Surely a man as clever as Chad could find work in a city as big as Houston. He could be a mechanic or run a garage while he finished his college degree, and then he could get a coaching job at a high school, or perhaps something a little more respectable.

Respectable. That was important to her, Julie realized. She wanted a man she could be proud of. That had been a part of Kevin McLaughlin's charm. At his side, she felt quite special.

Yet, in the ways that really mattered, Chad was a much finer human being than Kevin. But no one could tell that by looking. Her parents certainly couldn't. She doubted if her children could. And the Jody Zacherys of the world would laugh at her.

Damn, Julie thought. *I should be ashamed of myself for caring what shallow people like Jody think.* And by way of penance, she turned off the hot water and finished her shower with a blast of water from the cold water tap.

She put her robe back on and went to the kitchen to fix herself a quick cup of instant coffee *with* caffeine. Steve came rushing in to have his bowl of cereal. Sherry stumbled in behind him wanting a glass of juice.

"There isn't any," Julie said.

"No juice," Sherry whined.

"And there isn't any milk for my cereal," Steve said as he stood peering into the open refrigerator.

"It seems that no one went to the grocery while I was gone," Julie said, refusing to feel guilty. "Or mowed the lawn. Did any laundry. Emptied the trash."

"Hey, Mom, don't sound like that," Steve said, taking on a kidding tone. "Sherry and I both have jobs and active social lives. And we're just kids. What can you expect out of a couple of spoiled kids?"

"I think it's time for a little unspoiling, guys. I'm selling the house for whatever I can get. And I'm selling a lot of other stuff to pay your college expenses in the fall. You'll have to get part-time jobs in Austin, but I want you both to go to UT like you always planned, at least for a year. Then we'll have to see."

"Does this mean you've decided to dump Kevin for the guy in Nicaragua?" Sherry asked.

"It means I have decided that, regardless of whom I do or do not marry, this family will make it under its own steam."

"But what can I have for breakfast?" Steve asked, choosing to deal with a more immediate problem.

"I thought you loved McDonald's breakfast biscuits," Julie said.

"After two straight months, I can't handle fast food any more."

"There are oat-bran muffins in the sack," Julie announced, pointing to the sack on the table. "They have only three grams of fat and will lower your cholesterol.''

AT THE BANK, Julie's colleagues seemed surprised that she had returned from her trip unscathed. She explained repeatedly that she had not faced any danger, that foreigners visit Nicaragua all the time, that there was no shooting in the streets, that the country was impoverished but orderly. Then she stopped explaining and simply said she had a very interesting time, that the beaches were fantastic. She'd be glad when the questions stopped. She wanted to sink back into normalcy, to take comfort in the familiar routine of the bank, to concentrate on her work.

Claudia Martin, an old high school classmate and Julie's closest friend at the bank, was the only one who understood the true circumstances of her trip. "I see the third finger on your left hand is nude. How about it? Shall we, your female colleagues at First Texas Commerce, go forward with the surprise bridal shower we had planned for next week or not?"

"Why don't you put it on hold for now," Julie advised.

"If you decide to discard the gorgeous Mr. McLaughlin, please tell me first," Claudia said. "I can understand a woman carrying the torch for her old high school beau. Lord knows I did that for years until I finally saw Garret again, and he wanted to sell me a tax-sheltered annuity and brag about being president of the Rotary Club instead of talking about old times. I swear there wasn't a romantic bone left in that man's body. But Chad was a darling boy back then and apparently he hasn't invested all his passion in civic clubs. Obviously some of the old spark still lives, but honestly, kiddo, I'd sure think twice about calling it quits with Kevin McLaughlin. Men like him are rare.''

Yes, rich, successful single men were rare, Julie thought as she punched a deposit into her computer. But so were noble ones.

Julie found it hard to concentrate. Her mind kept wandering. At one point she found herself trying to imagine Chad working in a structured place such as this bank and failed. An image of Chad in a necktie behind a desk or teller window simply would not come to her. But images of him barefoot on the beach with his dog at his side or at the wheel of his battered old pickup were easy to conjure up. And Chad smiling at her across a table, Chad holding her in bed, Chad kissing her....

Midmorning, the bank receptionist handed her a note. ''Mr. McLaughlin requests that you call him at his office between twelve and twelve-fifteen. He will wait for your call.''

Julie felt a flare of irritation. *He would wait for her call.* In other words, she had no choice in the matter. She must call, and she must do so at precisely the time he had designated.

But he was only being efficient, she supposed. He knew she was not supposed to make personal calls while she was at her window. And he was often tied up and unreachable. However, he *was* mandating her call. Julie wasn't at all sure she wanted to talk to him and felt a knot of nervous dread at the thought.

Still feeling peevish, Julie waited until twelve-*twenty* to make the call from the pay phone at the delicatessen where she and Claudia were having lunch.

''I want to see you,'' Kevin said without preamble. ''We need to talk. I'll pick you up at seven.''

Yes, she supposed they did need to talk. Julie heard herself agreeing to dinner. But no, she didn't want him to come for her. Her kids didn't need to know she was going out with Kevin. They'd read too much into it.

"I'll meet you," she told him without bothering to explain why.

There was silence for a beat or two. Kevin was not accustomed to having his arrangements questioned. "Fine," he said briskly. "The racquet club at seven. I'll be in the bar."

Back at her window, Julie found herself worrying about what to wear, wishing she had time to do her nails, wishing she knew what Kevin wanted.

She wondered if her cream-colored silk was clean, if she had any decent stockings.

But why was she getting so worked up about how she would look for Kevin?

She stopped at the grocery on the way home, racing up and down the aisles, grabbing milk, juice, bread, lunch meat, ice cream, sodas, bananas and some frozen pizzas for the kids' dinner. And, of course, there was a line at the checkout counter. Impatiently she waited, reading the headlines on the trashy tabloids to calm herself. "Two-Year-Old Reads College Textbooks." "Seattle Man Revives After Being Dead For Three Days." Her favorite proclaimed "Eighty-Six-Year-Old Kansas Woman Gives Birth To Twins." Who writes such stuff? she wondered as she anxiously looked at her watch. She should have sent the kids to the grocery, but apparently she was on a guilt trip and needed to prove she was still a good mother after running out on them for a week. Dumb. Why did she always pick the slowest line? She wanted to have time to change clothes and redo her makeup. For whatever reason, she needed to look her best to face the formidable Kevin.

Make up your mind, she told herself with irritation. *You either want this man in your life, or you don't. You have to choose.* Chad, the beloved dreamer who would only make her life more complicated, who could not solve any of her problems, but with whom she was in love. Or Kevin, who could give her so much, whom she respected, enjoyed, admired, but did not love.

But perhaps she was being premature. Kevin might want to tell her firmly, face-to-face, that he was finished with her. Yes, that was what she hoped for. Absolutely. Then she wouldn't have to make the decision herself.

She was out of checks—an embarrassing state of affairs for someone who worked in a bank—and kept a line of people waiting as she went racing over to the automatic teller.

She hit every red light on the way home, and as she rounded the corner by her house she saw her parents' car in the driveway.

Damn.

She struggled in the door with two sacks of groceries. Her parents were sitting in the living room instead of their accustomed places in the family room. This was to be a formal session, it seemed. Both were wearing their stern, we-are-very-disappointed-in-you faces. Julie glanced at her watch. Five past six.

Julie called out a greeting as she raced by, taking the sacks to the kitchen. "I'll be just a minute," she said from the kitchen. "I have to put away the frozen things."

Leaving the kitchen in disarray, she hurried into the living room and dutifully kissed her parents and presented them with the souvenir gifts from her trip. Her father scarcely glanced at his wallet. Her mother said a polite thank-you for the belt. Julie didn't bother to explain about the exotic leather.

"I have plans for dinner and am really in a rush," Julie said, perching on the edge of the coffee table. If she told them who she was having dinner with, they'd get out of her way in a flash.

"We had lunch at McDonald's," her father said, ignoring her comment. He was standing in front of the fireplace, his hands behind his back. His General Patton pose. "Steve tells us you're planning to sell the house."

Thanks a lot, Steve, Julie thought. "Yes," she told them. "I need the money."

"I won't let you do this," Taylor announced.

Angela, sitting ramrod straight on the sofa, nodded her head to show her agreement with her husband. Her lips were pressed in a firm line. Didn't she know that caused wrinkles?

"Daddy, *my* name is on the deed. You really can't stop me, but I would greatly appreciate your advice and support. Now, if you will excuse me, I'm running late."

"No, I will not excuse you. We have driven over here to have this out with you, and I think you owe your parents the courtesy of listening to their advice." Taylor cleared his throat for emphasis. "You would not realize half the value of this house if you sold now," he said firmly. "It would be a foolhardy thing to do."

"At this point in time in Houston, Texas, given the conditions of the domestic oil industry, my house isn't worth very much," Julie explained with far more patience than she felt. "I realize the Texas economy will rebound at some point, but I have two children to educate, and I can't wait around for that to happen.''

"But what about Kevin?" Angela asked.

"I was very uncomfortable with allowing him or any other man to step in and pay for my children's education. If I marry again, I want it to be with a clean slate. I want to do it for me and me alone and not for what a man can give me and my children. In a way, I'm quite fortunate—a lot of women don't have that luxury. But because I have worked very hard and done without a lot of things and have wonderful parents—who have helped and stood by me since my husband died—I have made it this far without using marriage to solve my problems. I'm very close to having Sherry and Steve raised, very close to being able to make decisions about my life that are not based on financial need or what is best for my children.''

"You are making a mistake," Taylor declared, "about the house, about Kevin, about that Chad person.''

"Oh, Julie, honey," Angela intoned. "Chad almost ruined your life before, now you're giving him a chance to do it again. He's just not suitable for you, dear. He wasn't twenty years ago, and he isn't now. If you married him, you'd be marrying down.''

"Marrying down. I wouldn't have used those words, but I'll admit I've had some misgivings along those lines. I think it's time, however, for this family to get our heads out of the clouds. Things are not the way they were. We no longer have social standing in this community. I haven't been to a Junior League meeting in years. You guys can't afford to belong to the country club anymore. Our friends who still have money have forgotten we exist. I can't afford to live and maintain this house in a 'good' neighborhood. It will be a struggle to get my children educated.''

''All the more reason for you to marry carefully,'' Taylor insisted.

Again Angela nodded her agreement. ''I'm sure Chad's a nice young man,'' she said, ''but I think you are involved with him for the wrong reasons. Apparently there is a...well, a strong physical attraction for you to go all the way to a foreign country with an unstable political environment to spend a week...'' She looked away, embarrassed.

''A week making love,'' Julie said, finishing the sentence. ''And what's the matter with that, Mother? It's not a 'wrong reason.' It's a very important consideration. But aside from physical attraction, I happen to be sincerely in love with Chad Morgan, just like you've been in love with Daddy all these years. Tell me, Mother, if Daddy had been a young man of lesser prospects and from a family of lesser circumstances than the Harpers, wouldn't you have still married him, regardless of what your parents said? Wouldn't you have?''

Angela looked at her husband, her face softening. ''Why, yes,'' she admitted. ''I would have married Taylor Harper no matter what.''

''This is all a bunch of romantic nonsense,'' Taylor spouted. ''Your mother fell in love with a man who had been raised a certain way and had something to offer her. If I had been otherwise, we never would have dated in the first place. I never would have courted a girl who wasn't acceptable to my family.''

''Why, Taylor Harper,'' Angela said indignantly, ''you fell in love with me at that U.S.O. dance, and neither one of us had a notion of each other's families or anything else. You could have said your daddy was a carnival worker, and it wouldn't have mattered a bit."

Taylor rolled his eyes heavenward to show his exasperation.

"Are you saying if I had been from the wrong side of the tracks," Angela persisted, "you wouldn't have insisted on dancing every dance with me, insisted on walking me home and taking me out every night until you were shipped out, then written me a letter every day for the next year? Is that what you are saying?"

"I thought we came here to talk Julie out of selling this house," Taylor said defensively.

"Answer my question," Angela demanded, her green eyes blazing.

Taylor sighed. "No, of course not. It didn't matter whether you were rich or poor. I could see you were a lovely young woman of quality just by looking at you and talking to you. But it's different for a woman. She has to marry well. Her life is dictated by the man she marries, not the other way around."

"So, are you saying it's all right for a woman to be a gold digger?"

"Not a gold digger, *dear*," Taylor said pointedly. "Just mindful of what marriage means."

"Marriage means for better or worse, Taylor. You and I—we've have had it both ways now. We were rich, and now we're not. We still try to put up a good show, but it's getting less and less important to us both. And I think we're closer now than we've ever been. We've had to talk and plan and worry together. And you know, this little conversation has made me realize that we'd better leave Julie alone and quit trying to live her life for her."

"But..." Taylor sputtered. "But we're her parents. We need to look after our girl."

"'Our girl' just turned thirty-eight," Angela said, reaching for Julie's hand. "How can we help you, honey?"

"Daddy?" Julie said tentatively, looking at her father.

Taylor looked from one woman to the other. "I guess—as usual—your mother is right. I still think you are making an unwise decision about the house—and about Kevin McLaughlin—but I suppose we all have a right to make our own mistakes. But promise me, Julie, that you will seriously weigh your feelings for those two men. Don't automatically discredit McLaughlin because he's rich."

"I promise," Julie said. "And the way you can help me is by cleaning out your attic and garage. I'm having a Sherry and Steve Rhoades Benefit Auction. Do you know any auctioneers, Daddy? And Mother, if you could help me find a place to hold it..."

Julie tried to reach Kevin to warn him she would be late, but he'd already left the office and all she got at his home number was his answering machine. She left a message for him at the racquet club, which he obviously didn't get, judging by the scowl on his face when she walked into the bar forty-five minutes late.

Chapter Eleven

Acutely aware that Kevin would already be waiting for her at the racquet club, Julie had taken time only to freshen her makeup, change her low-heeled work shoes to high-heeled pumps, and put on flashier earrings and a wide red belt with a large silver buckle to dress up her sedate navy shirtwaist. That would have to do, she decided as she took one last look at herself and rushed out the door.

Even on evenings she had plenty of time to get ready, Julie never felt quite chic enough for the elegant upper level bar and dining room at the Houston Racquet Club. The informal lower level was for players coming in off the courts, but upstairs was where the ladies showed off their designer clothes and jewels, and the men showed off their ladies. Once Julie might have been able to compete, but no longer. Strangely enough, however, she found that she didn't mind so much tonight. Maybe it had something to do with her earlier conversation with her parents, or seeing conditions in Nicaragua first-hand, but she felt more accepting of who she was—a bank teller, who had neither the time nor the money for competitive dressing. She couldn't afford to shop at Neiman Marcus, and most of her jewelry was of the costume variety. And if she was ever able to afford nice things again, she would appreciate them, but having them would not make her happy. *People* made her happy.

Lola in Nicaragua probably got more joy out of one cheap bracelet than the women around here got from their diamond tennis bracelets.

Julie stopped in front of a mirror in the lobby to fluff her hair, then squared her shoulders and walked into the bar. Kevin was sitting at a table, his usual Manhattan on the table in front of him.

Kevin rose and formally kissed her cheek. "Hello, Julie," he said, his voice carefully neutral.

"Hi. I'm sorry I'm late," she said as she sat down. "And I can tell by your expression that you didn't get the message I left for you with the club secretary."

"No," he said tersely. "I didn't get a message." He motioned to the white-jacketed waiter. "A sherry for the lady, please."

"No," Julie said, shaking her head at the waiter. "I don't like sherry. Bring me a light beer."

Kevin scowled. "If you don't like sherry, why have you been allowing me to order it for you for the last six months?"

"You assumed I was the sort of woman who sipped sherry. I never told you otherwise, even though it was difficult to keep from making a face at every sip. Have you ever tasted the stuff? I wonder how it got elected as the proper drink for proper ladies. I just kept telling myself that I'd learn to like it. It was stupid of me."

"And what other things have you been hiding from me?" he asked, his head cocked to one side, eyeing her with a speculative gaze.

Julie considered the handsome, commanding man across the table from her. So impeccable, he was in his tailor-made silk sport jacket, his Dior necktie, his Hermes pocket square, his Gucci belt. His thick gray hair had been styled, not cut. His well-buffed fingernails were professionally manicured. The proverbial "catch." She had indeed been hiding things from him so that he would continue to think of her as an appropriate companion for a man of his tastes and means. But until now she wouldn't have admitted her deceit even to herself. "Well," she began, "I'm not terribly fond of ballet," she acknowledged. "I much prefer baseball to polo. I like Mexican food better than Continental cuisine. I think big, expensive cars are ostentatious. And I only read the chapter synopses in all those books you gave me 'to improve my mind'—and I found the authors as narrow-minded as you sometimes are. And I don't understand how a man who is apparently proud of being self-made could have turned into such an elitist—no, that's too gentle a word. You're a snob, Kevin. Okay. Now it's your turn. What have you been hiding from me?"

"Not a thing," Kevin said, using a smart gold lighter to light a long, thin cigarillo. "I've been totally up front in this relationship. I admired your looks, your agreeable nature, your innate elegance. I realized we weren't passionately in love, but I decided that was probably for the best. I wanted to negotiate the terms of a satisfactory marriage with a clear mind and work on passion later. I thought I'd found a woman who would bring grace and charm to my life, who liked the things I liked and would be appreciative of what I had to offer her. The fact that you were needy added to your appeal, I suppose. I would rescue you from the abyss of financial ruin, and you would, of course, be forever grateful. Apparently it was all a sham.''

''No, not all of it. I certainly was needy, and I did a pretty good job of convincing myself I was sophisticated enough to move on to the 'finer things in life.' And I admire you very much. I thought you were a prince on a white charger and found it very exciting to be courted by you. I just didn't stop and ask myself if I really wanted to be a princess.''

''And the man in Nicaragua?'' he asked, taking a draw on the cigarillo and carefully blowing the smoke away from her.

''It was unfinished business dating back many years.''

''And is it finished now?'' he asked, staring at her through narrowed eyes.

''Yes and no. I'm still in love with him, but I can't see myself sharing his life.''

''And can you see yourself sharing mine?'' he asked, his voice suddenly more gentle.

Julie shook her head no and felt a tug of genuine regret. Kevin was intelligent, kind, generous, charming. ''I'm not the woman for you,'' she said, finding it hard to look at him. ''I tried awfully hard to convince myself that I was, and actually, it probably would have worked out all right, except . . .''

''Except you're in love with another man,'' Kevin said, finishing the sentence for her.

''Yeah. Isn't that the pits?''

''Yes, it is rather. You know something strange. I find the real you more exciting than the one I manufactured.''

''Thank you,'' Julie said. ''That's quite nice of you to say. You're a true gentleman.''

They were silent while the waiter put a tall glass of beer on the table in front of Julie and asked if Kevin wanted another Manhattan. Kevin waved him away and took a sip from his half-full glass. Julie took a swallow of her very cold beer and realized how dry her throat was. The words of truth had not been easy ones.

"Will you call me when you've sorted things out?" Kevin asked.

"Maybe. I'm not sure. Don't wait around for me, okay?"

"Steve and Sherry didn't have to return the cars, you know."

"Return the cars?" she asked, stunned. "What do you mean?"

"You didn't tell them to?"

"No. I'd been wrestling with the problem of what to do about the cars but had been too much of a coward to discuss it with them."

"Well, they came to my office this afternoon and formally presented me with the keys. Sherry said they both hoped that you and I worked things out okay. Steve said that, for now, you and they had decided that the family needed to make its way under its own steam."

The thought of her children marching bravely into Kevin's imposing office and returning their precious cars was too much for Julie. She started desperately fishing in her purse for a tissue, but Kevin quickly supplied her with a monogrammed linen handkerchief to catch her tears. "They're good kids," she sniffled. "You can't imagine how hard that must have been for them."

"Yes," he agreed. "They were so grateful when I gave the cars to them. I would have been proud to be their stepfather, to help you educate them. I am a generous man.''

''I know. But it's better this way. Really.''

They had a fabulous lobster dinner expertly served by attentive waiters and accompanied by a magnificent wine. Outside the windowed walls of the room, the beautifully landscaped grounds of the club took on a fairy-tale look, with well-placed spotlights illuminating the lush foliage of the many trees. Subdued voices of other diners blended with background music provided by the nimble fingers of a tuxedo-clad piano player. Gershwin. Berlin. Light classics.

Julie smiled as she compared her lobster dinner in San Juan with the one here at the Houston Racquet Club. Worlds apart. But vive la différence. Different strokes for different folks. Except where did she fit in? She wouldn't be tough enough or patient enough for Nicaragua even if it weren't so far away from her parents and children. And she certainly didn't belong here at this exclusive private club. Funny though, as she sat there sipping her wine she felt more at ease than she had ever felt with Kevin before. Amazing, the magic of a little honesty. She wondered if she would now feel differently about him if she had been honest from the very first about what sort of a person she was, but probably Kevin never would have asked her out if he hadn't perceived her to be discriminating and mindful of social ranking. So she had slipped into the role of sherry-sipping lady that he had created for her and worked hard at convincing herself the role was real life.

After a dessert of flamed cherries jubilee, they returned to the bar and lingered over brandy. Really good brandy. Incredible how much better it was than the cheap stuff she kept at home. Kevin told her about the wedding trip they would have taken to Monte Carlo. She told him about the impoverished conditions in Nicaragua.

"I hate poverty," he told her. "I've lived my entire adult life to erase its nasty taste. I give to charity, but I will never go among the poor again. Monte Carlo is one of my favorite places. People who go there are wealthy. There are hundreds of yachts in the harbor, gilt on the walls, flowers growing everywhere and not a single weed. But I suspect now that my favorite place would not have suited you."

"It might have made me uncomfortable," Julie admitted. "I've never liked casinos or enjoyed gambling. I'm more into villages and countryside. I like to stay in little inns and eat in family-owned restaurants. I like to visit quaint little churches and walk through centuries-old cemeteries."

Reluctantly she declined a second brandy. "I'm a working woman, remember. But it has been a lovely evening."

"Yes, one of the loveliest," he said.

He walked with her across the parking lot to her car and held her for a while before allowing her to get inside. "I guess you know I'm feeling a lot of regret about this. Maybe I was a bit arrogant, a bit pushy..."

She shook her head. "No regrets. Let's just chalk it up to experience and get on with our lives."

"You will call me and let me know when you've come to some firm decisions."

"Yes. But don't wait around for me to change. We don't have the same values, Kevin. I think we'd be asking for trouble if we tried to put things back together."

"Maybe so," he said and kissed her, a lingering kiss but not intimate. The man had class.

THE NEXT MORNING it was the ringing of the telephone that woke her in the wee, small hours. She said hello and listened to a strange hollowness punctuated by a distant popping sound. "Hello," she said again.

"Julie," a distorted voice said.

"Chad," she called out, her heart turning a somersault in her chest. "Oh, my darling. Are you all right? Where are you?"

"At the telephone exchange in Rivas," he explained. The connection was terrible, with every fifth or six syllable getting lost, but she didn't care. It was Chad! Her precious Chad. Her heart righted itself and began beating like an excited tom-tom.

"I talked the operator into opening early so I'd have a better chance of getting through," Chad said, "but even so, we've been trying for an hour. I miss you. My bed seems awfully empty."

"Oh, God, I miss you, too. Terribly. I think about you constantly. Will you come to see me? I can't just walk away from this, Chad. I want to see you again. As soon as possible."

"How about Christmas?" he said.

"Oh, yes. My kids will be home from college. You can meet them. Yes, please come Christmas."

"I love you, Julie, more than you'll ever know."

"AND WHAT AM I BID for this sterling silver chafing dish?" the auctioneer called out. "Gimme fifty dollars, fifty dollars, fifty dollars, *five*! Sixty dollars, sixty dollars, sixty dollars, *five*! The little lady in the red hat. Are you fanning yourself, dearie, or is that a bid? I have sixty-five dollars. Do I hear seventy for this elegant, handcrafted creation in solid silver. Not *plated*, folks, but *solid silver*. A real family heirloom. Just look at the workmanship. A genuine work of art. Me and the missus, we used to have a chafing dish like this, but I traded it for a hound dog and like to got me a *di*vorce in the process. The missus, she died, God rest her soul, but I still got that old hound. Laziest dog that ever walked. And I mean walked. That dog don't even run when he chases rabbits—just strolls along. Gimme seventy-five dollars, seventy-five, seventy-five *eighty*!''

The auction was going incredibly well. Julie tried to concentrate on her good fortune and not on the fact that those were *her* possessions being sold. The colorful auctioneer was auctioning away a part of her life to a crowd of strangers. But at least there was a crowd. People had started arriving well over an hour before the auction began at eleven, and at four o'clock there was still a crowd. Some had left and others come, but many had been here the whole time. A snack bar at the back of the hall was doing a brisk business. And people were bidding—sometimes more than the item was worth. An electric blender that Julie was certain had cost less than forty dollars new had gone for fifty. A tattered quilt that Julie had considered throwing away had been labeled an ''antique'' by the auctioneer and sold for seventy-five dollars.

Julie owed most of the auction's success to her parents. Her father announced ''if she was going to do this thing, she'd best do it right.'' Both parents had scoured the city finding the right hall, the right auctioneer, looking into the best ways to promote the event, having fliers printed, taking out ads in newspapers as far away as Corpus Christi and Galveston. Julie was surprised when her parents started making decisions about some of their own possessions, deciding that this would be a good time to rid themselves of forty-two years' worth of clutter.

For the past three Sundays, Taylor and Angela had accompanied Julie and the realtor, looking at town houses, duplexes, smaller houses. At first her parents were just helping their daughter find a place to live, but they had fallen in love with a town house in a nicely landscaped complex that offered a security guard, coffee shop, pool, putting green, recreation hall, aerobics classes and Thursday-night bingo games. "But we won't do anything hasty," Taylor kept saying. "We're not going to give our home away. In a few years, the market is bound to come back." But Julie knew her parents were doing a lot of figuring, trying to decide if they were throwing good money after bad to keep up the large payments on their sprawling home in a status neighborhood.

For Julie, selling her home was not an option. She knew that on paper she was taking a beating by selling it at this time, but any money she got for her equity would be money she could use *now*. She counted herself fortunate to have found a buyer very quickly, but of course, she had drastically reduced the price, and her father kept pointing out that it was easy to find a taker when one was giving property away.

She found a house to rent in an older part of town. It was much closer to downtown than her present address and would cut down her time commuting to work. Of course, the house was older, with only one bathroom and antiquated plumbing, but there were newly refinished hardwood floors throughout, and the yard had wonderful oak trees and several tall pines. Julie decided not to sell her Oriental rugs, and she would keep the redwood picnic table to put in the shady backyard.

All the tears she had shed during the last days as she dismantled her home of more than fifteen years had left her exhausted, and as she sat in the back of the hall, watching her possessions being carted away, it was almost more than she could bear.

On the auction block now was a set of lawn furniture. She remembered shopping for it with Ross to put on their newly covered patio. She didn't have room for the set on the tiny back porch of her new home. The picnic table would more than suffice.

Sometimes, after dinner, she and Ross would carry their coffee to the patio and sit together, enjoying the evening and admiring the beautiful yard. Of course, Ross had an after-dinner drink more often than after-dinner coffee, and they probably hadn't sat there of an evening as many times as she would like to remember.

She wouldn't miss the yard furniture as much as she'd miss her yard. She had been responsible for every tree, every shrub, every flower bed. And now it would all be left for others. The realtor said the new owners planned to tear out most of the backyard to put in a pool and deck.

Nothing stays the same, she kept telling herself. *The only thing certain is change.* Even if she had married Kevin, her time in her beautiful home would have been over.

But it was painful.

Sherry and Steve had begged her to wait until they had left for Austin before she executed the move, but she needed their help. And it was time for them to face reality.

When the three of them took one last walk through their empty house, they all held each other and wept.

"I feel like we're leaving Daddy behind," Sherry had sobbed.

"No, honey. Your daddy lives in your heart," Julie told her. But her words hadn't helped. Many of the twins' memories of Ross were associated with this house. Hers, too.

The kids had gone on to the car. Julie stood in the doorway of the empty house and looked back one last time before she locked the door. A jumble of happy and sad memories came rushing back. Her children would indeed carry their father with them always, but for her, it was a time of farewell. She would never forget Ross, but his influence over her life would diminish. Her memories of him would be selected ones—the good times. "Goodbye, my love," she whispered into the empty living room.

It was only a house, she reminded herself as she walked blindly down the front walk. *Only a house*. People were what made a house a home.

When they got everything put away and the furniture placed, the little old house on Belle Street looked kind of cute—much better than Julie had expected. She felt a bit guilty about keeping the Oriental rugs, which probably would have brought a nice price at the auction, but they really dressed up the decor. Sherry and Steve each fixed up their own rooms, which were quite different than before. Steve's new room didn't have model airplanes hanging from the ceiling and Corvette posters on the wall. Sherry's room didn't have a huge bulletin board full of high school memories, and the posters of her favorite rock and roll stars were absent. The rooms looked strangely adult. Steve said they planned to save all the "jazzing up" for their dorm rooms. Home for them would very soon be someplace else. The bedrooms in this house would be just for visits.

After Julie had settled with the auctioneer and the owner of the hall, she felt almost rich. She clutched the check in her hand. Over seven-thousand dollars. With this and her house money, she could educate her children. The pain had been worthwhile.

The week after the auction, it was time to load up the car and a small U-haul trailer for the trek to Austin and the University of Texas. Julie realized she got to be part of this day only because Steve and Sherry no longer had their smart new Pontiac Cameroes. Julie regretted the loss of their cars, but she was proud that they had returned them to Kevin of their own accord. It was the most adult thing they had ever done.

The university brochure said that approximately half the students had their own cars, with the others relying on the campus-area transit system. At least Sherry and Steve wouldn't be alone in their carless state, and Melissa would be more than generous in sharing her car. But Julie knew how disappointed Sherry and Steve were after spending the summer visualizing themselves scooting about Austin in flashy Cameroes.

Even Chad, as poor as he had been, had had a car at college—an old beat-up Pontiac. Ross had driven a sleek BMW.

Driving into Austin, past all the old familiar places, was a trip down memory lane for Julie. She thought of her difficult year as a student here, with Chad wanting her to quit and go off with him and Ross and her parents pulling the other way. And after they had moved back to Houston, she and Ross had enjoyed the excitement of returning to Austin for fall football Saturdays.

After he died, Julie hadn't come to football games anymore.

The campus was as beautiful as she remembered with its handsome Spanish architecture and carefully tended grounds. They went first to Sherry's dorm, where Melissa was waiting, already settled into her side of the room. The four of them made short the work of carrying all Sherry's possessions in from the car and trailer, then they repeated the process at another dorm for Steve. Melissa went along while they turned in the trailer and shopped for philodendrum, extension cords and shoe racks.

Julie ate with them at the housing center cafeteria, and too soon it was time for last hugs and motherly reminders about weekly phone calls and not letting the laundry pile up. Then she was alone, driving down the highway to Houston, more lonely than she had ever been in her life.

"Damn you, Ross, for skiing off the mountain," she muttered in an attempt to ward off the tears that kept blurring the lights of oncoming traffic.

God, she was going to miss those kids.

God, she missed Chad.

As she drove she fantasized about how lovely it would be if Chad were waiting for her at her new little house. They'd have a beer and he'd rub her tired back. Then they'd make beautiful love.

But Chad was in Nicaragua, and besides, he didn't even know where she lived.

Old habits died hard, and Julie found herself heading for her old house. She had to retrace her way back to the expressway to take the correct exit. It was well after midnight when she pulled into the little house on Belle Street. It looked as dark and lonely as she felt.

But once inside she turned on the lights and the radio and poured a glass of wine to sip in her small but cozy living room.

"Okay, Julie Harper Rhoades, what now?" she asked herself.

JULIE MADE SEVERAL phone calls to the University of Houston and located a computer hacker in the math department who said he would send a message for her to the computer address of Chad's friend in Rivas.

"And the message?" he asked.

"It's for Chad. Tell him that my children left for college, and I am facing the rest of my life. Ask him if he has any suggestions about how I should spend it."

Then she changed her mind. "No, strike that. Just say that I miss him and think of him all the time."

"That's it?"

"Yep. That's it."

OVER THE NEXT WEEKS, Julie worked hard at being busy and happy. Even though her own children were gone, she still had family dinner Tuesday evening with Donnie and Betty Jean. Kit usually came, too. Monday, Wednesday and Thursday she went to aerobics class before going home to dinner in front of the television. She went out with her colleagues from the bank for T.G.I.F. She had dinner Sunday evenings with her parents, who at her pointed request finally stopped asking her if she'd talked to Kevin. Friday or Saturday night she would go out with Betty Jean and Kit, even though the more she was around Kit, the more Julie decided he was a conceited bore. He monopolized every conversation while Betty Jean sat there, agreeing with every pronouncement he made. If the two women initiated a discussion of their own, Kit interrupted them. Julie was irritated at Betty Jean, resentful of Kit.

Twice Kit and Betty Jean had arranged a blind date for Julie. Julie was reluctant, but as Betty Jean kept pointing out, she was not engaged and she'd made no promises. "Going out with other men might clear your head a bit," she claimed. "You'll either fall out of love with Chad or realize he's the only man for you."

The first blind date was an exercise physiologist from Baylor Medical Center. He and Kit talked about the benefits of B-complex vitamins most of the evening. Julie was afraid she would fall asleep. The second blind date was with a cycling enthusiast who ran a bicycle shop and was the individual organizing the cycling trek across France that Kit and Betty Jean were planning to take in the spring. Once again, Julie felt left out.

In fact she sometimes wished Betty Jean had never gotten tuned into the whole food and fitness routine, or at least had taken a more moderate approach. But Betty Jean turned their every conversation to food and exercise. Kit had apparently convinced her that most of life's problems could be solved by proper diet and adequate exercise. A disturbingly large percentage of Betty Jean's sentences began with the words "Kit says." Finally Julie told her she was tired of hearing what Kit said. "What about Betty Jean? Doesn't she have opinions anymore?"

"But Kit's so smart," Betty Jean said defensively.

"So are you. And you used to be fun. But now all you want to talk about is fiber content and muscle tone. And I'm sure getting tired of tofu. Surely a nacho every now and then isn't going to kill us. What say we sneak off and have something sinful?"

"But what if Kit found out?"

"Betty Jean, are you afraid of him?" Julie demanded. "You are, aren't you? You, who used to give me such a hard time about not being myself around Kevin."

"I am not afraid of him," Betty Jean said. "It's just that he's right about everything. How can you argue with an expert?"

"There's a difference between an expert and a fanatic. Sometimes I think you traded one fanatic for another—Bobby the sports addict for Kit the health nut, but I think you had more fun with Bobby. At least you got to go someplace other than restaurants that serve carrot juice cocktails and put alfalfa sprouts on everything. And I don't know about you, but that weight-lifting meet we went to last weekend was an all-time low for me. Remember baseball? Remember beer?"

"Yeah, and sometimes I miss the old couch potato."

"Does Bobby ever call?" Julie asked.

"Not anymore. But he did for a while after I stopped seeing him. He promised he'd do better. Said he would reserve television privileges for Monday-night football, the NCAA basketball tournament, the Masters Golf Tournament and the World Series but forgo all other televised sporting events unless I wanted to watch them, too. And if I'd come to all the Oilers home games with him, he'd take me anyplace that I wanted on Saturday night. Even dancing. He said he had enrolled in a ballroom dancing class. Imagine that. Kind of sweet, isn't it?"

JULIE ENROLLED in a night class to study landscape architecture. It was something she'd always promised herself she would do when the kids were grown, and now suddenly they were grown. And gone.

The class proved to be a godsend. She looked forward to the sessions, rushing home from aerobics, showering and grabbing a quick sandwich before rushing off again. She liked the teacher, liked her classmates, liked the learning and the books and the prospect that maybe someday she might be able to have a little business of her own. After all she did have a green thumb and was something of a self-taught botanist. And she needed to start thinking about the future. But mostly the class was better than sitting home alone.

She went out with a man from the class, another bank teller like herself. He was nice, and while she enjoyed her evening with him, Julie knew after one date, he would not be the one to make her forget Chad—and did she really want to?

Julie considered from time to time the possibility of closing up her house and going to Nicaragua on a trial basis. But she'd lose her job. Even though she had enough money salted away for her kids' college, she felt very insecure about her own future. And she simply couldn't imagine living down there on a permanent basis—even with an innerspring mattress and an exterminator on retainer.

She thought of all the romances she'd read as a girl where the young Englishwoman gives up her safe life as a nurse or nanny and goes off to live on a sheep station in Australia or on a remote military outpost in India to find true happiness with a strong, older, dashing man. The stories hadn't seemed strange to her at the time, but now she wondered what kind of lives those women had after the first blush of marital bliss wore off and they had to face the prospect of years away from family and friends and their homeland.

Or maybe for a young girl, it would be different. The young are more resilient, more adaptable to change. Julie wasn't sure she could ever adapt to the hardships in Nicaragua. She would probably always be comparing, always thinking of how much better life was back home. Beautiful beaches were not enough to offset the lack of consumer goods, health care, communication. And the thought of having to learn another language was overwhelming.

Her roots, her family were here. She had lived her entire life in Houston. She wasn't sure if it was time for a change or too late for one.

But, oh, how she missed Chad. How she ached for Chad. In her bed at night her physical need for him was a painful thing.

Could love conquer all for an American woman approaching middle age who used to think she was pretty tough but now was not so sure?

She often dreamed of Chad, beautiful dreams full of softness and love. She could almost feel his caresses, his kisses. When she woke from the Chad dreams, she was full of longing, not only for his body, but for his voice, his smile, his presence.

She felt as if some sort of spell had been cast over her person. Intellectually she knew she should put Chad behind her, try to find someone to replace him, someone who could be here in this city, in this house. She wondered about Kevin. Was he dating someone else? Did he think of her still? Maybe she'd call him someday and ask how he was. Kevin was only a phone call away.

But she never called Kevin. And when the teacher of her class asked her out, she declined.

Chapter Twelve

A handsome, rather elderly Hispanic gentleman came to Julie's teller window.

"Mrs. Rhoades, I am Pedro Moreno of the One World organization. I have a letter for you from Chad Morgan."

"From Chad?" Immediately Julie felt her heart pumping more furiously in her chest. "Oh, how wonderful! Were you in Nicaragua? Did you see him? Is he all right?"

"Chad seems to be well," Moreno said. "But alas for our organization, a visit by a certain green-eyed American lady has made him rather discontented with Nicaragua. But perhaps he explains that in his letter."

"May I send a letter back with you?" Julie asked.

"Oh, I will not be going back for many months, but we send a courier packet on Tan Sahsa Airlines at least once a month. We have recently opened an office here in Houston, and if you would like to send your letter there, I'll see that it goes down with the next packet."

Moreno gave her a card and left her to her customers. Chad's letter sat there propped against her computer, looking at her until her break. It had her name on it and was marked "personal." She had forgotten Chad wrote like that. Round, open letters. Easy to read. She remembered the message inscribed with that handwriting in her high school yearbook, a message thanking her for the most beautiful year of his life and expressing the hope that they would spend every year of their lives together.

At her break, Julie took her precious letter to her car in the parking lot in order to have absolute privacy while she read. Before she opened it, she held it pressed prayerfully between her hands. *Discontented with Nicaragua.* Maybe he was coming home.

Using a nail file, Julie very carefully slit open the envelope. There were two pages written on plain white typing paper. The date was over a week ago. November first.

My darling Julie,

Strange after having you here such a short time so many months ago, this house still seems empty without you. I feel empty without you. Joe still looks around for you, I swear.

He's sitting on the floor beside me now. I'm at the table facing the bay. The moon is reflected in the water of the bay. The night is very still, and the waves seem louder, closer. The night birds are calling, the crickets chirping. Such a peaceful place. I have been very fortunate to live in this house with its beautiful view. And I had the pleasure of sharing it all with you—even if for a very short time. I'm grateful that you are part of my memories of this house and of this special little corner of the world called San Juan del Sur.

And I'm very fortunate that when I once again came face-to-face with the dream of you I carried in my heart for so many years, it turned out to be as sweet and lovely as I remembered.

I have decided to wind down my operation here. As soon as the two orphans who are now staying with me go on to the States, I will be coming there myself—if you are willing to have me. As much as I love this town and my work here in Nicaragua, I love you far more. Please consider this a formal proposal of marriage. Nothing would make me so happy as for you to become my wife. I probably haven't the right to ask—I keep thinking about that McLaughlin guy and all he had to offer you. If you want to wait and see if I get a decent job before you give me an answer, I would certainly understand. I have saved a modest amount of money over the years that I could perhaps use as a down payment on some sort of business. I feel like a babe in the woods when I think of running a business in the States with all the regulations, restrictions, codes, taxes—city, state and federal. I guess what I'd really like to do is continue with One World, working out of the Houston office. But it would mean a lot of travel, so perhaps that isn't such a good idea, either.

I know we face many problems. Maybe too many. But would you be willing to try with me? I will work hard for us and love you like no other man can.

I have no idea exactly when I could leave here. I need to finish up some jobs I've promised and decide what to do with the house. And I'd like to wait until my two current orphans are on their way to their relatives in the States. U.S. Immigration requires birth certificates and other documentation that are unattainable in the case of these two boys, and their relatives in the U.S. are having a hard time convincing the Immigration authorities that the children were born and do exist, even though the facts have never been formally documented. What we need down here is a special center where such youngsters can live while they are being processed, where people who are more clever than I in working through the maze of bureaucracy can work with the children and their relatives.

I guess I'll leave Joe with Lola and her family. He wouldn't be a very good city dog. Maybe we can come back to San Juan from time to time to visit him and all my good friends here.

Even as I write this, I feel so insecure. I'm thinking, what if you've taken McLaughlin's ring back? Or found someone else? I keep wishing we'd made the promises we agreed not to make that last night in Managua.

All I have is my love for you. And I really don't think it would be possible for anyone else to love you like I do. You are my first thought in the morning, my last at night. I eat every meal wishing you were with me. I drive down the road holding imaginary conversations with you. When the sunset is magnificent over the bay, I am filled with such longing to have you at my side sharing the beauty. I dream of you, and in my dreams I can touch and see and taste and feel you.

I don't expect an answer to my proposal until I come to see you at Christmastime. I've made reservations for the twenty-first—on the same Sahsa flight out of Managua that you flew on. If I have a change of plans I'll contact you via the electronic mail service. The telephones are as frustrating as ever. I drove to a friend's house in Rivas two nights ago and tried most of the night to get a line out of the country, but to no avail. Maybe it will be more of a relief to come home than I realize.

Home. I want one of those—with you.

All my love forever,
Chad

Julie cried. Her darling Chad, he loved her that much! To give up the job and the place he loved the most, a place where he felt useful and wanted and could see each day the difference he was making in people's lives.

Could she let him do such a thing—leave his house, his dog, his job, his life and come to live in a place that had become alien to him?

She pressed the letter against her breast and ached with her love. She wished she had never planned that damned reunion, wished she were in love with Kevin McLaughlin. Wished Chad were here right this minute to kiss away her tears.

JULIE HURRIED ACROSS the parking lot to her car. This evening was her and Betty Jean's regular Tuesday-night dinner, and she needed to stop by the grocery on the way home for a couple of last-minute items.

Betty Jean had called last night to say that she would be coming alone. "Donnie has play practice. Kit's giving a lecture."

Julie was surprised that Betty Jean had not begged out of dinner in order to attend Kit's lecture. She could almost feel Kit's irritation. As he went around being important, he liked to have the pretty, perky Betty Jean on his arm to nod sweetly and agree with all his comments. Julie was delighted at the prospect of having Betty Jean all to herself for a change. In fact, she was so delighted that she decided to buy a nicer wine and save the inexpensive jug she had at home for another occasion.

When she got home, she put her chicken casserole in a low oven and the wine in the refrigerator to chill, set the table for two and washed a beautiful bunch of plump grapes. Ordinarily she would have put the grapes in a purple glass bowl, which she no longer seemed to have. She'd bought the bowl in an antique store in Colorado Springs. On her honeymoon. The bowl had either gotten broken in the move or sold in the auction. It's only a bowl, she had to remind herself. She had others.

Donnie dropped his mother off at six-thirty, and Julie greeted her at the door with a hug. "I can't believe it. I get you all to myself without Kit contradicting every word I say."

"You don't like him, do you?" Betty Jean asked, following Julie into the kitchen.

"Oh, I like him about as much as you liked Kevin. But if Kit is your choice, I'll live with it. Just once, however, I'd like to have the last word. When I said that Glenda Jackson won an Academy Award for *Touch of Class*, he announced that she'd never won an Academy Award. I swear, if I told him the year of my birth, he'd probably say I was mistaken. What does Donnie think, now that he knows Kit better?"

"Oh, Donnie's snowed," Betty Jean said. "Kit has got him hooked on vitamin supplements and bench-pressing. Donnie says the girls are starting to notice his biceps, and he's certain he got the second lead in the senior play because he's become such a hunk."

"Did we notice boys' biceps in high school?" Julie asked as she tore the lettuce.

"I honestly don't remember. Chad was so skinny, he didn't have enough muscles to shake a stick at. Mitch did, but I think I was more enchanted with his mouth than anything else. Lordy, how that man could kiss!"

"How does Kit kiss?"

"Okay," Betty said, marching to the refrigerator. "Golly, is this wine for us? Isn't it a bit grand for two old ladies?"

"It's intentionally grand for two good friends who never seem to get to spend quality time together anymore. The corkscrew's in the drawer."

Betty Jean poured them each a glass and sat on the kitchen stool, watching while Julie tossed the salad.

"Your mom called me today," she announced.

"Oh?"

"She wanted to know if I still had my Aunt Lura's recipe for apple brown Betty, but what she really wanted was to pump me a bit, see if I knew anything she didn't know about the state of your mind these days."

"In other words, is Kevin a lost cause?"

"I'm not so sure. I think she'd almost like to give you her blessing about Chad but doesn't want to do anything to tip the scales in case you're still interested in Kevin. Have you heard from Mr. Fortune Five Hundred?"

"No."

"Regrets?"

"Of course. I regret I wasn't more honest with myself when he first started courting me. I regret that I've lost the friendship of a man I admire."

"But no regrets in the night? No regrets when it comes time to rob Peter and pay Paul at the first of every month?"

"No. In the night, I think of Chad. And moneywise, for the first time in years, I'm current on my bills. And I solved my financial dilemma myself. I feel really good about that. Of course, I'd like to have more money, but I guess even millionaires say that. The money for my kids' college education is safely tucked away, and that's what I care about the most right now. And I have a hedge against emergencies. I'll worry about putting money away for my old age after I figure out what I want to do when I grow up."

"Have a landscaping business?"

"Maybe. Let's eat."

Julie waited until they'd finished dinner and were enjoying their coffee—decaffeinated in deference to Betty Jean's newly acquired preference—before she told about Chad's letter.

"Wow! That's heavy duty," Betty Jean said. "Giving up everything to come *here*. Of course, I love Houston myself, but from what you said about Chad, it's going to be rough for him."

"But we'll have each other. Maybe we can start a business together."

"Yeah, that'd be nice," Betty Jean said, but she sounded dubious. "Isn't it funny how the older you get, the fewer easy answers there are? Remember the song we sang at our high school graduation about believing, about candles always burning in the darkest night. We believed that if we wanted something enough and worked hard enough, it would be ours. And here we are—both widowed, both struggling, both unsure of what we should believe in."

"Which, I think, is my cue to bring Kit back into the conversation," Julie said, warming their coffee. "Do I sense a bit of disillusionment about Houston's own guru of health and fitness?"

"Yeah," Betty Jean said, helping herself to a cluster of grapes. "I'm getting tired of having my fat calibrated."

"Your what?"

"He has these little pinchers with a gauge that he measures the fold of fat on my arms and torso with," Betty Jean explained, making a face as she extended her arm and took a fold of flesh between her forefinger and thumb. "I feel like I'm a racehorse in training. He checks on my diet. He times me when I jog. He counts my sit-ups. He measures my fat, my blood pressure, my pulse, my ratio of fat to muscle, my weight, my waist, my flexibility. I think he's waiting to propose until I meet all his criteria. You know, I was never a ten, but I wasn't all that bad before. And usually I only ate nachos on weekends. I would have been perfectly happy with myself if I had taken up walking a couple of miles two or three evenings a week and lost a few of pounds."

"So...?"

"So, Bobby is picking me up tonight," she admitted. "I told him to come about nine. It's a test. If he can actually get up from the sofa in the middle of an Astros game, then maybe he's not hopeless. He's promised to enroll in co-ed softball next summer. In fact, he's promised all kinds of things."

"And you think he'll really change?" Julie asked.

"I think he's well-meaning when he says he will, and yes, he'll occasionally come out and play with me, but I realize that basically what I'm getting is a spectator, a couch potato. Just like if you married Chad, you'd be getting a grown-up Boy Scout who's still hooked on doing good deeds.''

"So why the change of heart?" Julie asked.

"Bobby loves me—just the way I am. In fact, he said I'm a treasure, that he's happiest when I'm with him. He doesn't expect me to devote my life to his interests. And when he's not watching television, he's awfully sweet.''

"Do you love him?"

"I'm not sure. I know I've missed him. Kit's done a wonderful job of making me have a great appreciation of Bobby's attributes. Before, I didn't think he had any. And if that doorbell doesn't ring at nine o'clock, I'm probably going to cry. Does that mean I love him?''

"It means you could be on your way," Julie said, lifting her almost-empty wineglass to her friend.

"But how come we're in love with men who aren't perfect for us?" Betty Jean asked with a frown. "If we were filling out one of those dating service questionnaires, I sure wouldn't request a man who's addicted to televised sports. And you wouldn't request a saint who's off building windmills in Nicaragua.''

"I think we both figured out a long time ago that few things are ever perfect whether it be our children, our jobs, our bodies, our hair, our friends. The only things that are perfect are minutes, like when we see something beautiful in nature or have a special moment with someone we care about or hear a piece of music that touches our soul. Hey, that was really good, wasn't it? Like something out of a book?''

"Or out of a bottle of wine," Betty Jean said, resting her chin on her hand. "But wine wisdom or not, Bobby and Chad aren't perfect and neither are we. Perfect for Chad would be a woman who wanted to selflessly devote her life to the downtrodden of the world. Perfect for Bobby, I suppose, would be a woman who would share his sofa with him."

"But if we were those women, they'd be bored to death with us," Julie said, laughing.

"Yeah," Betty Jean said, nodding. "We'd be like those couples you see eating in the cafeterias who never say a word to each other except 'pass the salt.'"

"I suppose the best anyone can do is examine one's options, make decisions based on what seems best at the time—and hope for the best. And maybe instead of looking at the things that aren't to our liking about our relationships with Chad and Bobby, we should be listing the things that are. We've both found out that we don't want to be involved with men who are domineering. We want to have a say in our own lives. And we want a man who is sweet and kind and likes us just the way we are. Both men seem to fill the bill in those departments."

"But Bobby will never be a dynamo, and no one needs windmills in Houston, Texas."

"No, but there has to be a middle ground."

"For you, sugar, I think the middle ground would have to be an island in the Gulf of Mexico."

AT EXACTLY NINE O'CLOCK the doorbell rang. Bobby was wearing a sport coat and tie. His round face had the glow of a fresh shave, his hair was newly cut and his shoes looked as if they'd just received a military spit shine. His smile for Betty Jean was as shy as a schoolboy's.

When Julie asked him if he'd like some of the lemon cake Betty Jean had brought, he declined. "I'm working on my spare tire," he explained.

"You look like you've lost a lot of it already," Julie said.

"Ten pounds," he said with a grin.

Betty Jean looked as proud as if he said he'd climbed Mt. Everest.

Julie stood in the doorway watching Betty Jean and Bobby hold hands as they walked down her front walk to Bobby's car and dared to hope she'd seen the end of Kit Carson.

She poured the last of the wine into a glass and carried it out to her picnic table. The moon was full and round. It must look spectacular hanging over San Juan Bay.

An imperfect world. It was indeed, populated by imperfect people involved in imperfect relationships. But the world still had a lot to recommend it.

The trouble was, she had been thinking too much about what was wrong and not enough about what was right.

She was healthy and had wonderful children. Her parents were well. She had solved her immediate financial problems. And she was in love with a man who wanted to marry her.

That was a lot of good. A damned lot.

The only problem was, could she stand the guilt if Chad came here to live? Any more than he could stand the guilt if she went to live there?

She thought of the story she'd read in college about the woman who sold her hair to buy her husband a chain for his pocket watch only to find that the husband had sold his pocket watch to buy combs for her hair. Their sacrifices had been for naught.

One had to watch out for sacrifices.

If she gave up her home and moved to Nicaragua, she'd be giving up precious times with her family—and she'd be doing all the sacrificing. If Chad came here, he'd be the one giving up too much.

Betty Jean and Bobby were trying to negotiate a compromise. Each would change a little. Neither one would do all the sacrificing.

As CHRISTMAS DREW NEAR, Julie threw herself into a frenzy of preparation. She made bathrobes for her children and her parents and a blouse for Betty Jean. For Chad, she had Betty Jean take her picture in the rocking chair. Actually she made Betty Jean take a whole roll of pictures, then she picked the best one and put it in a nice frame.

She had a wonderful time making Christmas goodies while singing along to the Christmas music on the radio. As she put up her tree and decorated the mantel with boughs of evergreen, she was bursting with anticipation. And nervousness. Chad would be here soon. And her children.

Sherry and Steve arrived first. "Where will Chad sleep?" Sherry asked bluntly at dinner their first night home.

Julie gulped. "With me," she admitted.

Sherry eyed her speculatively. "You never slept with Kevin, did you?"

Julie went to the kitchen for more rolls.

CHAD ARRIVED the Monday before Christmas. When he exited from the customs lounge at Houston International, Julie was waiting. She looked as nervous as he felt.

They kissed awkwardly around his suitcase and duffel bag. She insisted on carrying the duffel bag to the car.

In the car, they kissed again. Much better. "God, how I've missed you," he said. The feel of her was sweet beyond belief. He kissed her again and again in the dim light of the parking garage. His hand strayed to her breast. *Oh, my!* His body reminded him how much he wanted her, how much he had longed for her these many months. He wanted to ask her right that minute if she had an answer for him. Did she want to marry him?

But he would wait until a better moment. After they'd made love maybe. When he felt a little more sure of what she would say.

As Julie made her way through the heavy Houston traffic—last-minute Christmas shoppers, she explained—they both admitted they were nervous wrecks at the prospect of being together with her children. "I'm pretty uneasy about seeing your folks again, too," he admitted, "but it's the kids I'm really dreading. How are they feeling about all this?"

"Strange. My gentleman callers have never spent the night before."

"Are they still agitating in favor of Kevin McLaughlin?"

"I think they've given up on Kevin. They returned their cars to him after I got back from Nicaragua."

Chad whistled. "I must be as popular as a polecat in the outhouse."

Julie laughed. "Well, not that bad. But they definitely were not overjoyed at your reentry into my life. They've both had to get part-time jobs in Austin to earn their own spending money. Steve washes cars in the university motor pool. Sherry shelves books at the main library. They wouldn't have had to work if I'd married Kevin. We're all better off because I didn't, but it's hard for them to understand that now."

"You could be leading the life of leisure now," Chad said, feeling the dual pain of guilt and doubt once again assaulting him. He had so little to offer her. It ate at him. If he were as noble as she thought he was, he would have bowed out of her life instead of encouraging her to chase away a man who could give her everything.

"It wouldn't have worked," Julie said firmly. "He wanted a paper cutout of a woman to grace his life. I let him think that's who I was for a time, but it got to be a real pain in the neck. And in all fairness to Kevin, I must add that he was a real gentleman about the breakup. No scenes. No recriminations. Only good wishes for my happiness. Now, let's change the subject. Tell me about Lola and her family. And your business."

He updated her on San Juan gossip. He'd talked One World into paying Lola's tuition at a boarding school in Managua. She wanted to become a schoolteacher. Her younger sister now worked mornings at Chad's house. The padre had dislocated his shoulder while ringing the bell in the church belfry. The bus to Rivas had started running again—on Mondays and Fridays. The midwife had broken her arm. Everyone was hoping no babies were born while she was recovering. Joe had adopted a kitten. "He came home with it in his mouth. A newborn with its eyes still closed. Lola and I gave it milk from a dropper. Joe provided the cuddling. He'd lick that little thing until it was wet and carry it from one place to another in his mouth. Now it's about two months old and sleeps curled up on top of him."

Chad babbled on awhile about the dog. About his idea to put in a field of windmills and generate a backup power source for the town.

"I want to see a professor in the engineering school out at Rice University while I'm here about my plan. Moreno has arranged for me to give a One World recruitment speech to nursing students at Baylor Medical Center, and call on some older physicians and dentists to see if they wouldn't like to give a year or six months of volunteer service at one of our clinics. The older docs can often afford to take off and do volunteer work more easily than the younger ones. And we could use mechanics, agricultural experts, large animal vets."

"Then you're going to stay awhile?"

"Several weeks, although I'll be on the road part of the time. Moreno wants me to do the recruitment bit in San Antonio and El Paso and Austin. One World has gotten a couple of terrific grants from private foundations and will be expanding services in Central and South America."

Julie pulled in the driveway of a Twenties vintage Tudor cottage with a very slanted roof and arched doorways and windows.

"Kind of looks like the gingerbread house in Hansel and Gretel, doesn't it?" she asked as she unlocked the door. "And I'm the resident witch."

"Best looking witch I've ever seen. The house is charming," he said as he walked into the tiny foyer and surveyed the cozy front room. Easy chairs and a sofa instead of rockers. Rugs instead of bare floors. Ceiling fan. Fire place. America. It was nice.

A Christmas tree graced the bay window, live green-ery the mantel. The house smelled of evergreen, bay-berry, cinnamon. Christmas. His childhood. He felt the tug of nostalgia. It would be nice to live like an American again.

He knew it had been hard for Julie to give up her larger home, but Chad was glad to be visiting in a house that was not associated with Ross. He wondered how much smaller this house was than the other one. Lots probably. He wondered where she would have lived with McLaughlin. Someplace grand, he was sure. Why did she give that all up for him? Did she love him that much?

The twins were working this week as Christmas-rush temporaries at Sears, Julie said, explaining her children's absence. They'd be home for dinner. Shortly. "Betty Jean and her son and boyfriend will be here, too. I thought it would be easier to have their buffering presence while you got acquainted with the kids. I may make them come with us when we have dinner at the folks' tomorrow night."

"Dinner at your parents' house?" Chad said in disbelief.

"It was Mother's idea. They're trying, Chad. Really they are."

Chad followed her into the bedroom and stared in the mirror over her dresser as though trying to see what it was about himself that had attracted Julie. It was a sentimental attachment, he was sure. A reaching back to a more innocent, less stressful time of dates and kisses and basketball games.

But was that *real* love?

He wanted to take her in his arms. Lift her onto the bed. She returned his kiss, but her manner said *not now. Wait until later.*

Pictures of her kids were everywhere. And several of Ross. His old nemesis. Chad had hated him for so long, and now he was dead, and that made him feel very peculiar.

The daughter, Sherry, looked an uncanny lot like her dad. Steve, with his dark hair and green eyes, favored his mother.

He knew he couldn't make love to her, but he needed to hold her. Cling to her and feel assured that she really wanted him to be here. That he wasn't intruding.

Over her shoulder, he spotted her Nicaraguan rocking chair in the corner, a sewing basket on the table beside it, a colorful afghan thrown over the footstool that sat in front of it. And suddenly he knew that she sat there and rocked and thought of him.

"You really do love me?" he asked into her hair.

"God, yes. So much it hurts. I'm so relieved that you're finally here."

He wanted to say it then. *Will you marry me?*

But he had to meet her kids. He had to be with her in her house. *Una prueba*, it was called in Spanish. A trial run.

Julie put a casserole in the oven, then showed him where to put his things. "Only one bathroom," she apologized. "I hope you can stay on after Steve and Sherry go back to school. We can have more privacy and relax a bit more then."

He went with her to pick up the twins at Sears. They were polite. "How was your flight?" Sherry asked. "How's the weather in Nicaragua?" Steve asked.

He asked them about their jobs. Sherry wrapped packages. Steve worked at package pickup.

He asked about their majors. Steve didn't know. Maybe journalism. Sherry wanted to be a vet, but she'd have to transfer to Texas A & M, and she didn't want to do that.

"We need veterinarians in Nicaragua," Chad said too enthusiastically. "For the farm animals. We're trying to get a cattle industry going in the part of the country where I live. Dairy herds, too. But it's been rough going. We need a better water supply. Better breeding stock. Vets. Medical supplies."

A protracted silence somehow said that Sherry Ann Rhoades had no intention of ever administering to animals in Nicaragua.

"Chad was all-state in basketball when he was at Allen High," Julie said. "He went to UT on a basketball scholarship but hurt his knee."

No response.

"How was work?" Julie asked.

"Busy," Sherry said.

"You, too, Steve?" Julie prodded.

"Yeah," Steve said.

"I wish Melissa didn't have to work tonight," Julie said. "We'll miss her at dinner. Melissa is Steve's girlfriend, Chad, and Sherry's best friend. You'll get to meet her tomorrow."

Silence.

"You guys hungry?" Julie asked with forced brightness.

Both twins grunted noncommittally.

Chad closed his eyes. It was going to be hell.

BETTY JEAN SWOOPED into Julie's living room like a breath of fresh air, kissed Chad on the mouth, introduced him to Bobby and Donnie—who were both attired in Houston Oiler sweatshirts—assessed the situation and, when everyone sat down to dinner, tapped with her spoon on her wineglass.

"Attention. It's time for Betty Jean's speech. I'll make it short so the food won't get cold, but I think we'll all enjoy dinner more if I do this now. Okay?"

She cleared her throat. *"Lighten up, everyone,"* she began. "That's l-i-g-h-t-e-n u-p! As far as I know, we are not facing imminent nuclear holocaust, famine, flood, or a loss in the Super Bowl. I know this all seems a bit awkward for you, Sherry and Steve—Mom's got a lover. She's going to go to bed with him tonight. But she is of consenting age, and she and Chad are serious about each other. And Chad, stop looking like you're walking on eggshells and acting like you've taken a vow of silence. It's all right to talk. You used to talk just fine. I remember when you talked policemen out of parking tickets, principals out of study hall, waitresses out of extra portions. And Julie, with those frown lines between your eyes, you look as worried as a long-tailed cat in a roomful of rocking chairs. It will be all right...eventually. Chad and Steve and Sherry *will* find their way into a working relationship if for no other reason than that all three of them happen to love you. As I do. In fact, I love you all. So now, I want everybody to pick up their wineglass and take a nice big sip. Then I want you to take a deep breath, because we are going to sing a little song to get ourselves in the Christmas spirit."

She watched while all did as they were told. Then she smiled approvingly and began to sing.

"Deck the hall with boughs of holly,
Fa la la la la, la la la la.
'Tis the season to be jolly.
Fa la la la la, la la la la . . ."

Everyone joined in, the young people reluctantly at first. Then with more enthusiasm.

"That was lovely," Betty Jean said, clapping her hands when the song was sung. Then she reached for her glass again and lifted it high.

"Welcome, Chad. And Merry Christmas, everyone. Let's all love each other and count our blessings, and God bless us every one."

"Here, here," Steve said.

Then Sherry rose. She was blushing a bit. "Be happy, Mom," she said hastily, lifting her glass, taking a quick sip, then abruptly sitting back down again.

"Well, while everyone's being so nice," Bobby said, scooting back his own chair and rising to his feet. "Here's a toast to Betty Jean, the best little peacemaker in the state of Texas. Isn't she something, folks?"

Things got a bit noisy while everyone clapped and hooted their approval of Bobby's words.

Then Donnie looked around the table expectantly. "Is that it, I hope? Everyone looks reasonably happy. The crisis seems to have passed, and I'm starving! How 'bout let's eat?"

AFTER DINNER, Betty Jean directed the doing of the dishes and the cleaning of the kitchen, giving orders like a straw boss.

"I guess that about takes care of it," she said, surveying the kitchen and dining room. "Now, Sherry and

Steve, get your jackets. You're coming to the movie with us. Rambo. I can hardly wait,"

"I don't like Rambo," Sherry protested.

"Sure you do, sugar," Betty Jean said. "He's your favorite."

"Oh, yeah. I forgot," Sherry said, meekly accepting her jacket from her brother.

And suddenly Chad and Julie were standing in the middle of the living room, the house quiet around them.

"You've got the world's best best-friend," Chad said as he grabbed Julie to him. "I think we should build a monument to Betty Jean. Or write a song in her honor."

"Or be happy," Julie said, burying her face against his neck.

They undressed on the way to the bedroom. Like a miracle, the tension was gone, and there was only love.

Chapter Thirteen

"So this is the mystery man from Nicaragua," Melissa said with a big smile. "I'm Melissa, the nonmysterious girlfriend from Houston. Welcome."

Chad shook hands with Melissa and seemed relieved at her open friendliness.

"Where are the twins?" she asked Julie. "Do they know what time it is?"

"I think they're almost ready. You're nice to get up early and take them to work. I know you don't have to be at your dad's office until ten."

"Glad to." She cocked her head and regarded Chad. "So, how's it going? Did Steve and Sherry behave last night? Or did they do their twins-from-hell routine?"

"Things were a bit awkward until Betty Jean arrived," he admitted. "She broke the ice."

"Great. Betty Jean's probably the world's best ice-breaker. Please excuse Steve and Sherry if they were a bit standoffish, but they're still in shock, you see. They'd planned to party four years at UT without a care in the world, and now they not only have to work, but they have discovered that studying is required at the old university. All us spoiled kids who got through high school on charm are having to face up to the big bad world. But I suppose we're getting our characters built in the process."

Melissa walked over to the hall door and gave a whistle. "Come on, you two. You're beautiful enough."

Sherry still had sleep marks on her face. Steve's hair was wet from the shower. They hovered by the table drinking the orange juice that Julie thrust at them.

"How was the movie?" Chad asked.

"Rambo saved the world from Communism without ever once putting on his shirt," Steve said. "Sherry swooned through the whole disgusting performance."

Sherry made a face at her brother. "If Rambo wore a shirt, it'd get greasy. He must have used a vat of muscle grease making that film."

Then she poked Steve and gave him a knowing look.

"Oh, yeah," Steve said as he reached for a piece of toast. "Say, Chad, Sherry and I were wondering if you and Mom would like to go to Galveston the day after Christmas. We'll have to take Melissa along, but she's not too much of a drag."

"We'd thought we'd take a picnic lunch," Sherry said, "and maybe hang around long enough for dinner at one of the seafood restaurants and then drive around to check out the Christmas lights on all those old Victorian buildings. I read in the paper that the Christmas decorations on the islands are really neat."

Melissa winked at Chad as she hurried the twins out the door. "See. They're not hopeless."

Julie had taken the rest of the week off, so she and Chad luxuriated over their second cup of coffee and eventually lured themselves back to bed.

"Lovemaking in the morning. How decadent," Chad said as he pulled aside her robe and began kissing her breast.

Julie felt herself smiling. *How lovely. How very lovely.* She closed her eyes to better enjoy the sensations he was causing, and murmurs of appreciation rose deep in her throat.

She could tell by Chad's deliberately languid movements that he was planning on making things last a good long while, which seemed like a fine idea to her.

"Oh, don't stop," she groaned when he pulled his mouth from her nipple.

"I don't want to play favorites," he said as he moved to the other breast.

No. She certainly wouldn't want him to do that.

It was late morning before they finally managed to get themselves showered and dressed and out in the world. A trip to the supermarket had never been so enjoyable. They touched constantly, stole kisses when an aisle was empty, whispered sweet reminders about the lovemaking of the morning and last night, planned even more delicious escapades for the evening. Julie was certain she had forgotten half of what she came for, but she really didn't care. They could come again.

Together they prepared lunch. "I considered beans and rice but decided when you're in Texas you should eat *our* national dish and decided on tacos instead," Julie said.

"Tacos are Mexican," he said.

"Well, we've elevated them to a higher art. Tex-Mex, we've started calling our cuisine since you've been gone. You chop up the lettuce and tomatoes. Very fine. Afterward, I think we should go down to Baskin-Robbins and splurge on a banana split. You have this strange affect on me. I feel incredibly greedy."

After the trip to the ice cream store, they bought a potted plant for Chad to take to Julie's mother this evening, then paid a call on Pedro Moreno, the man who had brought Chad's letter to Julie at the bank. The One World offices were upstairs in an old house whose first floor was now a beauty shop. But the offices were freshly painted and had some wonderful photography on the walls showing various One World projects throughout the world. Moreno gave Chad some brochures to pass out when he gave his recruitment speeches and offered some suggestions about how to handle questions that would arise. The elderly man obviously was very fond of Chad. "Just tell them your own story," he said. "Why you joined up, what it's meant to you, why you believe in it. And don't be disappointed if you don't get anyone to sign up. Just telling people about our work is good publicity. That last grant we got came about because a young woman told her father about a speech I had given, and he set the wheels in motion."

Back home, while they were changing for dinner, Julie switched on the bedroom television so they could hear the evening news. A fire destroyed a warehouse in the city's dock area—arson was suspected. The president and first lady were spending Christmas with their children and grandchildren. An unseasonable tropical storm was brewing in the Caribbean.

The evening air was warm and muggy. Jackets were unnecessary as they stood around Taylor's huge brick barbecue, watching him grill hamburgers.

"The smoke draws well," Chad observed.

"The barbecue is my own design," Taylor said.

"No kidding. Do you still have the plans?"

Steve produced a Frisbee and tossed it at Sherry. Soon Chad joined in.

"Hey, where'd an old guy like you learn how to do that?" Steve asked.

"My generation invented the game," Chad said, making a tricky behind-the-back throw. "I've got a dog who's world-class at catching."

"Hey, I've always wanted a dog that could catch a Frisbee," Sherry said. "Next time, why don't you bring him along."

"How'd you get it to hover like that?" Steve demanded.

Julie went to help her mother in the kitchen.

"You know, I was thinking today how we never had Kevin over for dinner," Angela said. "I thought about it a lot, but I felt like I'd have to redecorate the house and hire a woman to serve. And we certainly never would have served hamburgers and potato salad."

"Chad's nice, isn't he?" Julie asked.

"Yes, I suppose he is. The twins seem to have warmed up to him. But you make that boy move up here. Maybe your daddy can help him get some sort of decent job. Don't you go off down there to that awful country anymore. Your family needs you here in Houston."

The late news reported that the tropical storm was threatening to become a full-blown hurricane. Rare for December. As was the weather in Houston. Highs in the eighties were predicted for tomorrow, with more of the same through Christmas Day.

The next morning, the reports about the storm were more foreboding. Nicaragua and Honduras were expected to take the brunt of Hurricane Natalie.

Chad explained that most hurricane damage occurred on the east coast of Nicaragua, which was mostly jungle and sparsely populated. "That's a bit of good news and bad news. Not as many people are threatened, but the roads are bad or nonexistent. It's hard to get help to people. And sometimes the hurricanes sweep right across the isthmus. The last big one caused some problems in Managua and along the west coast.''

Chad hovered around the television throughout the next day. As he feared, the hurricane damage was reported to be severe along the east coast of Nicaragua. Worse than the '88 hurricane. Widespread flooding. Hundreds feared dead. Water supplies contaminated. Food shortages. No medical supplies. No communication. No electricity. Roads washed out.

Julie brought Chad food that he hardly touched.

''You want to leave, don't you?'' she finally asked.

''I hate to do that to you,'' he said, burying his face in his hands.

Julie was unmoved by his anguish. She was too preoccupied with her own. ''I hate it, too,'' she said and went to call about reservations. She wouldn't make him stay against his will. But damn him for wanting to go. *Damn!*

Flights were expected to resume to Managua in the morning.

Chad called Pedro Moreno to see what medical supplies were available.

He packed his bag before they went to bed.

''I'm sorry,'' he said as he held her.

''I know,'' she whispered, trying to figure out just how understanding she felt. She wanted to be angry. But how could she feel selfish when people were dying, when Chad could help organize rescue efforts? But she was. She stung with anger. She would feel differently if he were racing back to help his friends in San Juan, but he would be helping strangers. Julie wanted him to put her first, to be here on Christmas morning with her and her children, to go to Galveston with them on Sunday, to shop the after-Christmas sales, to be a family with her and her children, to drive with her to Austin to take the kids back to school, to stay here with her in this house forever. But even if he gave up his job in Nicaragua, she feared that Chad would always be a do-gooder. He'd always be racing off in the aftermath of hurricanes, floods, earthquakes, volcanic eruptions. He would always feel that it was his job to feed the hungry, clean up after wars, find homes for the homeless.

Damn him and his goodness. She didn't want to be in love with a saint. She wanted a man who would be there for *her*, whose heart was only big enough for her and didn't encompass the whole damned world.

"We haven't talked," he said in the darkness.

"No, we haven't. Maybe there isn't anything to talk about."

"I'm in charge down there," he tried to explain. "I need to see the One World resources and personnel are best utilized in assisting the people who need help. We have emergency gasoline and medical supplies and portable generators. People are without food and water and shelter. People need medical help. They need to know that the rest of the world cares. I feel so—"

"You don't need to explain," Julie interrupted. "I understand. What we have here is a case of a selfish woman being in love with a selfless man. I wonder what advice Ann Landers would have to say about that particular incompatibility."

PEDRO MORENO had arrived to take Chad to the airport, the back of his station wagon loaded with crates of water purification tablets to be sent on Chad's flight. "We're trying to get the U.S. government to lift the embargo long enough for us to bring in a shipload of food and supplies," he said over a hurried cup of coffee at Julie's dining-room table. He glanced pointedly at his watch. It was time to go.

Moreno went to stand impatiently by the front door, while Chad pulled Julie back to the bedroom for their last embrace.

"I love you, honey," he said. "Please don't forget that. I'll get in touch with you as soon as I can."

She nodded automatically. The phone system hadn't recovered from the last hurricane. It would probably be years before she got a phone call from Nicaragua.

"I'll make this up to you," he said earnestly. "And I'll get back up here when I can. Soon."

He peered into her face. "Julie? Don't close me out. Please."

Her kiss was perfunctory. "Take care of yourself," she said. "Merry Christmas."

The tears started as soon as the front door closed behind him. "Oh, hell," Julie said out loud and went racing after him for a real kiss.

Moreno put on the brakes. Chad leaped out of the front seat.

"I do love you," she said, throwing her arms around his neck. "I wish I didn't, but I do."

Their kiss was clinging, desperate, like the last kiss for a lifetime.

And then he was gone. Once again, no promises had been made. No plans for another visit. Nothing.

SOMEHOW SHE GOT THROUGH Christmas. She tried to be cheerful for her children. They tried to cheer her up. But she kept having to sneak off to her bedroom to compose herself. She felt empty inside, like a shell ready to crumble.

Maybe she should have given Chad an ultimatum—made him choose. *Nicaragua or me.* Would he still have gone?

But that would have been unfair, like making a mother choose between her children. He was who he was. If he were otherwise, she probably would not love him so much.

She didn't want to go to her parents' house for Christmas dinner. She didn't want to hear her mother looking on the bright side, telling her it was best to know what sort of a person Chad was now than waiting to find out. But she heard anyway. "Mother, it's not like he was a criminal sneaking off to rob a bank. He went back there to help people in need."

"A woman needs a man she can count on," Angela said, then made a thin line of her mouth as she went about her chopping and stirring.

Taylor was even worse. He had "called around" to find out if Kevin McLaughlin was seeing anyone.

Julie blew up. "Damn it! Will you two lay off! I'm miserable enough without my own parents making me feel worse. I resent your I-told-you-so attitude. I resent your assuming that Chad is now out of the picture. And if I ever hear anyone mention Kevin McLaughlin's name, I will never speak to that person again."

At dinner Angela drove her crazy continually putting ice cubes in her glass, passing her bowls of food when she hadn't eaten what was on her plate, asking her if she needed anything.

When the meal was finally over and Julie could get out the front door, she felt like she'd been let out of prison.

Sherry and Steve went their own way with Melissa for an evening with friends. Julie was grateful finally to be alone.

She took a hot bath, poured a glass of wine and semi-watched a movie on television. In the living room. She didn't want to look at the damned rocking chair in the bedroom. Maybe she'd give it to the Salvation Army.

She had gotten along just fine before Chad came back into her life, and she'd get along just fine without him now. At least she'd wised up about Kevin. Chad had done that for her. Maybe that had been his function in her life—to save her from a stifling marriage. She was better off alone than married to Kevin, of that she was certain.

Alone. She could handle it. In many ways it was better. How did the song go? One less man to pick up after. Except Chad was neater than she was.

But her life would be tidier if she remained alone. She could do as she wanted when she wanted.

NEW YEAR'S DAY, Julie provided moral support while Betty Jean went through her house removing pictures of Mitch. Only the ones in Donnie's room were left in place.

Betty Jean lovingly stored her dead husband's pictures in a trunk, crying over each picture, remembering when it was made, clutching it to her bosom for a last embrace. Julie helped her put the trunk in the attic.

"I did love that man so," Betty Jean sobbed over a cup of coffee. "But I love Bobby, too. Mitch was bigger than life—the football hero, war hero, my hero. But Bobby is comfortable. Bobby will never be shot down flying fighter planes. Bobby will grow old with me. Mitch would have had a hard time growing old. And now, Julie, my friend, how would you like to help me plan my wedding? Valentine's Day would be nice, don't you think?"

"You're sure?" Julie asked.

"Absolutely," Betty Jean said.

The wedding was a godsend. Julie was so busy helping Betty Jean, she didn't have as much time to brood.
First, the two women spent a week's worth of evenings
shopping for Betty Jean's dress. Betty Jean was determined to look bridelike but mature. "I don't want to
look like I'm trying to be twenty-one again," she told
one saleswoman, "but I don't want to look like the
mother of the bride, either." Finally they decided on an
ecru lace tea-length dress with a Victorian collar and
graceful long sleeves.

Julie decided she wanted to make the wedding cake
herself and took a week-long course in cake decora-
tion.

The wedding and reception both were to be at Betty
Jean's house, and Betty Jean decided she was going to
start her new life with everything shipshape. She
scrubbed the inside of every cupboard, cleaned out
closets, gathered up old clothes to be given away. Julie
helped her wallpaper her bedroom. Bobby and Donnie
painted the living room, shampooed carpets, washed
windows, trimmed shrubs.

It took Julie two days just to make and decorate the
cake, a task that was far more formidable than she had
envisioned. But she took pride in the reasonably acceptable results. She could do things. She could make
things happen. It was nice to know that about herself.

Julie and Betty Jean made all the food for the reception, much of it prepared ahead and frozen.

The day before the wedding Betty Jean's parents had
arrived from their retirement home in Phoenix, her
brother and his family from Chicago, and Steve, Melissa and Sherry from Austin. Julie had cooked dinner
for everyone at her house. The morning of the wedding, she and Betty Jean arranged flowers and dusted
the furniture one last time.

"The old homestead has never looked so good," Donnie said as the three of them surveyed the house.

Betty Jean's mother and Angela helped arrange the food on trays and platters.

And suddenly it was time to get ready. "Nervous?" Julie asked as she buttoned Betty Jean into her dress.

"A little. But not about what I'm doing. I just want everything to turn out all right. We've worked so hard."

Julie was Betty Jean's only attendant. She watched the proceedings with misty eyes. Any cynicism she had developed about the institution of marriage didn't go very deep, she realized. The traditional words of the service touched her.

Bobby and Betty Jean made their promises in voices that were clear and sure. And when it was over and there were hugs all around, Bobby kissed Julie's cheek and said, "I know you're like a sister to Betty Jean, and I don't want that to change because of me. I'll just have to be your brother."

"I'd like that very much," Julie said, dabbing at her eyes.

After the food had been eaten, the cake cut and praised, the last pictures taken, the rice thrown as the bride and groom left for their wedding trip, Julie stayed to help Donnie clean up. They both stood in the middle of the living room looking around at the disarray. "Geez, it looked so good this morning."

"Well, let's get started. Looks like it's just thee and me."

The twins and Melissa had already left for Austin, hoping to get back in time for an important Saturday-night party. Sherry had a new boyfriend, it seemed. An Austin boy. Sherry had casually mentioned that maybe she'd like to go to summer school. Steve and Melissa had applied for summer jobs at a dude ranch in Colorado. Her children were flying away.

Once the house was finally in order, Julie and Donnie made a meal out of wedding leftovers. She stayed and watched television with him for a while. He seemed a bit forlorn, now that the excitement was over. "Want me to stay over?" she asked.

But Donnie assured her he was fine. "I'm happy for Mom. I just wish sometimes that things hadn't turned out this way. I can hardly remember my dad."

"I remember how much he loved you," Julie said. "Come over for breakfast in the morning. I'll fix waffles."

On the way home Julie realized she'd probably drunk too much champagne toasting the bride and groom. Her head throbbed, her satin pumps were pinching her toes, her body ached with weariness and letdown. The wedding was finished. What would she do now?

She kicked off her shoes as soon as she was in the front door and left them there. Who would see them anyway? She took a couple of aspirin and padded off to take a hot bath. Then, wearing her old chenille robe, she fixed a cup of tea and carried it to the bedroom.

When the phone rang, she offered a silent prayer.

It wasn't Chad.

For a minute she didn't realize whom she was talking to. Bill Somebody? Who had been in touch with Michel. Then she remembered—the computer hacker from the University of Houston.

She made him start all over again with the message.

"I need two to three months, then I will once again become a citizen of Houston. So sorry about Christmas. Terribly. But my being here made a difference. I'll make it up to you if it takes the rest of my life. You have my heart. Will you marry me? Always, Chad."

In two or three months, she could have him as a permanent resident of this house, in her life. So why didn't she feel absolutely terrific? Why wasn't she dancing a jig around the room?

My being here made a difference.

There weren't many Chads in this world. He was special. He made a difference.

With only the light from the hall, she rocked and sipped her tea.

Then she went to the kitchen for a second cup. The house was so quiet. But that wasn't bad. In fact, after the busyness of the last couple of weeks, she welcomed some peace and quiet. When she came home from work now, she no longer felt like she must immediately turn on the television. She was adjusting to living alone. She could survive a quiet house as long as she knew it wasn't permanent.

She wondered if they'd let her take a leave of absence from the bank. If not, she'd find another job when she got back. It wasn't like the bank paid her all that much. Slave wages. And she was a good employee. Damned good. Maybe she could start freelancing landscaping jobs. Open a yard-care service. Be her own boss. Or start a wedding service. Plan people's home weddings. Garden weddings. Special location weddings.

Could she do that? Take charge. Take risks.

She'd managed to get her kids to the college of their choice. That had worked.

Chapter Fourteen

The trip didn't seem like such a hassle this time. Maybe it was all in knowing what to expect. She took fewer clothes in a smaller bag. She had a Spanish dictionary in her purse with a list of words and phrases she knew she'd have to use carefully copied in the inside cover for easy access. She had a plastic container of water and a couple of granola bars in her purse—just in case.

The flight was uneventful. She sat by a woman with a toddler and a baby. The woman didn't speak English but, using her dictionary, Julie managed to ask the ages and names of her children. She helped keep the little boy occupied while his mother tended his baby sister.

From the Managua airport, Julie was able to direct the taxi to the little hotel where she and Chad had spent the night in Managua. Luis and Consuelo recognized her at once and insisted she share their dinner.

The next morning, Luis took her to the bus station and helped her buy a ticket. "Rivas," he said pointing to the ticket. *"Otro autobús por San Juan."*

Julie nodded. She understood. She would need to change buses in Rivas.

If she hadn't been sitting by a window on the bus, she wondered if she could have survived the close quarters. At least a hundred people were packed on the bus.

Maybe more. At Rivas she purchased a second ticket, but had to wait several hours in the square for the bus to San Juan. Roofs were being repaired on several buildings. From hurricane damage, she assumed.

The bus, when it came, was almost as crowded as the first one.

Finally she was standing on the familiar street that hugged the shoreline of San Juan Bay. Shifting her suitcase in her other hand, she started up the hill. The ruts in the road were worse. The pigs seemed skinnier. And there were definitely fewer chickens. Nothing seemed damaged, but she wondered if the hurricane had taken its toll in other ways.

When she arrived at Chad's house, a pretty young woman greeted her at the door. Not Lola. Lola was in school in Managua. But Lola's sister was a younger carbon copy.

"Dónde está Chad?" Julie asked.

The girl led her to the railing of the veranda and pointed to the beach far below.

A half-grown cat wrapped itself about Julie's legs, and she stooped to pick it up. "Did they run off and leave you?" she asked rubbing her cheek against the animal's soft fur.

Julie took a shower under a pitiful dribble of cold water and slipped into Bermuda shorts and tennis shoes. Chad was still not back.

So, with a light heart, she made her way down the cliff. She couldn't see man and dog, but their footsteps were easy to follow.

She walked for a long time before she saw them. It was just dusk. Chad was sitting on a rock. Joe was lying at his feet.

Joe saw her first and instantly came loping in her direction, ears flopping, tail wagging.

Surely the dog didn't remember her. It had been nine months, and she had been here such a short time. But the dog danced around her until she knelt in the sand and gave him a hug.

And then her precious Chad was beside her, pulling her to her feet, kissing her, crying with her. Joe ran in circles around them, whining and barking.

"Why?" Chad asked.

"Because I can't live without you, silly. But even fools in love can be sensible. I'll live here with you when I can. You come to me in Houston when you can. We'll ride the tide and see what the future brings."

"It seems so simple," he said.

"It is. I don't know why we were trying to make everything so complicated. All I know is that my heart belongs to you, and I'll take any piece of your life we can manage."

Chad lifted her off her feet and spun her around and around. "I love you, Julie," he called to the wind. "I love you. I love you."

Then the three of them, for lack of any better way to express their joy, raced down the beach and into the ocean. Joe leaped in and out of the waves, luring them further and further until both gave up and dove in after him.

One with the water, with the world, man and woman embraced and laughed and dove again and again.

Until finally, wet and happy, three wet creatures trudged up the hillside.

"Guess what's for dinner?" Chad asked.

Julie laughed. "Beans and rice and champagne."

"Champagne?"

"I brought a bottle left over from Betty Jean's wedding. She owes me an entire wedding complete with cake, but I'll collect the rest later."

Tonight would be a wedding of sorts, Julie realized. The first night of the rest of their lives. They would say the words they both longed and needed to hear, making their commitment to one another an irrevocable bond.

Chad felt obligated to warn her that they would face many problems.

"Nothing could be a bigger problem for me than the limbo I've been living in. I need a ring on my finger and your love in my heart."

"What made you decide?" he asked.

"Betty Jean getting married, I guess. It seemed so right, so appropriate for two people who love and care for one another to stand up publicly and take their vows, to face the future as man and wife. And I realized that getting married doesn't mean that two people have to live in the same house every day for the rest of their lives. Getting married means commitment. Sailors are only with their spouses part of the time. Salesmen. Entertainers. Lots of people. Commuter marriages are a sign of the time."

"Those kinds of marriages are more difficult," Chad said.

"Probably. But there doesn't seem to be an option for us at this point in our lives. I'll put up with your cold water and roosters some of the time. You put up with my smog and traffic some of the time. And we'll both pursue our own livelihoods as best as we can on a part-time basis."

"I used to be jealous when you made better grades than I did in high school," Chad admitted, "but now I'm really grateful you're so damned smart."

"Not smart. Just in love. People in love are crazy enough to try anything."

They lingered at dinner, talking, making plans, touching, smiling, laughing. Then Chad opened the bottle of champagne, and they stood by the veranda railing, the bay below them, a golden saucer of a moon overhead, and lifted their glasses, pledging their lives to each other forever and ever.

Then, arm-in-arm, they went to make love.

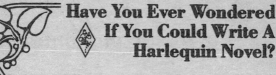

Have You Ever Wondered If You Could Write A Harlequin Novel?

Here's great news—Harlequin is offering a series of cassette tapes to help you do just that. Written by Harlequin editors, these tapes give practical advice on how to make your characters—and your story—come alive. There's a tape for each contemporary romance series Harlequin publishes.

Mail order only

All sales final

TO: **Harlequin Reader Service**
Audiocassette Tape Offer
P.O. Box 1396
Buffalo, NY 14269-1396

I enclose a check/money order payable to HARLEQUIN READER SERVICE® for $9.70 ($8.95 plus 75¢ postage and handling) for EACH tape ordered for the total sum of $_____*
Please send:

☐ Romance and Presents   ☐ Intrigue
☐ American Romance   ☐ Temptation
☐ Superromance   ☐ All five tapes ($38.80 total)

Signature_____

Name:_____
                                                (please print clearly)

Address:_____

State:_____ Zip:_____

*Iowa and New York residents add appropriate sales tax.

AUDIO-H

HARLEQUIN
American Romance®

THE LOVES OF A CENTURY...

Join American Romance in a nostalgic look back at the Twentieth Century—at the lives and loves of American men and women from the turn-of-the-century to the dawn of the year 2000.

Journey through the decades from the dance halls of the 1900s to the discos of the seventies ... from Glenn Miller to the Beatles ... from Valentino to Newman ... from corset to miniskirt ... from beau to Significant Other.

Relive the moments ... recapture the memories.

Look now for the CENTURY OF AMERICAN ROMANCE series in Harlequin American Romance. In one of the four American Romance titles appearing each month, for the next twelve months, we'll take you back to a decade of the Twentieth Century, where you'll relive the years and rekindle the romance of days gone by.

Don't miss a day of the CENTURY OF AMERICAN ROMANCE.

A CENTURY OF
AMERICAN ROMANCE
1900's

The women...the men...the passions...
the memories....

CAR-1